Bluebird
ON THE
Prairie

HEARTS OF THE MIDWEST • 1

TASHA HACKETT

ELECTRIC
MOON
PUBLISHING

©2021 *Bluebird on the Prairie: Hearts of the Midwest Book 1* / Tasha Hackett

Published by Electric Moon Publishing, LLC

Copyright 2021 by Tasha Hackett

Paperback ISBN-13: 978-1-943027-51-4
E-book ISBN-13: 978-1-943027-52-1

Electric Moon Publishing, LLC
P.O. Box 466
Stromsburg, NE 68666
info@emoonpublishing.com

Cover and Interior Design by Lyn Rayn / Electric Moon Publishing Creative Services

Cover Design by Doug West ZAQ Designs / Electric Moon Publishing Creative Services

Printed in the United States of America

www.emoonpublishing.com

For Robin

Prologue

Ockelbo, Nebraska
April 1879

The thick darkness of her bedroom pressed in until she cried out. She was suddenly awake. And alone.

With a gasp, she sat up in bed. Drenched in sweat with her legs tangled in the sheet, Eloise threw her pillow against the wall. Nausea rolled in her stomach. Scrambling out of bed, she leaned over the washbasin and retched.

At only twenty years old, she felt ancient. She had lived a lifetime already. Eloise Davidson, the widow, had woken up alone for the past fourteen months—months filled with weeks that felt like years.

The horrid nightmares had returned.

Gruesome though the dreams were, it was his warm arms, to have him hold her again, his kiss still burning her lips, that brought a new flood of tears. She woke to grief as strong as the day he was taken, and knew he was gone forever. Crossing her arms around her middle, she sank to the floor and let the tears run unchecked. She succumbed to the sobs that overwhelmed her.

Oh, Philip.

Her mind clung to the beauty of what was, yet Death tainted the corners of every memory.

A door creaked; a warning preceding the footsteps coming down the hall. They stopped outside her door.

"El?" The soft voice of her brother called to her.

Chapter 1

Z eke fought to keep his eyes open, though he moved his head in rhythm to the song he whistled. He had memorized all five verses to the new folk song "My Western Home" and annoyed his adopted family with it repeatedly.

The tune did little to pass the time today. Nebraska was endless. Grassland for all eternity. Mile after mile, forever and ever and always. Three weeks had taken him only halfway across the state. He'd been advised to take the train. Three weeks ago, traveling by horse had appealed to him as the adventure of a lifetime. But now the expanse of the endless sky only mocked him.

There was a fascinating beauty in its emptiness, to be sure. Moving to the edge of Iowa with the Donnely family last year had introduced him to western life—it had also sparked his desire to keep moving west. As far as he could go. He wouldn't stop until he fell into the ocean.

Another yawn stretched his sun-browned and dust-covered face. It was embarrassing how tired a man could be from doing nothing all day. Well, not embarrassing exactly since there was nobody else around. He wondered where Suzy Girl would take him if he fell asleep.

Probably nowhere. She was a lazy horse he'd bought from a farmer in Iowa only four weeks ago. Given the chance, she would find a shaded patch of new grass near a creek and live happily ever after. In hindsight, he should have asked a bit more why she went for the low price.

"Sing, Hooooo!" He called out to the prairie.

The prairie didn't answer. He continued singing unchecked.

> *Oh, give me a home,*
> *Where the buffalo roam,*
> *And the deer and antelope play.*
> *Where seldom is heard a discouraging word,*
> *And the skies are not clouded all day.*

He drawled out each word and switched to a whistle for the chorus until he lost interest halfway.

When he'd imagined his life out west, he hadn't considered the isolation of traveling alone. For three weeks, he'd followed streams, railroads, and bumpy paths from town to town. The next town should be beyond the next rise, or the next one. Three days ago, he'd looked at a map that someone had nailed to the wall of the diner and discovered he could trim five miles if he left the main road and cut straight to Ockelbo, a Swedish settlement with a population near a thousand. A town that size would have employment opportunities. Which he needed since his money and food supplies had dwindled. Again.

There was evidence of smoke some distance beyond the creek where it curved ahead. He would keep heading toward it and hope for the best. This prairie, though, the empty loneliness was enough to drive him out of his mind.

Suzy Girl slowed to a plodding pace, but Zeke hardly minded. Grass, grass, and more grass was all he could see.

"Hey, horse. Can you imagine living without eyelids?" Anyone's voice, even his own, was a pleasant sound these days. A few weeks of travel and he was ready to rethink his whole life plan. "Fish don't even have 'em. I think. Maybe. Do fish have eyelids? If they do, I've never seen 'em. Frogs have extra." He'd handled enough of those for close inspection.

Suzy Girl dipped her head to snag a bite and slowed again.

Zeke popped open his eyes. "Hey! What do you take me for? I didn't say it was snack time. Keep on, girl. Let's go."

She turned her head to look back at him with one large brown eye. She blinked and snorted before picking up her walk.

"See, if you didn't have eyelids, how would you so expertly express yourself?"

She ignored him.

"I know you can hear me." He clicked his tongue and slapped the reins, but his heart wasn't in it.

And she seemed to know it.

After another half-mile of silence, Zeke filled his lungs and was about to burst into an encore when he heard it.

Splashing. And . . . giggling?

The noise grabbed his attention, though he wasn't near enough to see the water through the scraggly line of trees. Zeke did not see a settlement nor a homestead, but the sloping hills could hide a town a quarter-mile away if a man didn't know where to look. Which he didn't.

"We're not alone, Suzy Girl. Think we should check it out?"

She didn't respond.

"Good plan. Me too."

As he came into the brush where the prairie met the creek, he flipped the reins over a branch of the nearest cottonwood. The splashing continued, and he heard a woman's voice.

"Ope! Was it cold? Here goes. Weeee!" She laughed again and Zeke wondered if this woman was deranged.

"Suzy Girl, guard my back, will ya?" The horse snorted and picked at the lush green grass. "Wonderful. I knew I could count on you." With a pat against her neck, he left her there.

He was pushing aside the low hanging branches when a scream froze him mid-step. Instantly reaching for his gun and searching for danger, he scanned the creek. A steep bank separated him from the sandy creek bed. Other bushes and shrubs grew around the water's edge. Looking below, he took in everything quickly. He was confused by the blue cloth hanging from a tree root waving in the breeze.

A woman stood knee-high in the water and held a naked baby as if to use him as a shield. Her arms were wrapped around his middle, hugging him close to her chest. Baby arms and baby legs wiggled, trying to get back into the water to play. Her eyes, on the other hand, large and serious, did not waver. Staring at him, she froze. Her brown hair hung loose down her back, and her pale arms were bare. The skin of her shoulders was visible through her wet underclothes. The child cried out; he begged to be released from the iron case of her arms. The thin muslin of her shift and pantaloons was plastered tightly to her legs, leaving little hidden. The woman's face was quickly turning bright red.

Ah, I'm the reason for the scream.

Apparently, she was not expecting company. She shivered in the Nebraska wind. The sun shone brightly, but spring was still new. The baby was unafraid and continued to windmill his arms and legs all around. One chubby hand flapped up and down at him. Both she and Zeke stood still, staring at each other for a few more seconds. He scratched his scalp under the side of his Stetson. He guessed he did look a little gruff these days. A bath would have been a good idea before entering a town.

"Stay back!" She dropped into the water, scrambling away as best she could with the boy in her arms.

Zeke paused and cocked his head at the sight. *Good grief.* He hadn't meant to frighten her. Here he was, yearning for company, for some other human voice, and the first one he sees screams at him. He holstered the gun. Raising both hands as a sign of peace, he planted his feet. A squall from the child sliced through the air.

"It's okay!" Zeke said. "I'm terrible sorry to come across you this way, if you wouldn't mind just—"

"Go away!"

He'd seen that look in her eyes in wild animals before. In startled chipmunks. And rabbits. He had once seen a chipmunk turn so quickly it bounced right off the nearest tree. His laughter rang out when he pictured a half-dressed wet chipmunk holding a naked baby.

She was furious.

"No! I'm sorry," he said. "Please don't be frightened. I'll stay over here, promise."

She grabbed a handful of wet pebbles and threw them in his direction. They showered the ground near his feet. Her chin jutted out in defiance. *Braver than a chipmunk.*

"You should not be here," she said.

She was right. What was he thinking? Suddenly he felt like the greatest cad this side of the Mississippi. He spun around and turned his back to her. "How's this?" he asked. Another shower of pebbles bounced off his boots. Dutifully, he covered his eyes with his hands and turned slowly back to her. "See? I'm not looking. I can't see a thing. Ma'am? Miss? I'm not intruding, but I heard a noise. Just passing through. Funny thing happened, actually, maybe if you'd just like to point me to the nearest town."

"What's the matter with you!" she said. "Leave me alone!" A fist of pebbles rained on his chest and neck, a few settled on the top of his wide-brimmed hat.

Her aim was improving.

He kept his eyes covered and ducked. "Okay! Okay! I'm going." He turned his back to her again, hands on his face, when more pelted him. "Would you stop that? Don't you listen? I said I was leaving."

His foot slipped off the edge of the bank. Caught off guard and distracted by flying pebbles, Zeke tumbled onto the gravel by the water's edge. The woman screamed again as he fell. His arms and legs flailed about and he landed in a heap, headfirst. Cold gravel pressed into his cheek.

He didn't move. *Ow! That's one way to get her attention.*

If he stood and climbed the bank without speaking, maybe he could forget this whole miserable encounter had ever happened. Slowly, he uncrumpled himself and lay on his back with one forearm tossed over his face. His heart pounded in his forehead. He would get up. Soon. He just needed another minute to catch his breath.

Great. Now I've bashed in my head. You really know how to impress the ladies, Zeke. I don't know how you've remained unmarried this long . . . it's probably the horse. No woman wants a man with a lazy horse.

More splashing signaled her return across the water. She was no longer running away or throwing rocks.

He groaned. She probably felt sorry for him now that he was wounded, blind, and ridiculous. He didn't need her help. He'd be on his way. Just as soon as he could get up. He attempted to stand.

"Please," she said, "sit and rest a moment. You're bleeding."

"Yup." Zeke slumped back against the bank in a more refined position. Keeping his face downcast from her, he gathered his wits.

His head throbbed. And he wasn't sure where the blood came from, but it was on his hands.

Fell off the stupid bank.

Nothing's broken.

Mostly naked woman standing nearby.

Her bare feet sank into the pebbles, and the water caressed her ankles. Not that he noticed. He didn't know where to look now that she stood right next to him. Suddenly, her face appeared in front of his, and she looked directly into his eyes. She still held the baby close to her chest.

"You okay?" she said. "You have blood all over your face."

Zeke stared at his hands. They were covered in mud, bits of grass, and some blood. "I'm sorry." He looked at her, then turned his eyes toward the creek, the trees, the bank, the clouds, and anywhere else but her. And then he started talking.

"I'm Ezekiel. Zeke. People call me Zeke. Ezekiel James. Whatever you want. My mother used to call me Zekey James, which is just kinda weird if you ask me. Which you didn't, I mean, you asked me to leave. Earlier. Which I didn't. But I was—I would have—I was. Leaving. I was leaving. I didn't mean to, I tried not to, I wasn't even looking. I mean, I looked some, just because I came across you so suddenly on accident." *Shut up, Zeke. Stop. Talking.* He squeezed his eyes shut.

"Why don't you stay here for a minute. I'll be right back." She adjusted her shift, pulling at it so it flowed over her backside. She put the baby in the sand a few feet away from the water. Finding the end of a rope, she tied it securely around his waist. The other end was already tied to the nearest tree.

The baby scrunched up his face and stuck out a lip, then noticed a bag near him and began pulling all the things out of it. "Naa? Naa?"

"Yes," she answered. "It's in there." By the time she snatched the bag from him, he had dumped half of the contents out. A brush and hairpins lay scattered at the boy's feet. "Here." She handed him a large muffin, and he sat down to eat it.

Reaching for her dress and stealing a glance back at Zeke, she hid behind some shrubs. Zeke felt his face warm and pretended to be interested in looking downstream.

"Hi!" the baby called to him.

Zeke smiled and waved his hand. "Hi." It was the best he could do while keeping his other hand pressed against the cut on his forehead.

The woman returned, damp but dressed, and leveled her eyes at him with her chin held high. She didn't trust him. He found that ironic, given that he was the one who fell on his face trying to get away from her. He turned his head. How much more could he humble himself in this situation? She swished something in the water and came toward him, stopping a yard away.

"I don't understand you," she said.

"Well," he said slowly, "I was just as surprised as you. I need to ask; like I said, I'm lost, and you're the first person I'd seen in a while. When I set off, I was told Ockel-something was only a day's long ride." He waved his hand toward the west. "That way. And then you and your baby threw rocks at me and pushed me off the bank." He flashed a cheeky grin at her.

She didn't find humor in it. Instead of smiling, she shoved a wet rag at him. "Here. Let's see how badly you hit your head. And you look terrible."

"Thank you. The bleeding has stopped, I think. I'll mend." He patted his face gingerly and then washed the dirt and mess from the rest of his face, neck, and hands. The rag turned brown.

"There is a town," she said in a measured tone, holding his gaze, "downstream a few miles. Keep following the creek, and you'll find a bridge. You can't miss it. Don't mind the rag; I'll wash it. You can be on your way." She took the stained rag from his outstretched hand. "I'm glad you weren't seriously injured when you . . . fell."

He stood, testing his legs. Everything was functioning again. He tipped his hat. "Ma'am." Without looking at her again, he climbed the bank with as much dignity as the situation allowed. He grappled for roots, and sand gave way beneath his feet. His ears burned, knowing she was standing there watching his backside. Reaching the top, he strode through the dry grass to his horse. She waited patiently where he'd left her. She snorted a greeting as she munched the grass around the bit.

"Hey, Suzy Girl, you'll never believe what just happened to me." She ducked her head and then knocked his hat off with her nose. "Real smart. Clever. Just because you had to stay up here and eat the best grass you've had all day doesn't mean you can mistreat me." With a grunt, he swung into the saddle.

"Come on, girl. We're on the right trail." He nudged with his heel, and she walked through the brush into the open prairie again. "When you have time later, I'll tell you all about the chipmunk I met playing in the creek today."

Suzy Girl dipped her head again.

The sky was empty and blue. The sun was shining with the freshness of spring. The day was looking up. Despite his humiliating meeting.

He smiled, thinking of the woman's concern when she'd knelt in front of him. It was sweet. Unnecessary. But sweet. It had been a while since anyone cared whether or not he had blood on his face. Her deep blue eyes showed strength. Her soft round cheeks held a blush of color on each side. He pictured her mess of brown hair, wet and dripping onto her dress.

He shook his head to clear his thoughts, pushing aside images of the woman. He reminded himself how glad he was to be free, strong, and independent, while shoving aside all other thoughts of her. Especially how her legs appeared through her wet underclothes or the water swirling around her ankles. He thought instead of the ocean and how the waves would look cresting and falling. He'd read before the waves could be taller than a man.

With the wind pushing at his back and the promise of a bed and real food for dinner, he couldn't help but laugh at the sky for his good fortune. "Hy-aw!" he said to Suzy Girl, kicking in his heels.

She seemed to feel his shift in attitude more than his verbal command, and when he urged her again, she leaped forward and they sped across the prairie.

Chapter 2

The wind increased, bringing with it the chill of the evening as dusk settled on the prairie. Zeke shivered and pulled his over-coat tighter. Faint outlines of the homes came into view. The sun eased into the west and made quaint silhouettes of each building. He followed a narrow walking path leading into the edge of town.

Squinting in the fading light, he looked for a Main Street. The path from the creek was not the main road. Or a road at all. He trudged through the outskirts of town, leading his horse. He yearned for a real bed, but he needed a livery—hopefully adjoined to a smithy and farrier. And ideally, all of this would be near a warm supper.

He complained aloud in a high falsetto. "'A few miles down-stream,' she said. 'You'll find the bridge,' she said. 'Can't miss it,' she said." *Heavens and stars and all things holy, if I don't find a warm dinner tonight, I'll know who to blame.*

He looked up. "Sorry God, you know I don't mean it." Except maybe he did this time. The events of the past few hours had put him in a sour mood. *Blasted chipmunk.*

That afternoon, Suzy Girl had joyfully galloped through the grass for near three miles before she ran out of steam. The haze of smoke he'd been riding toward was now behind him. There was no way the girl had toted the toddler this far. Though her family likely lived on a homestead.

He must have missed the bridge already. After a quick turn, he headed back the way he'd come. That's when he noticed something wrong with Suzy Girl's gait. An examination revealed a missing shoe.

"I'm sorry, Girl." He rubbed her shoulder and leaned into her. "We'll get you fixed up." Taking the reins, he led her back along the creek, pushing through the undergrowth and searching carefully for anything that could be considered a bridge. They traveled back two miles at this slow pace when he saw a string of large rocks crossing the creek. *Certainly, this isn't a bridge.* But it was the most obvious crossing that included a lower bank on each side to accommodate an easy descent to the creek bed.

"This is spiteful. If a man asked you to point the way, would you tell him this is a bridge? No. You would not. You would never set out to intentionally misdirect a starving, lonely, incredibly handsome, courteous, witty . . ." He ran out of adjectives. "You wouldn't, would you?"

Suzy nuzzled his shoulder and snorted.

"I don't need your sympathy. In fact, I'm the one feeling sorry for you. You hear?" Zeke's stomach answered this time. He groaned at the thought of eating beans and hardtack again. The afternoon sprint had been fueled by his visions of dinner.

He now stared at the line of rocks and pictured himself seated at a table with a full plate of fried chicken. Freshly baked biscuits on the side. The kind with the crust that flaked all over the plate. Still warm from the oven, with butter melting off the edge. There'd be a heap of green beans and mashed potatoes. After scraping his plate clean, he would order a slice or two of apple pie. Or raspberry or cherry. Any kind would do.

At twenty years old, he knew better than to lick the plate. Only little boys who knew their mothers weren't looking would lick the plate. Very little boys.

Unless the pie was warmed with the gooey insides that spread across the plate, and if there just happened to be ice cream to melt on top of it, and if perhaps he wasn't in a very fancy establishment and there weren't too many people about.

Without waiting for his lead, Suzy Girl pushed past him, yanking the reins from his hand and waded into the water, stopping midway to drink her fill.

He picked up the line where it lay on the water and yanked her back. "You think you outrank me? I'm the brains of this outfit. If I say it's not a bridge, it's not a bridge. I didn't say for sure it wasn't a bridge." *But it's not a bridge.* But it was a crossing. If there was a path on the other side, he would take it. He tugged off his boots and socks and shoved them into the saddlebag. As an afterthought, he unbuckled his gun belt and strapped it to the saddle. Just to be safe. Carefully, he made his way across the rocks with Suzy Girl splashing along beside him.

"Fried chicken," he told her, "the kind you can sink your teeth into and come away with a bite that melts in your mouth. Crispy. Fresh. Juicy. You can peel the skin off if you want. Eat it first. Breaded and browned to perfection. The inside will be white and tender." He groaned. "What I would do for some fried chicken right now." His mouth watered.

Halfway across the creek, an owl hooted directly overhead, startling him out of his dinner dreams. He shot his gaze over his shoulder, searching for the bird that must only be a few feet away. The rock he stood on wobbled, and the movement of the water did nothing to help his balance. His arms flapped at the air, trying to stay on the precarious rock, which wasn't nearly as sturdy as a bridge. He teetered on the ball of his foot with one heel hanging off and the other leg wild and unsteady.

The horse decided it was a good time to jerk the other way toward the bank. There was no helping it. With a yelp, Zeke jumped. Landing on his feet in knee-high water, he gasped at the cold. Zeke's leg tangled in the reins, and they pulled tight when Suzy Girl clambered to the side of the creek. All at once, he found himself swept off his feet, submerged in frigid water that stole his breath. Splashing like a wild man, he was unable to keep any part of himself dry. The water rushed over his head and muffled his curse.

Suzy Girl stopped on the high bank and turned to look at him as he floundered.

He sucked in air when he came up before sending all of his frustration at his horse. "Dad-blame it, Suze! You tryna drown me? Sakes alive!" A shiver coursed through him involuntarily from his core to fingers. Irritation welled up, and he hollered accordingly, hitting the water with both hands. He trudged out and stood at the edge. The sand and pebbles pushed between his toes, and water streamed from his hair, down his face. Wiping his sleeve across his eyes, then shaking his arms and hands of the extra drops, he tried to cool his anger. Blowing and spitting the water from his face, he shook his head and flung drops in all directions like a shaggy dog. A tired, hungry, and wet dog.

He yelled at the string of rocks. "My boots are dry!" Heavens, but that water was cold. April was not the season to go swimming, in his opinion, and the afternoon heat had long passed. His trousers clung uncomfortably to his legs. Zeke didn't relish the idea of swimming fully dressed no matter the season.

He shrugged out of his vest and suspenders and began unbuttoning his shirt. Midway, he paused to wipe the water that continued to drip from his hair and into his eyes. *Where's my hat? Please, don't let it be gone.* A man needed a hat. Scanning along the shore downstream, he spied it in a tangle of branches.

"Suzy Girl," he began in all seriousness, "you will stay." After looking her in the eye, he shook his head and tied her to the closest tree. If she decided to wander off in the wrong direction, he was in no mood to go after her. A man needed a horse, and a horse that didn't mind was better than no horse at all.

Sucking in a breath, he waded back into the cold for his hat. A few minutes later, after drip-drying and changing what he could, he picked out a path through the trees and followed it over a rise in the prairie. From the top, he could view the whole town. Relief flooded him. *Thank you, Lord.* It was larger than he'd expected. He was arriving from the east. The main road, he could make out, led from south to north.

His hopes of a hot dinner were rapidly fading. He saw no people in the dim light and heard no sounds of village life. The shops were long closed, and folks were retired for the evening.

His head ached from the earlier tumble, and he was wet and muddy. He looked a mess. He was a mess! Days of patchy stubble protruded from his face. It was looking more like a beard every day; if only he could fill it in.

When he found his way to the livery, he was greeted by Frank—a balding man whose white beard made up for any hair that was missing from his head. He refused to negotiate a lower boarding fee.

"I'll take no less than three dollars," the man repeated.

Zeke scratched the back of his neck. "For one night? A week maybe would be fair for that amount. But I'll not pay it for a night. That's downright robbery." Not to mention he didn't have it. And even if he did, he wouldn't spend it boarding a horse and starve himself.

The man's stringy whiskers twitched out of the way as he shot a stream of tobacco juice onto the barn floor.

As was Zeke's habit, he'd saved just enough from the last stop to board them both and buy a few meals on the side with plans to find immediate work before starting west again. He'd begun the journey with limited funds and, for the most part, had enjoyed the eclectic jobs and people he'd met. He knew it would take an eternity to reach the ocean this way, but it was part of the fun for him.

Another shot of juice barely missed Zeke's boots.

"I'm not standing here all night watching you scratch your head," Frank said.

"Fine." Zeke sighed. "Can I work for it? I can do anything that needs doing." There was always work to be done. Three weeks of travel, and he had not been forced to shake the dust from his feet yet.

Chapter 3

"If I didn't know you as well as I do, I'd never believe a story like this. He really fell on his head?" Jessica doubled over with laughter.

Eloise elbowed her best and only friend, Jessica Palmer, who sat in the yard with her. "Honestly, Jess. It wasn't at all funny at the time." The sun couldn't have come up any sooner today. Eloise had been itching to share the story with Jessica. She'd brought Luke, her eighteen-month-old nephew, who went wherever she went. The three of them sat behind the boarding house where Jessica lived and worked with her mother. Jessica's father farmed a homestead they were still proving up miles out of town.

"And you were practically naked!" Jessica said. "Oh, I'm so jealous. Why you get all the fun, I'll never know. What a time that would have been. Were you terribly frightened?"

"I don't know." Eloise was not sure how she'd felt. "I was startled, of course. And I felt exposed in my underthings." She suppressed a giggle. "But Luke didn't pay any mind; he just went on splashing and kicking. But you know, when the man fell and lay there all stretched out with blood on his face, my mind didn't waver. I could have high-tailed it in the other direction, but where? My clothes and everything were on his side of the river."

Jessica, always the dreamer, fell back into the grass with her arms under her head. "Was he handsome? Rugged? Dangerous?"

"I just told you he had blood all over his face!"

"Yes, but after that." Jessica propped herself up on one elbow. "So what'd you think of him?" Jessica loved to embellish a story; she was worse than the best fisherman. By this time, Luke had lost interest. He toddled off to the chicken house and was in the process of poking dandelions through the fence.

Eloise watched him and smiled. "Luke loves chickens. Did I tell you he carried around a bit of clover all afternoon last week? Saving it to bring over. Such a funny boy. The chickens love him too. See how they're all lined up waiting for what he might have for them? Tobias wanted me to keep chickens. But I didn't need anything else to take care of."

Jessica poked a finger into Eloise's shoulder. "El, I know what you're doing."

"Hm?" Eloise knew her friend would try to pull every tiny detail of her. She had never been able to live up to Jessica's story-telling ideals. Sometimes it was more fun to let her work for it.

"I'm dying over here," Jessica said. "Did he have warts or something? Was he old? Hairy? Were his teeth rotting out?"

"You're disgusting," Eloise said. "He was . . . normal. Okay? He was young, well-built. Dirty. He was very dirty. Looked like he was trying to grow a beard." And failing. The scruff on his face had days of growth but patchy. She remembered when her brother Tobias had started growing a beard, he was so proud of the few hairs he'd sprouted, even when they didn't cover most of his cheeks. She eventually convinced him to keep it shaved for a few more years.

"So he wasn't good-looking?"

Eloise rolled her eyes heavenward. She was beginning to regret bringing it up. She knew what Jessica was hinting at, but it hurt more than she'd thought it would to play along. Pretending to be interested in other men held no delight for her. She tried to think of a topic to distract Jessica. But hiding something from her was like trying to hide fried bacon from a husband. Impossible.

She was saved by Luke's dash toward the garden plot in search of more greens for the chickens. There was nothing planted yet, except the sugar peas and radishes, but she wasn't taking chances with those. Despite the fun a toddler could have in freshly turned soil, it was not worth adding that mess to her workload for the day.

Helen Palmer's voice rang across the yard. "Jessica Mary Palmer! I sent you out for eggs nigh ten minutes ago. Are you laying'em yourself? Morning, Eloise. Such a nice day to be out. It's going to be another warm one. Better soak it in while you can. But keep your shawl handy, hear?" Helen stood at the back door with a wooden spoon in her hand. "You must have crawled right under my nose. Come eat with us. We've got three new boarders this week who

I simply must introduce you to." She scooped up Luke from the yard, and he squealed when she nuzzled his tummy.

"Come on in," Helen said. "I've told them all about you, and they are such a nice bunch of boys."

"Oh, Helen," Eloise said. "You didn't."

"Baby, don't you 'Oh, Helen' me. I told them what I tell everybody. Why you wouldn't want lovely things said about you, I'll never know. I mentioned you would be stopping by this week, and look, I was right. So here we are." Helen raised her eyes at Jessica. "I'm still waiting on eggs."

Eloise grimaced at Jessica, who mouthed a silent apology before she hurried off to the chicken house. "Helen," Eloise said, "I don't feel right eating so many meals here. You already work hard for your paying company. I can make my own food, honest."

Helen squeezed Luke, and he snuggled against her. "Nonsense, baby, you're family! Besides, you eat half as much as Mr. Palmer, and he's only around a few Sundays a month." She planted a kiss on the toddler's cheek. "And I've seen the food you cook, if you want to call it that."

"Helen!"

Helen ignored her retort. "I forget sometimes that you're not actually mine. Now get in here. I've got plenty of milk, and biscuits will be coming out any minute."

Eloise sighed. She dreaded meeting another round of Helen's boys. Most were day laborers who didn't stick around for more than a season. They were hard-working, true. They were young and friendly, and they had dreams and plans. They also spent most of their money at the card tables, while a few would come to church and pray for their sins to be forgiven each Sunday. Regardless of their faults, she wasn't interested in any man. Ever again. True love only came along once, and she'd found it. When Philip died, all her love went with him to the grave and there it stayed, a constant tugging on her heart.

Squaring her shoulders, she followed Helen to the house. "Helen, can I talk to you, please?"

"Sure, baby," Helen sat on the steps and snuggled Luke until he squirmed away. "I've got two minutes left for those biscuits."

Eloise leaned her shoulder against the wall. They watched Luke pick a blade of grass and bring it back to Helen's knee. "I would rather you didn't talk about me to any of your guests."

"Why ever not? They're all nice boys." She held out her hand to accept more gifts of grass and a twig from Luke.

"I know you don't mean any trouble, and that's why I haven't mentioned it before. But I just think," Eloise held in a breath, trying to find just the right words to bring understanding without hurting Helen's feelings. "I would like to be the one to share my history. When I'm ready. It's hard to know how to act or behave, always wondering if they know or if they don't know, or if it makes them uncomfortable. Honestly, it wasn't like he just . . . died. One of these days, I'd like to be known as Eloise again. And not Eloise the widow."

Luke picked a handful of the grass he'd collected and shoved his whole fist into Helen's apron pocket. She reached her arm around Eloise and hugged her close, catching Luke between them. "If it means that much to you, I promise to never speak of you again. I can hold my tongue when I've a mind."

Luke did not like being caught in the middle and made his presence known with another squeal.

The women laughed at him before Helen stood with him in her arms. "How about a second breakfast? I have just the thing for you." She easily maneuvered with Luke in her arms, swung open the door, and was inside before it slammed shut behind her.

"Try to keep his hand out of the jelly jar this time," Eloise called to her. Standing and shaking off the bits of nature Luke had gathered, she walked to the middle of the yard. The sun bathed the grass with fresh hints of spring. A few dandelions were making an early show, and little curled ears of the violet leaves clustered in patches throughout the yard. With another sigh, she slumped to the ground and lay back in the grass to wait for Jessica. She didn't want to do anything.

Breathe in. Breathe out.

She closed her eyes against the morning sun. A minute went by before it was blocked by a shadow. Jessica stood over her, egg basket in one arm and the other planted on her hip. Her face was stern and questioning.

"Jess," Eloise said. "You look just like your mother when you do that." Eloise couldn't help but smile at the resemblance and waited for the advice she knew was coming.

"Get up. There's no getting around it now. You just try to pull that boy away from her without a fight. I've never seen a kid eat so many biscuits." Jessica reached a hand to hoist Eloise off the ground.

"Jess, you promise he didn't come in last night?"

"Who? The normal-looking, well-built, dirty man who may or may not be rugged and dangerous?" Jessica winked and hooked arms with Eloise. "Nobody new for two days, and Professor Oakfield has already left for the school, so you're safe. You know how he likes to go in early on Tuesdays. It's watering day or something or other. Have you seen his classroom? He's collected over twenty plants in there. He tends them all, and nary a student can touch 'em. Says he doesn't trust grimy fingers with them."

Eloise steeled herself for another round of introductions to eligible young bachelors. She prepared to slap on a smile and say all the right things. But she didn't think she could do it today.

Jessica turned and looked her over. She pulled a piece of grass from Eloise's hair.

Unable to shove it aside any longer, it finally spilled out of Eloise's mouth. "Today is Philip's birthday."

Jessica nodded. Jessica and Eloise were two opposite pieces of a puzzle that fit together. They were always what the other needed. Jessica knew how to rejoice with those who rejoiced, but she never shied away from mourning with those who mourned. "I know."

"He would have been twenty-two."

"I know." Compassion filled her friend's face, and she pulled Eloise in for a hug.

"I'm not going in today," Eloise said. "Tell Helen I'll swing by after the morning bell to fetch Luke. I'll be at the shop with Pa. I'm sure he won't mind the company today. Maybe he'll let me sweep out the place."

"Okay. I'll tell her. I'm sure Mr. Davidson would love to see you today. Be good to yourself. Hear me?"

Eloise forced a smile and nodded. Brushing any extra grass from her skirts, she hopped off the steps and was around the corner and onto the Main Street boardwalk before the first tear fell.

Fresh hay. Horse blanket. Strong wooden walls. Zeke lay on his back, enjoying the quiet of the morning moments before the weight of responsibility sank in. He rarely had the luxury of rising when he pleased. Living with Paul and Beatrice Donnely throughout his adolescent years had been a godsend. But he became one of seven children on a farm, expected to pitch in with the rest of them. This meant rising with the dawn, even on the weekends. If Zeke didn't get up when he was supposed to, his adopted brother Mike, on more than one cold morning, yanked the blankets off him and threw them out the window.

He lay still, staring at the rafters, at least until his stomach grumbled a reminder that he had entirely missed dinner last night. Time to get up. He stood and rolled his shoulders while he mentally ticked off his priorities for the day. Because he was impatient to venture out on his own, he had not saved anything to fund his trip. Therefore, at the forefront of the agenda was to find a job that paid in hard cash. First, he must eat food, bathe, eat more food, and find a respectable place to sleep. With an air of determination, he shook the kinks out, stretched his arms over his head, and caught a whiff of himself. A bath would need to be a priority. He finished dressing and smiled at the stall next to him where Suzy Girl was eying him. Running a hand through his hair, he gave it a thorough tousle and finger comb.

"Morning, Girl. Sleep well?"

She snorted and moved closer to him.

"Yeah? Good to hear. I hope you didn't make too big a mess in there. Yours truly is on duty. So take it easy, will ya?" He braced himself with a hand on the stall to pull on his boot.

She nuzzled his hand and nipped at his shirt cuff.

"I like you too. Thanks for sticking around." Zeke crossed his arms and rested his elbows on the dividing wall. "You'll have to hang tight for a few days until I earn you a new shoe. And food." He ran a hand along the mare's jaw.

The horse nickered and turned away.

"Stinky?" Zeke asked. "Me? I knew I needed a shave, but I was under the impression that I smelled like a fresh summer rose. Fine. I will. But you don't need to be rude about it."

Making his way past the other stalls, Zeke poked his head into the front office, which doubled as a bedroom. The old man was not there. His bed was neatly made. Wondering what he should do, Zeke stared into the man's quarters. From behind, a voice made him jump.

"You stink."

Zeke turned and almost put his foot in the path of tobacco juice heading his way. "I am aware, sir. Thank you for so kindly bringing it to my attention. Glad to see you this morning. So hey, thanks for the bed last night. I was wondering if there was anything else I could do for you before I head into town. I was planning to walk around and see about a job. And food."

"Hmm." The white mustache on the man's lip bobbed as if it were continuing the conversation on its own. "I reckon you oughta bring in fresh water for the stock. And when you're through, you can wash yourself in the back room. Miz Helen don't take kindly to men of your type."

Men of my type? He was a type now. Zeke grabbed the man's wrinkled hand and shook it gladly. "Yes sir. I'll do that right away."

Pumping and carrying the water was not difficult work. He finished it quickly and ran to the back room. He was really starting to feel the lack of food gnawing at his middle. Sure enough, waiting for him was a washtub and a bar of soap. The tub was empty. But he knew where to find the water. He filled the tub halfway and sucked in a breath to brave the chilly water. It just took a bit of getting used to. At least that's what he tried to tell himself.

Finding his razor, he did the best he could with his meager bathing arrangement. The harsh soap did a number on his skin, and he nicked himself a couple of times. A rustling noise in the corner brought his attention to a medium-sized black and white dog. It sniffed around his bags and his pile of discarded clothes. "Hey!" Zeke said. "Go on, now!" He whistled, but the dog looked at him unconcerned. Zeke shook a wet hand at him. "Hey, mutt. Get lost! Those things aren't for you."

The dog took one more sniff of his saddlebags, and before Zeke could do anything to stop him, he lifted his leg and relieved himself on Zeke's pile of clothes.

"No!" Zeke yelled as he jumped out of the water. The damage was done. The mutt ran off in a hurry, having done his business. Zeke quickly sorted the pile though the straw and dirt stuck to his wet feet as he shuffled around. Luckily, his trousers were spared, with his vest on the top of the pile getting the worst of it. He tossed it into the tub to soak while he finished dressing.

Finding the cleanest of his three shirts, he dressed carefully. Making a good first impression would be important. He never knew who his next employer might be. Stumbling into town last night the way he did, it was just as well he never made it to a boarding house. If this Helen woman was as strict as Frank suggested, he should meet her on better terms. He wasn't the rugged cowboy type. He was simply tired and dirty and resembled more of a vagabond when he came off the trail. He was still easing into the rugged life of the trail, which was why he had made so many stops across the state. At this rate, it would take him a year to reach the ocean. He would make his way south this fall, if he was still traveling, in order to avoid a snow-covered winter. Rachel Donnely, his adopted sister, had insisted he had too many holes in his plan. She just didn't understand spontaneity and the sense of adventure he felt.

Zeke scrubbed and rinsed the vest and lay it over his pack to dry. Soon, he left the livery with a bounce in his step and a smile on his face, having finished one thing on his to-do list.

A gentle breeze brought attention to the damp brown hair that curled along the nape of his neck as it dried. He felt confident today was going to be a good day. Despite the dog mishap. *Avoid mangy dogs.* His list kept growing. But first, he would find a job and eat food. Real food. Fresh food. Warm food. From an oven.

Stepping outside the livery, he looked across the street and scanned for shops that looked or smelled promising. He stood on the edge of the town square. Four blocks of businesses and a church surrounded a lawn with young trees being well-tended. Someday this square would be completely shaded by the towering evergreens, oaks, and others that had been planted.

The town was awake, and it was glorious to see. The large painted letters over the facade of each business were easy to read from where he stood. He scanned them for a diner. He saw Rose's Mercantile, Anderson's Bakery, Abigail's Dress Shop, and the Sheriff's Office. Looking the other way, he noticed the Smithy down at the end of the block. *Good, I'll go there first thing after breakfast.* Quickly turning back to find food, he collided with another person.

"Ope!" she said.

He'd been so engrossed on his mission to find a place to eat that he hadn't seen or heard her coming. Her shoe was wedged between his boots, and her skirts caught around his legs. He grabbed her arms to keep her from falling as they stumbled a few awkward steps together before gaining their balance. Her wide-brimmed bonnet hid her face.

"Excuse me, ma'am," he said, "I wasn't watching where I was going."

"Never mind. It's my fault. I was preoccupied myself." She dusted her arms and straightened her skirts. Her voice was polite but distracted. As if crashing into him was a mere annoyance. It hadn't upset her, but she didn't look up nor offer more.

"You're not hurt then?" he asked. "I hope I didn't crush your shoe." The brim of her bonnet did its job well; each time he ducked to see her face, she turned her head.

"No, thank you. I'm fine." With a nod of her covered head, she walked on.

He placed his hands on his hips and watched her walk away. There was something about her that tickled him. She walked with a sense of urgency. As if she were trying to get away from something. Or someone. On a whim, he looked behind him. No one was following her. Looking back at her, the blue skirts mesmerized him. *Swish, swish, swish.* Hints of her white petticoat showed from the hemline.

His stomach interrupted. *Food, man.* But just before he turned to go, she stopped. He saw her face as she turned to look back at him. It was the woman from the creek. He didn't recognize her at first, with her hair pulled into a fashionable knot and a bonnet primly tied under her chin. And she was fully dressed. Stockings, shoes, gloves—everything appropriately covered.

A broad smile spread across his face, and he raised a hand to wave, but before he was given the chance, she turned and strode toward the smithy.

She doesn't recognize me. Was this good or bad? Definitely good because now he had the chance to start over. Yet also bad because she'd already caught him ogling her. He had muddled not one but two first impressions.

Either way, it was time for food. Heading the other direction, he followed his nose to Anderson's Bakery.

Chapter 4

Eloise had been prepared to grieve today with her father-in-law, Jacob Davidson. But when she entered the smithy, he welcomed her with a smile.

"Good morning," he said. "I'd hug you, but I'm already covered with the day's soot. How's my favorite toddler? He's not with you?"

"Oh, he's fine. I just needed to get away for a while. You know?"

"Of course, you're welcome here, you know that." He turned back to his work, pulling the rod of iron from the furnace with tongs. The rhythmic pounding of metal on metal rang out.

Eloise retreated to the corner and sat in one of the two chairs near the table. She'd often sat there and watched Philip work. She'd run over after school most afternoons and dally there before school in the early mornings. How many times had they sneaked a kiss in the back office? A picture of them from their wedding still hung in the office where Philip would tally the books. She'd had it framed and given it to him as a special gift after their first month of marriage.

Being here was cathartic sometimes and jarring at others. Familiar and strange. Comforting and painful. Memories of Philip accosted her senses. The sounds, the smells, even the taste of soot and smoke in the air. She saw him everywhere. His smug grin when he knew she was watching him; he was very good at what he did and knew it. Adoration didn't begin to describe what she'd felt for him and his talent. Not surprisingly, Pa turned half of the shop over to him, full partnership. There was plenty of work in town to keep them both busy.

She had been asleep when he'd come over, tossing pebbles at her bedroom window one night. After telling her he owned half the shop, he'd wanted her to come out with him and celebrate, to go swimming of all things. When she wouldn't, he grew angry and called her an old biddy. With Tobias and his wife Katie sleeping the next room over, she knew better than to sneak out. Because she'd shut the window in his face, he didn't speak to her for two days. He ignored her and pretended he didn't see her when she walked by.

Finally, she'd made amends with a basket of Katie's chocolate muffins. He'd brought her behind the shop to talk privately. After apologizing for his behavior, he kissed her for the first time. One kiss led to another—breathtaking kisses that were exciting and new and made her want more and more of him. He shared with her how he was going to build his own smithy someday. His ideas were wonderful, though different than Jacob's for how to grow the business. At the time, she'd thought her heart would burst with love and pride for him. She was ready to marry him then and there.

Sitting here wasn't helping. She snatched the broom from its hook and swept the floor vigorously, being careful of the many customer's tools to be mended that lined the walls and the coal bin that would smudge her dress. The bin had been moved to hide a hole in the wall where Philip had once thrown his hammer in anger. He'd been alone, trying to fix a chain that refused to cooperate.

The hiss of the water brought her attention back to Jacob. He tossed the finished horseshoe into a box of others like it, then looked at her. "Florence and I would like to take Luke fishing. Think Tobias would mind?"

"That would be wonderful. Just let me know when and I'll have him ready. You have to watch him like a hawk near the water, though. He has no fear."

"Oh, I remember how little boys are. Philip was incredible at that age. He just kept walking, even when the water came up to his mouth." Jacob chuckled. "It's like he didn't realize he was the one doing it to himself."

Eloise never knew what to say when Jacob talked about Philip so naturally. But that was one of the reasons she liked to come, to be around someone who knew and loved Philip as much as she did.

Jacob's face brightened when a man walked in behind her. "Eloise," Jacob said, "have you met Mr. Sage? I wanted to introduce you last week at church. Isaac Sage. He will be working with me from now on. Until I fire him or he quits." Both men laughed at the joke.

Mr. Sage had a stocky build with a dark mustache and trim beard. "Glad to meet you," he said. "I've heard good things about you. I was glad to answer Mr. Davidson's ad in the Omaha paper."

Eloise was surprised. "You placed an ad?" she asked Jacob without thinking. He had a right to hire anyone for his shop that he pleased. "Of course. I'm sure you will do well here." She reached to shake Mr. Sage's hand, and that's when she noticed he was wearing an apron she had mended for Philip after he tore it two years ago. Her hands grew clammy, and she forgot what to say. "Excuse me. I need to go." She handed Mr. Sage the broom and fled.

Get a grip, Eloise. It's just an apron. It's just a smithy. She knew that Jacob had not forgotten his son's birthday, but somehow, he was carrying on as if it were any other day. Perhaps she should too. If everyone else was able to live like it was any other spring day, she could too. If she stayed busy, perhaps she wouldn't have time to think about how broken she felt. She had plenty of ironing to do. That could take the rest of the morning. And then she had meals to prepare and regular chores. It wasn't hard to find extra things to do if she looked.

A goofy grin stuck to Zeke's face. Settled at a table near the front window, he felt he'd never been happier. He stared at the feast before him. A cinnamon roll almost too beautiful to cut into, and a pastry the baker called a Swedish cardamom roll lay on his plate. They were smaller than he preferred, so he'd also ordered the open-faced meat and cheese sandwich with sliced boiled eggs.

Something about the first meal off the trail always made him feel giddy—like finding a spring of cold water in the desert. Life was too wonderful for words. His lopsided grin remained, and he drew in a slow and easy breath, savoring the moment.

He sent up a prayer of thanks for his food, for this town, the steaming coffee, washtub and soap, for Frank, and even Frank's tobacco.

Now it was time to eat. He enjoyed every mouthful, appreciating the new flavors. His mother had been a delightful cook. Baking together was a pastime they both enjoyed before she died. Orphaned at twelve, he was old enough to continue experimenting and practicing wherever he found himself living. Cinnamon rolls were always a favorite. They were more of a mess to make and more involved than many other dishes, but the payoff was worth it. As a kid, he flipped through his mother's stack of recipe cards each Saturday and picked the one he wanted to try. She'd ruffle his hair and kiss his cheek, mumbling something about a sweet tooth.

He chuckled slightly, remembering the time they had returned from afternoon chores and the rising dough had more than doubled. He was nine years old. The sticky dough spilled onto the table and then the floor. Mama hadn't chided him or become angry. She froze in the doorway and looked at him in pretend shock.

"Zekey James!" It would have been an obnoxious nickname from anyone but her. "I do believe our dinner is trying to make a run for it. We'll not stand for that in this house." She set down the eggs, and he tossed a load of wood in its box. "You wash up now, and I'll scrape this off the table. Won't tell if you don't." Of course, there was no one to tell. But the two of them ate their fill later with sly grins as if sharing a grand secret. She explained about testing the yeast and the importance of keeping a closer eye on quick-rising dough in warm weather. She was the only kitchen authority he knew, and baking was their specialty. He learned everything she could teach about baking before he was twelve.

With six other children underfoot at the Donnely's, meals had been simpler. Multi-step baking projects were rare and saved for special occasions. Though he yearned for those times when he was allowed to play in the kitchen, as Mrs. Donnely called it, he wasn't often given the opportunity.

Breakfast at Anderson's Bakery was delightful. The roll had a tough outer crust and was glazed with egg whites. The baker knew what he was doing. The Swedish flavors were new to Zeke, but he enjoyed them.

"G'morning, Mr. Anderson," a young boy said. "The boss says he needs whatever you have left from yesterday. An' he needs at least enough for fifteen so's we'll have whatever you got to make up for the rest. You can box 'em, and someone'll fetch 'em later." The boy's head barely surpassed the counter. A glance told Zeke enough about the boy that his heart softened toward him. His trousers were too short. His shoes, though clean, were well worn. His shirt hung out the back as if he'd dressed in a hurry and nobody checked him over before he left the house. One of his suspender straps was twisted. He was eight years old, nine at most.

The graying man behind the counter came around with the fresh tray of cardamom rolls. "The boss beat you to it. He let me know your breakfast was to be added to the order."

Trying not to completely eavesdrop, Zeke was glad not to miss the boy's face when his eyes grew big, and his mouth dropped open.

"One of those?" He looked up into Mr. Anderson's face for reassurance before picking the largest off the tray. "The whole thing?"

An older woman, with a thick halo of white hair pulled into a wild bun, came from the kitchen, drying her hands on her apron. "Morning, Samuel. Hoping we'd see you today. Oscar, get the boy a plate."

Oscar pressed a kiss to the woman's cheek before he stood to his full height with the tray. "Leave him be, Agnes. He's off to school anyhow. He needs a paper sack. No matter how fast he chews, he can't eat that whole thing before the bell." He winked at Samuel. "Don't try it, Sam."

"Yes sir," he said, muffled around a mouthful.

Choking down his own full bite, Zeke remembered his manners and swiped the napkin across his mouth. Subtly watching the scene play out in front of him, he silently sent a prayer of thanks for this couple. It was people like these that helped Zeke get through the years after his mother died. There had always been someone to mentor him, to feed him, to give him work, to teach him new skills. Even after he took off on his own, everywhere he traveled, God sent him a grandma to admonish him about his hair and to remind him to put on clean socks. God knew what little boys needed to thrive. Among other things, like fresh air, frogs, dirt, and cookies—they all needed a grandma.

"Come, Sam." Agnes reached for him and put him to rights. She finger-combed his hair into a presentable state, turned him around to tuck in his tail, unhooked his suspender strap, and fixed the twist. He ignored her while doing his best to eat his breakfast, only scowling at her once when she wet a finger to wipe a smudge from his forehead. She only smiled in return.

Oscar arrived with a paper sack. "Run along now before the school bell catches you late."

"Yes sir." He exited the door and headed down the street, shoving the second half of his roll into the sack.

"Only fifteen this week," Oscar said. "I wonder who's run off this time."

"Uffta," Agnes said, attempting to tame the flyaways from her knot of hair. "I told you the Johnsons were flighty. You put the cheese in his sack for lunch?" She began to rearrange items on the display trays.

"Yes, and the dried apples. I think it was the Johnson brothers. They weren't too keen on working the clay pits from what I heard." Oscar absently wiped the counter with a dry rag.

"Bah! What did they expect? Lazy men get a lazy reward. They won't find better." She picked up the broom and swept the floor behind the counter. "Everyone starts at the bottom. They were only on the job for two weeks."

Zeke noisily cleared his throat. Using the crust of the roll to mop his plate, he took his last bite.

"More coffee?" Oscar asked.

Zeke stood. "No sir. You could help me with something else." Moving toward the counter, he tried to project an air of confidence and humility and topped it off with a friendly smile. Hoping that combination didn't make him look like a loon, his smile slipped. "I came into town last night. I'm searching for temporary work, and

I'd like to get a recommendation for a place to board for a week, if you know of one."

Before he could answer, a town bell tolled the hour. Nine clear notes echoed into the bakery. Outside, a few straggling children were seen sprinting down the street to the schoolhouse. The last sound had just died when a group of women jostled inside. There was a round of "good mornings" and "how d'ya dos" from all parties. Agnes, with coffee in hand, set out plates for the group. All of them were well into their prime, and all had much to discuss. Agnes pulled an extra chair up to them and joined their table, making it an even six. Their hats bobbed as they conversed, clinking their cups on saucers, and stirring with their spoons. The bakery had come alive now that they were there.

The two men stood staring, distracted by the animated way the women moved and flowed as one connected ring of skirts. Agnes lifted her head above the others. Seeing Oscar standing there, she raised her eyebrows and motioned her head toward the kitchen with a jerk.

Muttering something in Swedish under his breath, Oscar scuttled to the kitchen and returned with a tray of cookies. Squeezing through, yet staying as far away from the mass of skirts and bobbing hats as possible, he reached through and miraculously set the plate in the center of their table. Gloved hands descended before Oscar could remove himself. Agnes tugged Oscar's sleeve and whispered in his ear. Zeke didn't miss the smug look on her face.

Oscar returned with an exaggerated shiver before leaning on the counter where Zeke waited. "Barely made it out alive, man. I warn you, never approach a flock of this kind with a plate of cookies unless you have crafted a solid escape. Back to your questions, I gather the brickyard is hiring. Agnes has confirmed the Johnson brothers have left town." Oscar turned his face from the group and took in Zeke's full measure, weighing him against something or someone. Zeke tried not to squirm as much as the look made him feel uncomfortable. "Now, about you. What brings you through?"

"Just going where the wind blows," said Zeke, who was able to breathe again. "Currently, it's blowing west."

"Leaving family?"

Zeke hedged, never sure how much to share. Was the man asking because he really wanted to know, or just making pleasantries? The baker had no business poking into Zeke's personal life. He found it best to avoid direct conversations regarding his past, unless he was asked a specific question he couldn't get around. Nobody knew how to respond when given the truth. He didn't want their pity, and yet, it felt dishonorable to his mother to simply brush off the grief. For countless other men his age, the West was full of promise and adventure. The wind could blow him there as well as anywhere else. Whether or not he had family.

"No sir," he finally answered. "No family."

Oscar's gaze pierced through him.

Zeke felt guilty for a lie he hadn't told. He hadn't left his family behind. Not really. Rachel Donnely could nag all she wanted, but he was free to go where he pleased. He would always be grateful to Mr. and Mrs. Donnely for taking him in when he needed a home. But he was a grown man now. The West called, and he could go if he had a mind to. Rachel would be alright. She just worried too much.

"You look strong." Whether Oscar meant physically or mentally, Zeke didn't know. He didn't feel either at the moment. "The brickyard could always use a strong back. Especially so today. As for boarding, the best you can find would be Helen's. She runs the Palmer Boarding House with her daughter. They've usually got a handful of men underfoot. If she's got an open room, you'd be wise to take it. Her rules are strict. She doesn't put up with rowdy behavior. If you keep clean and never tramp your muddy boots through the house, you'll be all right. If she's full, there's the hotel on the side of the square, or the saloon has rooms for rent above the bar. But I don't recommend staying there."

Zeke grunted. He did not wish to stay there. A man could get into a lot of trouble in a place like that if he wasn't careful.

"You say you came in last night?"

"Yup."

"Did you meet Frank? At the livery?"

"Yup."

Oscar tilted his head. "You had coin for it?"

"Nope."

The answer ignited a full belly chuckle from Oscar.

Zeke smiled. "Have I missed the joke?"

"Good ol' Frank. He's the town sieve." He slapped Zeke's back, "Any man who comes through looking scruffy gets the Frank treatment. From looking at you, you must have worked your keep. Cold washtub this morning?"

"How'd you guess?" Zeke rubbed a hand along his nicked chin.

"It's his gift to the town in a way. Though it does get him a morning off work." Oscar chuckled again. "Well done." He offered his hand. "Oscar Anderson. Pleased to meet you."

"Ezekiel James. Friends call me Zeke."

"Zeke. You head that-a-way, and you'll see Helen's place. Palmer Boarding House. You tell her you had breakfast with Oscar and bunked with Frank, and you won't have any trouble. The boss will be 'round later this morning. I'll tell him you were inquiring. Temp job or no, any man with a strong back can work in the pit."

"Where is the brickyard?" asked Zeke, trying not to think of what working in the pit might entail.

"Southwest, you can see the kiln chimneys from the edge of town."

Zeke hitched his trousers around his waist and settled his hat back on his head. "Thank you, sir. You've been most helpful."

The bell above the door jingled when he left. In a hurry to get settled and locate the boarding house, he didn't notice the woman in his path until he crashed into her for the second time that morning.

Chapter 5

The bell jingled only a moment before Eloise found herself entangled. She stumbled and almost fell. Her hands flew to brace herself as a pair of strong arms wrapped around her. A mess of arms and legs too close together searched for space. She gained her footing, but the man held her close. It lasted only a second. A second too long. Long enough for her to catch a whiff of horse, barn, soap, and coffee. A familiar and comforting combination. The strength of him fully surrounded her as they mumbled apologies.

Eloise looked into his face. *Not him again!*

Quickly, she pushed away and hid her face beneath her bonnet. If only she could shrink into it completely and avoid confrontation. Keeping her eyes down, she saw two black handprints on the front of his shirt. She'd not paused to wash the soot from her hands or retrieve her gloves after meeting Isaac in her rush back to Helen's. There was no helping it now.

Serves him right for bursting out of Anderson's without looking. Again! Perhaps the blame did not fall only on him. Walking briskly with her head down, shielded by her bonnet, she had only been focused on her next step. *After all, it's the only way to get anywhere in this town without being forced to stop and smile at every passerby.* But to run into this man twice in the same day? The same hour. *It's completely his fault that he has soot marks on his shirt . . . even if they were put there by my hands.*

"Pardon me." She sidestepped to continue on her way.

He moved and blocked her path.

The nerve of this man! "I'm sorry. Did you need something?" She did not look up at his face. Sucking in a breath, she let it out in a huff. She counted to ten. Slowly at first, then rushing to the end. Honestly, how long did he plan to hold her hostage? Chancing a peek at him, she lifted her eyes to meet his.

He was grinning. A big stupid grin. As if he were the only one in on a joke, and he wasn't sharing.

"Hi, Chipmunk," he said. "Remember me?" He stepped aside but leaned his head to catch her eyes under the brim of her bonnet and refused to let her look away. Most people ignored her. They were used to her avoidance by now and let her be.

"Of course I remember you." *Did he call me a chipmunk?* "We met an hour ago in front of the livery. You have a habit of plowing into people. Now, if you'll let me pass." A fresh cut on his forehead puckered red with faint bruising surrounding it. Realization hit her like a rock. *Oh! Oh, no. He is the stranger from the creek.*

The one who fell and the one she thought she would never have to see again. The one she dreaded would ever see her again. Especially after giving him those false directions into town. If he had only listened! He should have been in Hadley Springs or past it by now. He would be gone forever, and she would never have to think of it, or him, again. Why was he here? How was he here, looking at her with his strong green eyes and his indecent grin? Warmth ran down her neck at the remembrance of their improper meeting.

"You look . . . clean," she managed to say.

"As do you."

That stupid grin of his. There was nothing funny about any of this. This man had all but seen her naked. There wasn't a man alive who had seen that much of her. He stood there smiling, rocking back on his boot heels, waiting for something, but what? She didn't know.

He did look clean today. And different somehow. He looked . . . nice. She knew from the heat pulsing in her ears that he was witnessing her face turn red. "Yes, well, I need to be going. Good day." *And goodbye.* She stepped around him. He let her pass this time. Thank goodness for that; she was in no mood for games. Keeping her eyes off the ground, she took measured steps, hyper-aware of being watched. She would not run. She would not appear to be at fault. She was guilty of nothing.

Goodness, what would Jessica say now? She would ask again about his looks. Dashing? Rugged? Dangerous?

No. Mischievous and smirky.

Good looking?

No.

Perhaps.

It was hard to say; she was so distracted. She lifted her hand to fan her face but shot it down again when she realized what she was doing. The heat she felt stemmed from her embarrassment, not his dashing appearance. If one were to go as far to describe him as such. He looked worlds better than yesterday. Yesterday, he was a dirty mess, covered in dust from the trail with sand in his hair from the tumble off the bank. The blood mixing with the dirt on his face had not been an image that brought girlish fancies to her mind—or heart.

No.

He was not handsome. Was he? Good grief, she didn't care! Jessica would find out for herself soon enough, and best of luck to her. Regardless, Eloise slowed her walk and glanced behind, then whirled her head back to the front and sucked in her breath. He was following her.

Ignore him? Confront him? Step into the next shop and pray for him to pass by?

He made the decision for her. The *thump* of his boots sounded lightly over the few paces he jogged to catch up with her. As much as she wished to avoid this man, there was not to be an easy escape today.

"I hear there's a respectable boarding house this way. May I walk with you?"

She simply nodded and kept moving down the walk. But she picked up her pace. *Two blocks.* She could be polite for two blocks, and then she could be rid of him.

He kept talking. "I'm new in town. Just rode in last night."

So he thinks he's funny. He wanted to make small talk, but she was never good at pleasantries. Often, she said too much or not enough. *Suppose I ignore him. He might forget all about me. Of course, that would never work. He was looking for lodging at Jessica's house. Oh, why didn't he keep riding? If only men would listen! He would have been far, so very far away by now. Uffda, why did I leave the house today?*

She blurted out the first thing that came to mind. "Did you meet Frank?" Sneaking another glance, she saw his grin disappear in a hurry. What a stupid thing for her to say. "At the livery? Frank owns the livery. You have a horse, yes? I thought you would have a horse."

"I have a horse. Suzy Girl. She is quite faithful. Honest. You know? She can be a little ornery at times, but I never question her intentions." He matched his steps to her increasing pace. "You always walk this fast?"

Self-conscious now, she slowed and let him set the pace. What were two blocks?

"A funny thing happened yesterday," he said. "Suzy Girl and I were riding along, minding our own business. When we came across—"

"I'd rather not speak of it," Eloise said.

"—a baby playing in the creek. He wasn't alone, of course. No, of course not. Everyone knows it's dangerous to let a baby play alone in the water. You never know what might happen. No, ma'am. He wasn't alone. This was wonderful news for me because, you see, I'd been lost on the prairie for three days. Though I suppose, 'lost' is a relative word. I had water and the sun. Eventually, I would have found the ocean, perhaps a town or two and a crust of bread in the meantime. But I was desperate for guidance. You can imagine my gratitude when a chipmunk pointed me in the direction of a town. Or so I believed. I had no reason to suspect that I was merely being sent on a goose hunt. And to my knowledge, April is a terrible time of year for hunting geese."

Eloise stopped abruptly. Boldly, for her, she stared at him, prepared to give him a strong piece of her mind. Though his grin was gone. It had been replaced with a hardness she hadn't expected to see from his light tone. She said nothing as she locked eyes with him, but her heart sped up, and she could feel it clawing at her chest. Her rebuttal died on her tongue.

She envied his strength. Reason warned her to be cautious, but oddly she felt no fear. Harm would have come to her yesterday if he was of ill intent. She shouldn't have lied to him. She knew that, but was he so very angry? *Does he think I lied spitefully?* Of course he would be angry. Words of apology caught in her throat. Lowering her gaze, she found herself looking at the buttons on his shirt. One stood out particularly. A different color of thread had been used to attach it. A repair. Such a small hint at who he was. Yet it made her feel less awkward; it reminded her that he was just a man trying to make his way in the world too. A man who had buttons fall off his shirt, like any other person.

"Miss? Is something wrong?" He reached out as if to grasp her elbow but stopped. His hand remained suspended in the air.

"I'm sorry," she said. Getting the words out first and quickly was always the most efficient way to move on from these situations. Waiting for Philip to apologize had been like waiting for the snow to melt in January.

"What for?" He shifted from one foot to the other, and she noticed his grin was back. "For my pleasant bed of straw, for my lack of fried chicken dinner, or for supplying me with ten horse stalls to muck out with no pay this morning. For which of those would you like to take responsibility?"

She shook her head. *Fried chicken?* Stilling her nerves, she answered. "I'm sorry for giving you misleading directions. For lying. But I meant no real harm. If you had kept going the way I suggested, there would have been a town . . . just not . . . this one." Sucking in her lower lip, she replayed her apology in her mind, wringing her hands. After all, he had been the one to ogle her in the creek. What more could he expect?

He rubbed his chin. "I told Suzy it wasn't a bridge," he mumbled.

Maybe it was the fresh shaving nick on his chin, maybe it was the bruise on his forehead from a fall she had inadvertently caused, or maybe it was the way his expression transformed from disgruntlement to compassion, but she found herself wanting to reach out and straighten his crooked shirt collar. *Stop staring at his shirt.* She offered a smile. "Hadley Springs is a lovely town another seven miles west."

He laughed. "Fair enough." His coffee-brown hair fell into his eyes. He lifted the corner of his Stetson and combed it back under his hat, offering a half-smile, "After all, you can't be too careful these days. I could have been anyone. Standing up there on the bank while you were, down there, less than—"

Her hand flashed to cover his mouth on its own accord. "Don't speak of it!"

Blocking her hand, he laughed and skipped out of her reach. His grin was back in full force, causing her cheeks to turn a beet red.

"And what if I do?" he asked, teasing. "There's no harm in having a freckle above your ankle."

"Why!" Eloise was stunned. She spied a pair of men across the road. Otherwise, the area was clear of people. Still, she lowered her voice. "Hold your tongue! If you ever speak of this to anyone, honestly, I'll . . . I'll . . ." She shook her head frantically.

"Woah! Hold it." He leaned toward her and put his finger to his lips. "If you ever, and I mean, ever, tell anyone that I slipped and fell off a creek bank and landed on my head . . . I will deny it to my dying breath. Are we clear?"

Now it was her turn to laugh.

"Shall we?" He motioned down the boardwalk.

"I'm on my way to Helen's. I can show you the way." She was overly conscious of him beside her. He'd seen enough of her to notice the freckle on her ankle. And what a silly thing for her to say. *Show you the way.* Like the man couldn't walk two blocks on his own? She could have pointed: *That way.* She reasoned he could use directional help. After all, what kind of a man loses track of a railroad? With homesteads every half-mile scattered through the county, she was always surprised to hear of wayward travelers. Nevertheless, walking beside him through town was unnecessary.

He, on the other hand, appeared to be perfectly at ease. He swung his arms comfortably and kept his pace measured to hers. The *click* of her heels sounded too loud next to the deeper *thump* of his boots.

She raised her eyes up the street and took in as much of the sky as she could see over the town. It was beautiful, as always. She had that at least. There wasn't a cloud in sight. Just solid bright blue in every direction. So open and free.

"Big sky you have here," he said.

"It's just the sky. It's always big."

"Not like this." He waved a hand up and around.

Her gaze followed.

"Have you always lived here?"

"Yes, I was born here, barely. We were one of the first families." His green eyes were so vivid. His patient smile compelled her to keep talking, "When I was a child, my family used to visit the Platte River during the summer. And I've traveled by train to the State Fair three times, once each in Omaha, Nebraska City, and Lincoln."

"The sky is smaller where I'm from," he said.

She let out a small laugh. Despite their undesirable meetings, she began to relax. A little. "I don't know how that could be true. It can't be any bigger or smaller anywhere on this earth." They had reached Helen's and stopped in front of the porch.

"Someday, when you've traveled outside of Nebraska, we can have this conversation. Until then, you'll just have to trust me."

"Explain yourself." She surprised herself by her own audacity to keep the conversation going. "If the sky is big here, how can it possibly be smaller where you're from?"

"There are too many trees in West Virginia. The sky has to fight for everything it's got. We have so many trees that you have to find a lake to know if the sun is coming up or going down. I used to climb on top of the house and push the branches out of the way just to check if it was going to rain."

She squinted at him. "I don't believe you."

"It's true! Okay, mostly true. The sky has more room to play here. It sure likes to show off when it can. Just trust me, West Virginia has a few things going for it, but the sky is smaller." He shrugged, so matter of fact, and then he winked. "I'd like to hear more about your State Fair."

Her heart leaped in her chest, not in a pleasant way. It was the slam of the deadbolt locking back into place, reminding her of who she was. That it was Philip's birthday. That he was gone and was never coming back. Not that she deserved any better. If she had been a better wife, and less selfish, he would still be here.

He held out his hand to her. "Ezekiel James. My friends call me Zeke." His warm hand held hers firmly and his steady eyes never left hers. A genuinely friendly smile graced his face. But he didn't know. He couldn't. If he had known about her, he wouldn't be wasting his time on her.

Everybody knew who she was. She could only imagine what they said about her when she wasn't around, which was most of the time. It was her fault her husband was dead and would forever be her fault. There was no going back or changing anything.

Ezekiel James. My friends call me Zeke.

He raised his eyebrows. "And you are . . . ?"

"Oh!" She startled. "El-Eloise Davidson." The wind gusted at that moment and blew her skirts around and tousled her bonnet. She pulled her hand away from his and tucked her hair back into place as best she could, and was reminded of her soiled hands. She wiped them together, attempting to remove any extra soot. It was useless. She stole a glance at his chest that bore the marks of two distinct handprints.

Zeke wanted to keep her talking and find out everything. What made a girl like her laugh, and what made her stop in her tracks and apologize for having done nothing but try to protect herself? Despite her reservations, she had spunk, though her whole countenance suddenly changed. She'd gone from aloof to a weary sadness. He could not figure her out, but he wanted to.

The gold of a wedding band glinted in the sunshine. Zeke studied the simple gold band while she held her wayward hair in place against the wind.

Married.

Disappointment stabbed his gut. It was odd that he would feel that way, or feel anything, for that matter. The fact came as a surprise that he cared one way or another about her marital status. What did it matter if Chipmunk, *Mrs. Eloise Davidson,* was married? Good for her. He had spent five minutes with her. And another five yesterday, but they weren't talking about that. He grinned at her.

Ockelbo was just a stop on the road. Just a dot on a map. Not even a noteworthy landmark. A means for him to find work, and cash, and food for the next section of his journey. Nothing more. Certainly not a place to get attached to someone, especially one who didn't even like him. *Especially one who was married.* All this silly talk about the sky was ridiculous. Still, she was sharp-witted and clever. He sure hadn't minded passing the time with her.

Zeke observed the house where they'd stopped, a two-story white wooden house. A large sign hung from the porch.

Palmer Boarding House

Respectable Guests Only

No Drunkards

He motioned to the sign. "Think I'll pass the entrance exam? I'm generally a respectable person. Most often." He was stalling. "Suzy Girl is available as a character reference, but unless Mrs. Palmer speaks horse . . ." He didn't want to go in. *Zeke, you're an idiot. Making friends with a married woman is a fool's errand.* And yet, he lingered.

She was cautious and closed up, and he wanted her to smile and laugh a little more. He wanted to tell her everything would be okay. Though he knew absolutely nothing about the *everything.* Maybe he had misjudged her. She was just wary of strangers, that was all. But no, there was something else about her that puzzled him. Something secret just below the surface. Not likely anything she would share with a complete stranger. His conscience stabbed him for lingering. He'd wanted to keep her talking, but she wasn't taking the bait. He knew horse jokes were a stretch, but he gave himself credit for trying. Following her gaze to his shirt, he saw two black handprints smudged on his chest.

"Woah!" He laughed. Looking at his own hands, he found soot on his right palm.

She lifted her eyes to meet his and wrinkled her nose. Shrugging an apology, she turned up the palms of her hands to show him.

"You did this?" He grabbed one of her hands and placed it on his chest. "Look at that. Perfect fit."

She slipped her hand away. "I've been at the smithy. Forgot to wash before I left. A terrible habit."

Secrets indeed. "You work at a smithy?"

She smiled, though it was only in her mouth. The sadness did not leave her eyes. "My father-in-law owns it. I stop in when I can to help out now that, um . . . now that he works alone. Sweeping and such."

The thumb of her right hand massaged circles into the other. As if that would clear away the soot. She sniffed and blinked back tears.

Oh, no. What had he done now?

His mother used to cry over the oddest things. Especially after his father died. A poem about a butterfly once choked her up. Tears didn't bother him, much. Girls would be girls. There were no butterflies presently, so this must be something else. Not knowing what else to do, he found his navy-colored handkerchief and offered it. "A little dirt never hurt anything. Here, let me." He gently took her hands in his and wiped them. Not much soot came off.

Zeke thought of Rachel and the particularly slow way she used to dismount from the wagon. He missed her. There was no hurrying Rachel, and she insisted that he stand patiently with his hand supporting hers until she was fully on solid ground. She would straighten her skirts and hat and double-check that she had everything she needed. And only then would she squeeze his hand and say, "Thank you, dear." As if he had done her a grand favor. Funny that holding her hand used to be such a chore, and yet, how he missed it.

The gold band on Mrs. Davidson's finger could not be ignored. "Your husband doesn't work at the smithy?"

Her hands stiffened, and she looked up at him. Her whole body went rigid as an array of emotions played across her face. His question had struck a chord. She pulled her hands away. But he held tight to one and wrapped her fingers around the handkerchief, offering it to her.

"No." Holding in her breath, she pulled at the kerchief, wrapping it around and around her hand in one direction, and then twisting it back in the other.

The screen door slammed. "Ellie! Hi! Who's your friend?" A young woman came skipping down the steps with a packet of letters in her hand.

Chipmunk startled and stepped away from him as if she had been caught sneaking cookies before dinner. At least, that's something he would get caught with.

"I saw you from the parlor, thought you were on your way in. Gave up waiting on you."

A blush covered Chipmunk's cheeks. He watched the flush travel even to her ears and down her neck. Was she thinking of their first meeting? When she looked at him, he barely shook his head, then winked at her. Her eyes widened, and he struggled to keep a straight face.

"Jess, this is—" She swallowed. "Mr. Ezekiel James. He's new. In town. I was showing him where to find a decent room to rent. Mr. James, meet Jessica Palmer. But I wasn't sure if you had a vacancy? Weren't you just telling me earlier that you had filled all the rooms this week?"

Miss Palmer approached Chipmunk with a smile and wiggled her eyebrows. "Oh no, we've room. Any friend of Eloise is a friend of ours."

Zeke offered his hand. "Please. Call me Zeke. My friends do. Mrs. Davidson and I were just discussing the State Fair."

"What fun!" Miss Palmer said. "Our fathers always went together and let us tag along for the adventure. They were always interested in new equipment. We were only girls the last time we went. What were we? Ten? Nine? No matter, it wasn't much fun, all told. A crowd of men all excited over a threshing machine isn't my cup of tea. But I suppose there is always something pleasant to do if you look for it. And the excitement of traveling by train. I daresay it's improved since then. Did you come by train, Mr. James?"

"I did not." Zeke looked at Chipmunk and cleared his throat. "I have a horse. She's with Frank. I may leave by train, but I have business in town first."

"What sort of business? Pardon me, but you don't look like a regular business-type man," Miss Palmer said.

Her mouth ran faster than the train, that was for sure. Zeke smiled pleasantly. "You're very right, Miss Palmer. My business includes taking care of a few basic necessities, namely a new shoe for the horse and restocking for my trip west."

"Excuse me," Eloise said. "I must see about Luke." Without a backward glance, she hurried up the steps and into the house.

He found himself staring after her. A cough from Miss Palmer brought his attention back to her.

"What happened here?" She twirled a finger at him, pointing to the handprints on his shirt. He looked down and grunted.

He would have to do something about that.

Chapter 6

Eloise found Luke in the kitchen. He sat on a stool playing with a handful of dough while Helen bustled around the kitchen. "I don't know how you get him to sit for you," Eloise said. "I feel I spend my whole day keeping him out of trouble."

Helen wiped her hands on her apron. "You just have to outthink them. No, baby, don't eat that," she said, gently wiping Luke's chin of the dough he spit out. "You bring him over any time. We'll find something to do together."

While Eloise scrubbed the soot off her hands, Luke scrambled off his chair and approached her.

"Bye!" he said to Helen. But once wasn't enough.

"Bye!"

"Bye!"

"Bye!"

"Bye!"

"Come on, you." Eloise took his hand and led him back through the house, calling her own goodbye to Helen.

Zeke was just entering and held the door for her on her way out. She nodded her thanks but otherwise avoided him. She couldn't believe she had almost cried right in front of him. What was wrong with her today? Who knows what she would have said or done if Jessica hadn't come out when she did. What must he think of her? Thankfully, he would be gone in a few days, and it wouldn't matter.

Since she had nothing besides the ironing waiting for her at home, she accompanied Jessica to the post office. Walking through town at a toddler's pace was about as much leisure as she could ask for today.

"Well," Jessica said. "He is not what I had in mind. He's sort of skinny, don't you think?"

"I hadn't noticed." Eloise had noticed his green eyes and the warmth from his hands as they held hers. She'd noticed his hair was still damp and the strength of his arms when they'd wrapped around her. She'd felt his energy in the easy way he conversed and the way he carried himself. She had noticed many things. Skinny? No, she hadn't noticed that.

"His buck teeth are awful," Jessica said. "Gives his whole face a terrible slant. No wonder you ran away."

"What?" Eloise was shocked. "His face is perfect."

Jessica laughed, and Eloise clicked her tongue, knowing she'd fallen too easily into her friend's trap.

"Okay, very funny," Eloise said. "Now, will you let it rest? So he's got a great face. So does Tobias, and nobody's making a fuss over him."

"I'd check your facts, ma'am. I know of at least one person who's been taking an interest. You can't ignore Maribeth any longer, you know. Just accept that they're sparking, and you'll find her to be a very nice girl."

"I know, I know. Tobias has been incredible about the whole thing, letting me brood about it on my own time. But I should go talk to her soon. She probably thinks I'm an old goat. I just don't know what I'll do with myself when he remarries, and Luke isn't mine anymore."

"You think it's inevitable?"

"I do. If I know my brother at all, he's completely enamored."

"Well, it wouldn't be a sin if you were to smile at a man every now and again. If Tobias remarries, there are other options for you."

"There are other ways of living besides marriage."

"Oh yes, very pleasant ways. You can move in with Mother and me and keep house for ten men instead of one. And not a one of them will kiss you goodnight."

"Fine." Eloise surprised them both.

"Fine? Fine, what?"

"Fine! I will smile."

"Oh my, Eloise. We need to mark this day in the books." Jessica grabbed her arm and pulled her to a stop. "You are aware that this involves making eye contact, yes?"

Eloise huffed at Jessica and pulled away. But she thought of Tobias and how often he came home whistling and the frequent handwritten notes that he thought she didn't see. Her brother was thoughtful of her feelings, but she could not continue to ignore the presence of Maribeth and the looming truth that he would remarry. Living as a guest in a new sister-in-law's house is not what she wanted.

"I will smile and talk politely with the next man we meet. Will that please you?"

Jessica stared at her with furrowed brows and gave her a curt nod. "It doesn't count if he's old or ugly."

"Not Frank?"

"Not Frank."

They linked arms and watched Luke march on ahead of them.

"Roy?" Eloise asked, smirking at Jessica.

"Now you're just being mean. If you dare lay a claim on him, I'll disown you as a friend forever. I know the man is clueless, but one of these days, he will look up and see me. And Lord help me if you're in the way."

"Everybody sees you, Jess. Do you ever wonder if he's not interested?"

"Thus do I pine, El. Thus do I pine."

Eloise began Shakespeare's sonnet for her. "So are you to my thoughts as food to life; Or as sweet season'd showers are to the ground."

Jessica sighed. "I'm sorry. You don't have to do anything you don't want to do, just because I bullied you. But have you considered a certain man who just checked into town? It could be great practice. After all, he's leaving in a few days, so what's a smile and bit of eye contact going to hurt?"

Eloise surprised them both. "He's not old."

Jessica smiled. "El, he's also far from ugly. And besides, you've already marked him." She licked her lips and widened her eyes.

"That was his fault." Eloise cast her eyes down, hiding her face. "Serves him right for barreling out the door like a child." She patted Jess's arm that was linked with hers, "Deal's a deal." Grasping Luke's hand firmly, she helped him navigate around a hitching post, where he wanted to stop and play.

Where did this bravado originate? Her instincts told her to crawl into a hole and never come out, but she yearned to run away and be rid of the chains that dragged her back to the cemetery. She was a prisoner possessing the key to her own cell. It was safe here. Nobody hurt her here.

Something about Zeke tempted her to keep the door propped open . . . just a little. Just in case. Was it because he had already caught her in a vulnerable situation? Why would that make her feel safe?

Eloise broke from Jessica to catch Luke a moment before he walked into the street. "No." She pointed a finger at his nose. "You will stay with Aunt Ellie."

"I'll be right back," Jess said over her shoulder and hustled into the post office.

Luke stuck out his lower lip and buried his head in Eloise's shoulder.

Zeke rolled his shoulders and reminded himself that he was a grown man. He wasn't used to being coddled. Helen had ushered him into the house, and within minutes, adopted him as another one of her boys, offering him food and showing him a room. She sent him to the brickyard with a basket of cold ham and biscuits to meet the boss. A homelike boarding house was comforting, but if she tried to tuck him in at night, he'd be out the door before morning.

Down the street, he saw Chipmunk squatting in front of the toddler, shaking her finger at his nose. He pulled away from her and tried to step into the street. She yanked him back and set him firmly on the boardwalk. He cried and made another run for the street.

Miss Palmer came out of the post office and rescued the boy from further discipline. She picked up the child, and when he pointed to the street, she took him there, allowing him to choose a few pebbles before joining his mother who stood with hands on her hips shaking her head.

When Miss Palmer saw Zeke, she pointed him out to the others and waved. Evidently, the apple didn't fall far. He'd only spent a few moments with her and her mother, but there was no mistaking her energetic personality traits. Joyful abandon. Her smile was big enough to show all her teeth, and her wave would have signaled him a mile away. *What interesting people there are here.*

Miss Palmer called out to him as he neared. "Hello again!" She was exuberant, and yet, it failed to hold his attention. He found quiet chipmunks much more interesting at present.

Mrs. Davidson's soft demeanor was in stark contrast to her friend's. She returned his smile and cast her eyes down, her cheeks turning pink. He'd need to be careful with this one. He glanced at the gold band on her finger to remind himself.

"Mr. James, I see my mother is sending you with a peace offering. I'd recognize that tea towel anywhere." She handed Luke over as he lunged for his mother. "Off to meet Boss?"

"Please, call me Zeke." He tipped his hat at the ladies. "I am on my way to the brickyard, yes. Does the man not have a name? You're the third, no, fourth, this morning to mention him. One whisper of the brickyard and me needing work, and all I hear is Boss, Boss, Boss. Makes me wonder what I'm getting into."

Chipmunk laughed at his question—a soft sound—and hitched the boy higher on her hips.

"You've nothing to worry about," Miss Palmer answered. "Eloise and I call him Tobias. But to many around town, even those he doesn't employ, he's Boss." Miss Palmer hardly stopped for a breath. "He took over the brickyard at nineteen. Took over for his father after he died. We had a great many die that year of a terrible fever. Anyhow, the name started as a joke since he was so young, but when he filled the role better than they bargained for, it stuck. We're used to it now."

"I was strapped to a plow in Iowa at nineteen. The oxen didn't even listen to me. I'm lucky if my horse listens to me."

The toddler wanted down. She let him but held tightly to his hand. He tugged at her, walking in front and then behind. Chipmunk easily transferred her hands on his as he walked circles around her. He hid his face in her skirts and then peered at Zeke, playing his own game of peek-a-boo.

Zeke squatted in front of the boy. "And what's your name? I'm Ezekiel James, but my friends call me Zeke."

"This is Luke," Chipmunk said. "He's not yet two. But he sure keeps us hopping."

"Hello, Luke." Zeke offered his hand.

Luke held out a fist to Zeke, showing what was in his hand. "Rock," he said before he swung his arm back and threw it at Zeke's face.

"Ope! Luke, no!" Chipmunk yanked Luke backward and pulled him into her arms. Her face flushed red. She scolded Luke for his behavior, all the while avoiding eye contact with Zeke.

Luke fidgeted in her arms, fighting to be put down.

Zeke only laughed, rubbing his forehead. "It's alright, Mrs. Davidson. Sometimes first impressions are hard to forget."

She flashed her eyes at him in warning, which only made him laugh harder. She jutted out her chin and pierced him with a glare, as if he were the misbehaving toddler, and added a subtle shake of her head.

Miss Palmer raised her eyebrows, but if she and Chipmunk were as good of friends as he guessed, she would soon hear the whole story, if she hadn't already. Girls were like that. Nothing was kept quiet for long.

"Ladies, g'day to you." He grinned. It shouldn't be this much fun, or easy, to make her blush.

"We'll walk with you." Miss Palmer made eyes with Mrs. Davidson. "Right, El? We have nothing else urgent. Besides, Luke likes to watch the boys work and see his dada."

Mrs. Davidson avoided Zeke. He knew he ought to decline. He'd made her blush enough for one day. Especially if *Mr.* Davidson was apparently at the brickyard too. "I'm sure I can find my way."

"Nonsense!" Miss Palmer said. "It's no trouble at all. In fact, we were going to El's house, and it's practically on the way. Eloise? Don't you agree?" Her direct statement could not be ignored.

Chipmunk tore her face from the toddler, but her eyes still didn't quite meet his. It was comical. Would they ever move on from that first encounter? *Not if I don't stop bringing it up.* And it didn't matter. He was leaving in a few days. As long as he stayed out of trouble with her husband before then.

"Of course," Chipmunk said. "We'd love to go with you." But she turned and walked away with Luke's hand in hers.

Miss Palmer fell in line next to him, and the four slowly made their way through the edge of town. Their pace was set by toddler legs. Miss Palmer pointed out everything of possible interest. She told him the names of the shop owners, what items were sold where, and the best places to get what. She even told him interesting snippets about those they passed along the way. Her chatter, though lively, did not interest him.

He absently watched the way Luke held tight two of Mrs. Davidson's fingers. He watched her thumb rub the back of the chubby hand. If Miss Palmer weren't here, would she have stopped to talk to him again? She had friends, she had a son, and she appeared to be in good health. He wondered why she was so reserved. Maybe he was reading more into the situation than he should have. Replaying their earlier conversations, he felt sure she would be easy to converse with if she would relax. Why did he get the feeling there was more to be discovered?

Once, he and Rachel were out exploring along the back acres of the forest when they'd discovered a cave. It wasn't big, and it didn't go far, but it was enough for a fourteen-year-old boy to feel like he'd found something worth finding. They'd excitedly shown it to Rachel's younger siblings, and over the next few years, it had been filled with a number of playthings, including cracked cups and grass-woven rugs. The boys had gathered large rocks for seats and marked the walls with chalk, and the girls kept it decorated with flowers and whatnot.

After he and the Donnely family moved to Iowa, they talked fondly of that cave and hoped more children would find it, especially since they had left it fully furnished. He wondered if animals had taken residence there before children reclaimed it.

He realized Miss Palmer had stopped talking. He glanced at her. She raised her eyebrows at him, expecting an answer. What had she asked? *Where are you from?*

"West Virginia," he answered, relieved she hadn't caught him too distracted.

She smiled and nodded. "Of course." Suddenly, she called ahead. "El! I need to borrow Luke. I promised we'd look at the toy trains. We'll catch up." She snatched Luke and walked into the apothecary, leaving the two of them stranded outside.

Zeke stood for a moment, unsure of what to do. He had the urge to offer his arm but knew that was inappropriate. How did one walk through town with a married woman that you saw in her unmentionables yesterday? *You don't, Zeke. You run away.*

She reached a hand toward the basket he carried. "May I?"

"This? I won't have a lady troubling herself on my account." He resumed walking nonchalantly, swinging his arms as if it were the most natural thing for a grown man to be carrying a feminine basket down the street. Neither of them spoke for a while.

"Anyhow, purple is growing on me," he eventually said, breaking the silence that Miss Palmer had not allowed. Chipmunk matched his stride, making up time now that they weren't hobbled by a toddler. Above, a hawk floated on the high winds, searching for breakfast—or perhaps out for fun.

"Lavender," she said.

"Lavender what?"

"The tea towel." She motioned to the basket. "Lavender. Not purple."

"This isn't purple?" He raised the basket, holding it with both hands in front of him.

"No."

He watched her, undecided if she was trying to pick a fight or making a joke. He couldn't see her face. The bonnet did its job very well. "Light purple then. Would that be fair?"

"I'd allow it," she said. "But it's risky. Would you say pink is a light red?"

He laughed. "Risky is okay with me. I'm an adventurer, after all."

Stifled laughter came from her, ending in a muffled snort when she covered her mouth with her hands. This was not the same blushing chipmunk he'd run into this morning. Her burst of humor surprised him. But that bonnet! Why did she insist on hiding her face? He skipped ahead and walked backward to face her. A smirk still lingered, though she cast her eyes away from his.

"What's so funny?" He kept up his backward stride.

"Do most adventurers make a habit of tumbling headfirst into creeks?"

"Aha! They do when accosted by fair maidens armed with all manner of pebbles. And babies."

She flashed him a smile. "Do most adventurers lose their way and require directional assistance of fair maidens?"

"Could be. How many adventurers have you met?" He tripped and high stepped into a backward jog to cover for it.

She rolled her eyes at him—a childish gesture that made him laugh. "Turn around. I don't want to watch you fall again."

He did, though he missed her face. There was much more to her than she let on in her words. It was hard to read her without seeing her face.

"So, West Virginia?" she asked.

"Born and raised."

"Do most adventures leave their bags in West Virginia?"

He was stumped. "What? No, I left my things in the stall next to Suzy Girl."

"Jessica asked where you left them since you didn't have anything with you when you checked in. You said they were in West Virginia."

He smacked his palm to his forehead. "I didn't!"

"You did." She turned her face to his and smiled. "I gather you're the easily distracted type of adventurer?"

"You've pegged me."

"Mr. James, how did—"

"Zeke," he said.

"Very well." The boardwalk ended as they left the square and continued through town.

He held the basket in the crook of his arm and peeked into it, digging under the towel. "How did I what?"

"I don't remember."

He smiled. "Now who's distracted, Chipmunk?"

They were still walking down Main Street but had left the shops behind. Miss Palmer and Luke were nowhere to be seen. An easy companionship had started to grow, and he yearned for more. Zeke felt something new. A fullness he hadn't experienced in a long time. He took a deep breath and smiled. This was what life could be like. He'd almost forgotten how enjoyable it was to simply be with someone. To banter over silly things for no purpose other than the pleasure of the company. Granted, they'd only just met. First, or second, impressions could be deceiving, but he liked her. And not just because he found her in the creek. There was a lot to like there too, but that wasn't the half of it. He wanted to ask her everything and tell her everything.

Married. He remembered like a cannon going off in his head.

Married. Married. Married.

Off-limits.

She belonged to someone else. She had a child with someone else, for goodness sake. Zeke stretched the space between them. He swung the basket there to be sure it stayed that way, and they made their way out of the heart of town. The beehive kiln chimneys appeared over the next rise.

"I've never worked at a brickyard before. Any tips?"

"It's a dirty job. Brickmakers and blacksmiths both keep a girl busy doing laundry." She turned serious. "Boss is fair, but he doesn't miss a thing. You shouldn't have any trouble if you are honest and put in your share of work. Don't expect to be able to keep up with the others when you start out, but he knows it takes time to learn. You'll need a good pair of gloves."

"Gloves. Check. Anything else?"

"Dee will show you the ropes, I'm sure. He's the foreman, the one you'll need to answer to most of the time. You'll get to dig clay from a pit, and in a few weeks, if you want to try something else, you can ask for it if they don't put you on another rotation."

"There's no need. A few weeks is plenty. I'm chasing the setting sun, if you've forgotten. 'Go west, young man!' That's me."

"West for what?"

She sounded disappointed, but surely, he was mistaken. "Why ever not? The West is as good as here. Better even."

"Oh."

One word. And yet, this single-worded statement unsettled him. An elegant speech highlighting the pitfalls of his plan wouldn't have had the same impact.

What was she to him? *Nothing*. That's what she was. Nothing.

She had no right to tell him he couldn't go west if he wanted to. The Donnelys had cared for him and taken him in, but he did not wish to spend the rest of his life strapped to the back of a pair of oxen or any other animal trained to plow a field. His rows were never straight because his focus was everywhere but the end of the line.

He had dreams, talents, and ideas. He wasn't strapped to a family, a horse, a job. Nothing. It was his life; his choice. He'd go where he wanted. And that was that. He didn't need another girl to tie him down. He didn't need someone else to cry and tell him he was reckless, foolhardy, or too ambitious. Rachel already filled that role. A married woman, no matter how intriguing, had no reason to tell him he was a fool. So he was easily distracted. So he lost his way a few times. That's why it was such a blessing to be alone. He didn't mind a few extra days, or weeks, or months. He was only interested in the adventure to be found along the way.

He pushed like a fish against the net around him, always searching for a break in the ropes—for a hole that would let him back out into the open. "Here." He shoved the basket into her arms.

"Ope!" she said.

"I can find my way from here. Don't need to give anyone ideas about us. Be seeing you." He stalked along the worn path. Alone. It was better this way. A grown man didn't need to feel guilty for making his own way in the world, and he sure didn't need to be escorted to work. Chipmunk—*Mrs. Davidson,* he chided himself— could go back to whatever it was young mothers did, like swimming in frigid creeks.

Eloise stood with the basket in her hands. What had she possibly done to upset him? She should have known better than to play games. To what gain? He would never be interested in her anyway. Not that she wanted him to be. Letting Jessica get to her was a mistake. Zeke was no different than any other man. Honestly, had she not learned her lesson by now? Men would never be interested in anything she had to offer. She hadn't been enough for Philip, even after years of courtship and then marriage. Making deals with Jessica was silly. She hadn't expected Zeke to fawn over her, but she hadn't prepared for a full rejection.

Jessica's escape with Luke threw her off guard; it was humorous listening to Jessica chatter to Zeke about the town. He'd listened politely to all of it, but she'd kept herself safely out of the conversation. That word again, *safe*. What was she afraid of? Being noticed? It was easier to let Jessica do the talking.

No, it went deeper than that. What if she was noticed and found lacking? What if she found love and it wasn't returned? That would be worse yet. If she wasn't enough for Philip, to whom she had given everything, what's to say any man would be satisfied with her? If she hadn't been enough to keep him here, there was nothing more she had to offer.

Jessica had rattled on about everything, and Zeke did not contribute. He hadn't been mute with Eloise when they'd walked earlier; then again, she left room for him. She'd bitten her tongue to keep from laughing out loud when Jessica asked him where he stored his things, and he'd said West Virginia.

After Jessica scuttled off with Luke, Eloise kept to her pact. She smiled. She talked. She'd surprised herself with the ease of companionship with him. It hadn't been a toilsome task after all. Zeke didn't mind moments of silence. He was clever and good-humored—until he wasn't.

A lot of good the effort had been. Here she stood on the outskirts of town, alone, watching the back of his shirt disappear down the hill. *Stupid shirt.* Men were impossible. She felt jilted—a cast-off from yesterday's bouquet. Next time he fell off a creek bank, she'd let him lie in his own mess.

What did she care if he dismissed her so easily? He was nothing to her. *Nothing.* Just a silly man, with a silly stupid wink. Except he'd woken something in her she hadn't realized she'd buried. A yearning for companionship. She missed Philip terribly.

You'll just have to trust me. Zeke's words ran through her mind from that morning. *Hardly.* She didn't even trust herself most days. She'd find Luke and they would eat Zeke's lunch, thanks to Helen. Mr. Ezekiel James could fend for himself.

Jessica was the best of friends; she had been a support through all of life's troubles and the first to share in the good. But sharing a joke with Zeke had caused a stirring of excitement that fluttered in her middle. The newness of a possible friendship. A gut feeling that they shared something. A hidden treasure. A connection. But no. It was better this way. She was better off alone.

Chapter 7

Eloise sat near the window in her favorite chair. Her mother used to sit in the same one in the evenings and mend, quilt, or read. Since her mother's death, Eloise had claimed the chair as her own. Tonight, she fought against the needle and thread, making a poor show of concentration. The needle wouldn't thread, the knots wouldn't hold, and the scissors wouldn't cut. And she blamed it all on a pair of green eyes that winked at her and the back of a shirt that marched its way down the path without her.

Tobias sat across the room, softly singing hymns and rocking Luke, who had long since fallen asleep. His chair creaked in rhythm, and Tobias rubbed his calloused hand on the toddler's back. He snuggled the boy and kissed his blond head. Luke sucked his thumb but was otherwise still.

The thread tangled again as Eloise tugged it through the fabric. She gripped it with both hands and growled her frustration at it. Resting the mess on her lap, she took a deep breath and attacked the knot with vigor. It was no use. She added another grunt for good measure. Grabbing the scissors from the basket, she snipped the thread, tied it off, and threaded the needle to start again. Angling her project toward the lamp for better light, she resolved to finish at least one seam before she gave up for the night.

Tobias stopped humming and stared at her.

"What?" she asked, biting off the word and the thread.

He only smirked. "Nothing."

"Then. Stop. It." She glared at him.

"I'm not allowed to rock my baby?" He was unafraid of her.

"Stop staring at me. I'd like to see you try—this stupid dad-blame thread."

"Language, sister. Not in front of my boy." He covered Luke's exposed ear.

"He's asleep," she answered, not looking up. Squinting at the needle, she attempted to re-thread it again. "I've heard you say worse."

"Can't prove it."

She eyed him for a moment until the creak of the rocker went back to its steady rhythm. Tobias sighed and snuggled Luke tighter. "El?"

"Yes?"

"You're upset. What is it? And don't tell me it has anything to do with whatever mess you're working on over there."

"Nothing." She held the two quilt blocks carefully and ran the needle through the fabric. Her running stitch was not as neat as her mother's had been. But it was functional. Eloise didn't take much pride in her sewing.

Or baking. Thankfully, Agnes Anderson kept her little family in good supply of baked goods. She frequently dropped off Swedish rusks, tea rings, and smörgås bread. Agnes had gifted the bread for years, but Eloise paid her now for a regular supply. Sure, she should be able to bake for her own family, but it wasn't worth the effort. She wasn't good at it, to begin with. Everything she tried was terrible, so she'd given up. Evening sewing at least kept her hands busy, even if she didn't love it. Every few weeks, she had something functional to show for her sewing efforts. On the other hand, she couldn't do anything useful with burned food.

Come to think of it, what was she good at?

She was good at loving Luke. She kept him busy, healthy, and loved. When Katie died and left Tobias a widow and Luke mother-less, Eloise felt useful again. She'd found purpose again. She missed Katie and the sister she'd found in her, but Luke was now the happiest part of her life. They spent much of their time wandering the country around town and visiting the Palmer family. She took him down to the smithy to watch Pa work, who had become a grandpa to him, even though there was no relation. And they visited Tobias and the other boys at the brickyard.

Not today. Mr. James had ruined everything. What right did that man have to come into her town and keep her from going to the few places she wanted to go? He and his good-looking face and perfect smile. And when he winked at her! Goodness. She hadn't felt her stomach flip like that since . . . since Philip. Today's emotions were as varied as the weather. She didn't know what might come next. She'd been appalled, embarrassed, and yet, he treated her like a friend . . . like someone he wanted to talk to. He made her laugh, but more than that, he looked at her as if he truly cared about what she had to say. *You'll just have to trust me.* Except she couldn't. *Wouldn't.* Why did she still hurt from when he'd brushed her off? What had she done wrong for him to shut her out so quickly?

It didn't even matter. They weren't friends. He was a stranger on his way west. Avoiding the brickyard for a few days would be simple. And Palmer Boarding House. Or any other place she might run into him until he left town. He'd told her himself he wasn't staying.

"El?"

"What?" She yanked the needle through the fabric hard enough to snap the thread.

Tobias frowned at her and shook his head. "Just put it down. It's not worth it."

She saw the concern on his face. But she didn't need him to worry about her. She was fine. He always made such a fuss. After all, she wasn't helpless. She wasn't a child. Even if he was her big brother, it was only by a few years. He'd never even been required to do his own washing thanks to her.

Bending over her work again, she muttered. "Don't tell me what to do."

"Okay." The rocker creaked, and he shifted Luke to the other side. "Arm's falling asleep."

"Why don't you put him to bed?" Clamping the needle between her teeth, she unwound another length of thread.

"Why don't you mind your business? Looks like you have enough to worry about over there. I'll hold him as long as I want."

Eloise rolled her eyes. "Fine." Wetting the thread between her lips, she poked it through the eye of the needle. She pushed it through the fabric and pulled it through slowly, carefully, backstitching a few times to secure the seam. She ignored her brother.

Tobias resumed his soft singing:

> *All the way my Savior leads me;*
> *What have I to ask beside?*
> *Can I doubt his tender mercy,*
> *Who through life has been my Guide?*
> *Heav'nly peace, divinest comfort,*
> *Here by faith in him to dwell.*
> *For I know, whate'er befall me,*
> *Jesus doeth all things well . . .*

He trailed off during the second verse and hummed through it, guessing at the words, then went back around to the first verse.

She wondered what Tobias was thinking about and if he knew he was singing the same parts over again. She didn't look up as she carefully weaved the needle through to finish her second seam of the evening. "Do you believe it?"

"Believe what?"

"The song."

Eloise and Tobias looked at each other in the evening light. The sun, almost gone, cast a soft glow over her hands in her lap.

"Which part?" he asked. "I wasn't paying attention."

"All of it. Being led? Him being merciful? In spite of all we've been through. Losing Katie. Mom and Dad? Philip? Can you say he does all things well?"

"Can you?" he asked her.

Eloise looked down at her hands. She secured the needle through the edge of the fabric, folded it gently, and tucked it into the basket with the other notions. Taking a deep breath first, she answered him. "I don't know."

"El, I don't try to understand him. But I've got to believe that he's guiding us. There would be no purpose for any of it otherwise."

The creaking of his rocker filled the silence. Eloise rested her head on the back of the chair and closed her eyes. It was good to live here. Safe. Easy. Accepted. Loved. She was only fifteen when her parents died. They were just two of the hundred who died that year of fever. Tobias had made it work. He took care of the brick-yard business and encouraged her to finish school. She picked up the other duties of the house, and they fell into a new sort of family.

"Did you hire Mr. James?" she asked.

"Zeke? How'd you hear about him?"

"We met. Bumped into each other, rather. Did you notice the prints on his shirt?" She chuckled. "Those were mine. He plowed into me on my way back from Pa's."

Tobias laughed loudly, disturbing Luke. "Shhh. Shhh. Shhh." Luke quickly settled. "I wondered about that. I didn't ask. Yeah, I hired him on the spot. Had Dee show him around right away. Guess he'll do alright. He worked the pit this afternoon. We'll see how long he lasts. What did you think of him?"

Images of him laughing at her when she scrambled away in the water came to mind. So did his repentant attitude and tumble, as well as his good-natured conversations and flirtatious winking.

What do I think of him? He's a flirt. Overconfident. Distractingly good-looking. He's seen me half-naked in the creek.

"El?"

"What?" She glanced at Tobias, startled.

"What's wrong with you? You're jumpy tonight."

"Nothing. I'm not. I'm fine."

"Yeah, okay. I asked you what you thought of him."

"Oh, he . . . um—fine." She pulled the sewing basket into her lap and dug through it absently. "We didn't talk much. Jess and I were busy."

"Mmhmm."

"What?" She clunked the basket back on the floor by her chair.

"I don't believe you. And don't leave that there. Luke will find the scissors again."

Eloise stood and feigned a yawn. "Well, I have nothing more to say. I'm going to bed." She put the basket on the high shelf.

"Good night," Tobias said. He followed Eloise up the stairs. She went into her room and he passed her down the hall to lay Luke in his crib.

Eloise sat on the edge of her bed to take the pins out of her hair. It fell down her back, and she shook her head to release the rest of the knot. Hearing Tobias come down the hall, she wasn't surprised when he stuck his head into her room, and leaned a hand against her doorframe.

"Your blush gives you away. It always has. There's more to this story." He untucked his overshirt. "No matter, you've got three days to worry about it. Good night." He ducked out and crossed the hall to his bedroom.

Three days? Three days for what? Eloise jumped off her bed and scattered hairpins to the floor in the process. Clicking her tongue at the mess, she bent and gathered the pins. She shoved them on the top of her dresser and scrambled to Tobias's room. Flinging open his door, she caught him taking off his shirt.

"Geez, El, don't you ever knock?" he asked.

"Sorry. Three days for what?"

Tobias hung the shirt on its peg and sat on the bed to remove his socks. "Oh, did I not say? I invited Zeke for dinner Friday."

"You didn't."

"I did."

"You did what?!"

"He's coming to dinner Friday."

"Why would you do that?"

"Because I live to make your life miserable. What's the big deal? I've had workers over before. I didn't know you liked this one."

"I don't like him. I don't even know him."

"Okay. Well, I didn't know you didn't like him. I thought it would be nice to get to know him. Besides, he looked hungry."

"But it's only Tuesday. He may not still be here Friday."

"He will. I don't pay until Friday. Shut the door on your way out."

Chapter 8

Zeke paused to wipe the sweat dripping down his temple. For the first week of April, he hadn't expected temperatures in the upper eighties. Shoving the handkerchief into his back pocket, he shouldered the mattock. Swinging it in a wide arc over his head, he brought it down into the earth wall.

He was working the clay pit. As promised. It wasn't much of a pit. The clay was found directly under a thin layer of topsoil and didn't require digging very deep. He tore at the side, widening the pit rather than digging down. Chunks of brown clay fell around his feet as he hacked at the wall. Sometimes small clods stuck to his mattock, while other times, large sections opened up and exposed worms and beetle tunnels that fascinated him. When the mess around his feet grew to the point of getting in his way, he used a flat shovel to transfer the clay into the cart behind him.

His job was to keep breaking down the clay and loading carts. Intermittently, another man came to take a cart and exchanged it with an empty one. While Zeke worked, he listened to snippets of conversation around the yard, hearing laughter and good-natured jokes. Occasionally, he heard a shout for attention. Though the labor was strenuous, the men enjoyed their work. A man named Jonas worked the pit nearby. Zeke watched how he maneuvered and took his cue from him regarding how to handle the tools and the pace to set. It wasn't complicated work, but it was tiring.

Zeke's back strained, lifting the mattock again. Weeks of travels had not prepared him for this type of labor. Riding in the saddle was tiresome in its own right, but it didn't require the strength needed for this career. The years of running behind the plow and pitching hay were not for the lazy, but the continual motion of lifting, swinging, pulling, and shoveling, had awoken a number of muscles he didn't know he had.

Swing. Thump.

His clothes were smeared with clay. *Chipmunk wasn't kidding about the laundry service.* He added *laundry service* to his growing list of expenses.

He wondered what she was doing right now. Miss Palmer mentioned that Luke's father worked here, but he hadn't yet been introduced to a Mr. Davidson. For that matter, the few men he'd met hadn't used last names.

Swing. Thump.

Not Jonas. He lived across the hall from Zeke at Palmer Boarding House. He was young. Stocky. For breakfast, he'd eaten three plates of eggs, tossed down a second cup of coffee, and was out the door in a hurry. Zeke hustled to catch him. Five other men were living at Palmer's. Her boys, she called them. They were polite to the ladies and courteous at the table. But on the walk over this morning, their talk turned to less savory topics. Zeke's ears burned thinking of the picture Charles had passed around.

Jonas, Bill, Charles, and Thomas lived at Palmer's, along with Simon Oakfield, whom he had already learned to keep a wide birth. All were young and unattached. He looked forward to their camaraderie for the few days he'd be in town. It was great to have a few fellows around, yet he was glad none of them belonged to Mrs. Davidson. She deserved better.

Swing. Thump.

She wasn't married to Dee Williams, the foreman. Dee's wife came by yesterday afternoon. She was well into the family way with a young toddler in her arm who sat on her round stomach. She passed the child to Dee, and two other boys played around her skirts. Jonas confided there were three boys of theirs already in school. Their seventh child would arrive sometime this summer.

The toddler left a wet mark on Dee's shoulder from where he'd been chewing on his shirt. Dee either didn't notice or didn't mind. The boy wanted down, but Dee held him firmly, pointing out the kiln and speaking into his ear. The little boy stared at everything but did not fight his father again.

Swing. Thump.

A few older men worked here. Most were scruffy and spit tobacco juice along the path. Their hands were gnarled from years of lifting and loading bricks. They were old enough to be Mrs.

Davidson's father or grandfather. Surely none of them were Mr. Davidson?

Swing. Thump.

The boss spent the morning in the office. A shipment of coal was due from the train this week. He'd assigned a crew in charge of transferring it with the horse carts. *Surely she's not married to the boss? If she is, you had better pray she keeps her mouth quiet.* Daydreaming about the boss's wife could get a man in trouble.

"What are you doing?" said Dee, startling Zeke, causing him to drop the mattock and yanking him into the present. "You've got so much clay piling around your feet that you're mashing it into the ground. We're not paying you to bring down the hill. We need the clay in the carts and moved to the yard for mixing." Dee mimed with both hands, motioning where the clay was to go.

Zeke leaned the mattock against the wall, switched to the shovel, and began moving the clay to the carts. Nervous about being scrutinized, clods fell off the shovel before making it to the cart. He mumbled an apology. "Sorry. Got distracted."

"Zeke. Look at me. This is the simplest job in the yard. It takes zero finesse or skill. Break the clay. Load the carts."

"Yes sir." He worked quickly and tried not to step on any large pieces around his feet.

"Stop a moment, will ya? You look like a frantic badger trying to clean his room before his ma sees it." Dee chuckled. "I've already seen it." He took the shovel from Zeke and jammed it into the ground. "Sit down. You're wearing me out."

Zeke obeyed. Sitting on the ground, he rested his back against the wall of the pit.

"Jonas!" Dee said. "Hold up. I'm putting you on water-boy duty. Make the rounds."

Jonas nodded. He was probably relieved for the break as he jogged to the pump and bucket.

Dee crouched beside Zeke and leaned into the little bit of shade still available from the wall. "I don't know your story— where you're going or where you're from. But I know Boss likes you." Removing his flat-brimmed hat, he finger-combed his white-blond hair, careful not to disturb the pencil tucked above his ear. "He hired you. But if you can't do this job, I can sure fire you."

Zeke looked across the brickyard. He could see the whole operation—the brickmakers pressing the mixture into the molds, a man working the mixer, the office, the coal bins near the three kilns, and the drying sheds. There was a lot of action for a small area.

A flash of blue caught his attention. *When did Chipmunk get here?* She was talking to a man near the sheds. Ralph? Ray? He couldn't remember the man's name. He was young, her age at least. They were laughing together. The man leaned toward her and whispered.

Her hands flew to her mouth, but they did not cover the squeal of excitement Zeke heard from across the yard. She bounced on her toes a few times like a schoolgirl. Ralph or Ray pulled a scrap of paper from his pocket and gave it to her. Pressing it into her hand, he didn't let go. He held her fist closed with both of his hands as he talked to her. She smiled and nodded before tucking the note in her pocket. The man brought her hand to his mouth and kissed it. *That ends the search for Mr. Davidson.*

Suddenly, Zeke realized his supervisor was still talking to him.

"—bring down the unicorns and mermaids will make the bricks with their magical powers, and we can all sit around like this the rest of the day."

Zeke tore his gaze from Mrs. Davidson. "Excuse me?"

"I was testing you." Dee clamped his hat back on his head. "You failed." Dee stood and offered his hand to Zeke. "Dream about girls on your own time. Miss Eloise is . . . just mind your work. My wife doesn't like it when I fire people, so I'd rather not."

The note from Roy Swenson burned in her pocket the rest of the morning and afternoon. Eloise fed Luke, then cleaned and started a pot of beans for supper while he napped.

Eloise was glad to be the bearer of such a message. Jessica would be ecstatic. Though Roy was oblivious to Jessica's attention, he had been a mutual friend of theirs for years. The town dance on Friday would be worth attending, just this once, to witness her friends' official first outing.

Thus do I pine. Eloise smiled, thinking of their school years when Roy chose Shakespeare's Sonnet 75 for his poetry memorization. Jessica's heart melted when he looked at her during his recitation and convinced herself he was speaking directly to her.

At nearly four o'clock, Eloise managed to get Luke out the door to Palmer's. They passed near the schoolhouse and were joined by Simon Oakfield, the teacher of the primary grades. He smiled upon seeing her. Eloise inwardly cringed and prepared for the chatter she was expected to participate in. She chided herself for not getting out the door sooner in order to avoid this exact situation.

"Miss Eloise. It is a pleasure to see you today. You are on your way to visit Miss Jessica? I have not enjoyed your company for some time. I am honored to walk with you." Simon quick-stepped to catch them. He was always proper. Always the gentleman. Since grammar school, she had begun the practice of biting her cheek and tightening her middle to keep from saying something she shouldn't when he was near.

"Yes," was the best she could come up with in reply. Luke dawdled, and she slowed to accommodate him. "I trust your students are behaving this week?"

Simon pursed his lips and pushed his glasses with his middle finger. He chuckled before answering, "Oh, Miss Eloise," he said, formal with names, though they had known each other for years. "It is April. Even the little girls misbehave this time of year."

"Honestly, can you blame them?" Eloise breathed deeply and gazed at the clear sky. "It's been a gorgeous week."

"Mmhmm," he said. "Hot, if you ask me. But we must learn to restrain ourselves, no matter the age or the weather."

Luke, walking between them, rubbed his handful of grass on Simon's carefully pressed suit. Simon eased to the far side of the boardwalk. The toddler laughed, thinking it was a game, and followed. Disdain showed clearly on Simon's downturned mouth. When Eloise saw his face, she tugged gently on Luke's other arm, and he resumed his walk. After a minute of uncomfortable silence, Simon began again.

"Miss Eloise."

She focused on the cracks between the boards and encouraged Luke to walk a little faster. She wished Tobias had splurged on one of those baby carriages that were so popular. For as often as she and Luke wandered around the square, it would have come in handy plenty of times by now. Provided the wheels could make it over the mud or dust once they were off the boardwalk.

Simon continued. "I have noticed your absence from the town socials for quite some time."

She refrained from rolling her eyes. *Of course I've been absent. Why would I go to a dance by myself?* Philip was dead, and she wasn't in need of dancing. No sense in dragging anyone else down with her.

"Yes," she answered.

Simon maneuvered in front of her, causing her to stop abruptly. Startled by his barricade, she was not prepared for his next statement. He snatched her free hand and held it between both of his. She immediately grew cold and clammy.

"Miss Eloise, I would be honored to escort you to Friday's social if you would be so inclined to go with me. There are yet two days to prepare. I know this may appear short notice. I understand how women can be, but you need not do much to please me. I enjoy you as you are. Miss Jessica may have something you could borrow for the evening if you have nothing on hand. Though I should not speak of such things. I do not wish for you to be put out if you have not anything prepared in the latest fashions."

He stood, beseeching a positive answer.

She looked over his slicked brown hair, parted perfectly straight and every strand in its proper place, even after a full day of teaching.

His appearance was perfect. The gold standard. And yet, everything about him made her cringe. He never did anything mean on purpose, and yet she'd always avoided him. In grammar school, he was the student who finished first. Who volunteered for everything. Who waited his turn. Who raised his hand for every question. Nobody liked that person. She wasn't interested in a man who continually proved his worth. He'd put himself in this position with her multiple times throughout the years. She'd hoped her stance was clear by now.

"Simon." She swallowed, tugging at her hand. "Why would you ask me this?"

He dropped her hand like it burned and stepped back, and his eyes grew large. "I have waited for an appropriate amount of time. You are the one who did not adhere to the etiquette of mourning dress for six months. Do I not have a right to extend an offer of my company? What am I to think of your behavior? I have seen you walk with Mr. Swenson and others. Even this new fellow who has taken a room down the hall? I was appalled to hear him speak of you."

Eloise narrowed her eyes. "What does he speak of me?"

Simon stuttered. "He—Not much, precisely. But when you were mentioned, he implied that you had met. I attempted to find out more, but he did not elaborate. Only spoke of walking with you from the bakery. But you should be ashamed to be seen with a man like that. One whom nobody knows? Where he's from and where he's going?"

"He's from West Virginia. He's on his way to the ocean. And what is that to you? Or me? Why are we even speaking of it?"

"We aren't," said Simon, exasperated. "We are talking about how you flaunt yourself at every available man, but when a respectable match like myself makes a go at it, you shove me away. What have I ever done to wrong you?"

Eloise shook her head. *I don't want to be with you! Flaunt myself! Has he been living in a foxhole? Where does he even come up with this drivel?* Her teeth bit into her cheeks.

"Miss Eloise. I apologize for whatever has upset you. If I may start over. I desire to take you to the social on Friday. It appears you are in need of an escort."

"Simon! If I want to go out, I will go out. With you or without you. Or by myself. Or with my brother. Or with Jessica. Or I won't! Maybe I don't want to go out." *Because of people like you!*

Simon straightened his shoulders and tugged on his coat as if he'd been personally insulted. "I am appalled. You refused to follow proper mourning guidelines, and yet you remain cloistered away from the world as if we are to blame for your misfortune. Philip is dead. You are free." He gestured with his arms wide, showing just how free she was. "Are you not at least a bit relieved? He was sick, Eloise. He was sick. And you of all people should know it. And now he is not. You do not have to live this way anymore, as if he is still waiting for you at home. Can you not put that time behind you? You do not have to put up with him anymore. Time to move on."

Lead fire flamed in her gut, and her chest felt like the life was being squeezed from her. She gritted her teeth. "I am *not* one of your students, Simon. If you ever speak to me again . . ." Her lip trembled. She bent and picked up Luke. Holding him tightly to her chest, she stalked around Simon.

"El! Miss Eloise! I spoke out of turn. Please, forgive me," he begged.

With her eyes locked on the end of the street, she marched past Palmer's, turning at the corner before the tears found their way out. Luke squirmed, but she held him fast.

Chapter 9

She wound her way through neighborhoods, unaware of anything but the fragmented stream of thoughts running through her mind.

How dare he!

He is right, though. Everyone knows. I didn't wear black long enough. Black is old, and I'm not old. I'm too young to be a widow.

Everyone dies.

How dare he! "Time to move on," he'd said. How can I move on when my dreams keep me a prisoner? There will never be a moving on. Is Simon only brave enough to speak what everyone is thinking? So maybe Philip was sick. But I could have helped him. Should have helped him. I could have been enough for him. If I had stayed with him that day. He'd begged me to stay.

Eventually, she found herself at the cemetery. The place where nobody ever bothered her. Luke wriggled down and she let him run. Her back ached as she stood in front of her parent's stone. Eyes closed, she calmed her mind and waited for a sense of peace to fill her. She'd been coming to this same spot for five years. Even after Philip was buried nearby, she found solace in the familiarity of this spot.

No peace came today. Only anger. A spring of hot tears leaked from her eyes. If only the pain could fall from her like tears. She knew it wasn't fair to blame Simon, but she hated him. Hated him for his appearance of perfection and what he represented. Hated him for the way he made her lose control of herself. She hated him for the stupid way he talked and for speaking out when he should be silent. She even hated his polished shoes. She hated him the most because everything he said pricked an element of truth in her soul.

Kneeling in the grass, she said aloud, "Mama, I'm sorry. I'm sorry. Sometimes, I just . . . I just don't know how to keep going. How to keep doing the right thing."

A footstep crunched in the grass behind her. She turned to see, of all people, Ezekiel James. He stood with one foot raised, in the process of backing out of the park.

"I was just leaving," he said. "Sorry. I'm leaving. I mean, I wasn't staying, just looking around. I wasn't trying to, I mean. Sorry. I'm going." He stumbled backward, knocking his shoulder against a tree. A pair of gloves dropped from where they'd been tucked in his trousers. He bent to pick them up, and in his haste, dropped one again. Once they were securely in his hands, he waved them at her, offering a sheepish grin. Turning to leave in a rush, he tripped over a bush between him and the path.

"Ope!" Eloise covered her mouth to keep from laughing while watching him flail around the bush. It was impossible to turn away from the spectacle. Once untangled, a hound with his tail tucked couldn't have crawled away more dejected than he did—after he found solid ground at least. She sniffed and wiped both eyes with the palm of her hand. "Mr. James!"

He turned, scratching the back of his neck absently. "Yup?"

"Were you looking for someone?"

His mouth moved, but no words came out. Finally, he shrugged. "No?"

"What are you doing?"

"Well, I was leaving." He jerked a thumb over his shoulder.

She laughed, despite the tears drying on her cheeks. "Before that. What are you doing all the way out here?"

He shrugged again. "I'm embarrassed to say, but I was hiding. I'm about as close to getting fired as a man can be, so I'm sulking, and the other boys usually fight for the washroom when we return. I was wandering around before returning to Palmer's."

"Fired? It can't be. How can you be fired from working the pit?"

"Daydreaming on the job is a good start. Dee doesn't mess around."

"Dreaming of your ocean, Mr. James?"

"Something like that. And it's Zeke. Just Zeke."

"Okay, Zeke. Tell me how someone with your skills can be fired from working the pit?"

"Shoveling clay is a poor example of my skills."

"How about wrestling? I'd give 50/50 odds to that bush."

He shook a finger at her and smirked. "Now, listen here, young lady." Making a show of carefully walking around the bush, he made his way to her. Pointing behind, he said, "I hate to make a scene in front of women and children." He tipped his hat to Luke, who was busy pulling the heads off dandelions. "But that bush should not be there. Whoever designed this place," he waved his hands widely, "should have taken into account that a man might have need of that space."

Eloise laughed at him. "I like that bush. It will have pink flowers on it soon." She wiped a stray tear with the back of her hand.

Zeke lowered his voice and cast his eyes to the ground. "I didn't mean to intrude. I'd offer to make it all better for you, but my guess is it's out of my skill set."

"Thank you." She gently dabbed at her eyes and wiped her nose, and watched Luke running around and around her parents' gravestone. Zeke tip-toed behind and jumped out at Luke just as the boy came around the corner.

Luke squealed and fell on his bottom. Placing his hands on the ground and sticking his end high in the air, Luke stood and ran around the other way, laughing. Anticipating Zeke to chase him, he wasn't disappointed. Zeke lurched as if to run, but when Luke took off one direction, Zeke surprised him by going the other way and caught him on the other side. Another squeal, another fall, and more toddler giggles. Zeke ruffled the boy's hair and glanced at Eloise. Suddenly, he hit the ground behind the stone and waited for Luke to find him. Luke didn't. When he didn't see Zeke, he wandered off the other way.

Eloise put her hands on the stone and leaned over. "You're off the hook."

Zeke flashed her a smile. Nodding to the stone, he asked, "Who are these folks?"

"My parents. They were taken the same year."

He held her gaze. Brushing himself off, he came around to her side to read the names. "What were they like?" Despite the sensitive topic, a soft smile in his expression encouraged her to share. He didn't say he was sorry. He didn't shy away or pity her. Instead, he got comfortable. He moved himself to the nearby tree, stretching out a leg and resting his arm on his pulled-up knee.

"They were wonderful." And they were. She had no reason to trust Zeke. Yet there she stood, nose still running, face blotchy from crying. She felt safe. His presence and humor made things feel better. She wanted to tell him everything, to pour out her heartache and troubles. She wanted to be seen and understood.

She sat opposite him, leaning against the stone. "They loved each other. They loved me. Mama always pushed me to have fun. To go out and do things with other people."

"You didn't want to go out?"

"No, I was content." Even at fourteen, Philip had been her world. She'd had Philip to occupy her every thought. Much as she did now, though he wasn't here. "I didn't think I needed anything more than I already had. Maybe Mama was right."

Zeke cocked his head and waited for more.

She watched him, remembering the long conversations she'd had with her mother. She would often brush her hair or work on mending while they talked late into the evenings.

"Right about what?" Zeke asked.

"About Philip." She knew Zeke was leaving, and her secrets

would be safe. Things she had never fully divulged to Jessica now came tumbling out. "The last day. It was February. Jessica, and a few of us, were going to see if the creek was still frozen. We didn't get the chance to play very often anymore. We were no longer children, but the sun was out, and the wind had stopped." She picked a clover in the grass and began pulling the leaves off. "Philip didn't want to go and begged me not to. I didn't listen. I was upset with him." She glanced at Zeke, and his face softened. She tossed the clover aside and picked another.

"Was there an accident on the ice?"

"No," Eloise said. Her answer was almost too soft to hear, and she added a slight shake of her head. "It happened afterward." She pulled her knees to her chest, wrapped her arms around them and rested her chin on her knees. "Philip needed me. More than was natural. Nobody understood him like I did. I was his light. He'd said I was God's special light, his gift, and he didn't know how he'd go on without me." She shook her head. "Mama died before things were serious, but I think somehow, she knew how it was between us and tried to protect me. Perhaps to keep me from taking on that kind of responsibility. How I loved him." She sighed, picking the bits of grass from her skirts. "But I wasn't enough. I don't know how to explain it." Luke came over and fell into her lap. Eloise snuggled him and kissed his hair. "But I have you, little guy!" She squeezed him tightly. "What would we ever do without you."

Zeke cleared his throat, "Philip is . . . ?"

"Dead." Eloise set Luke on his feet and brushed a leaf from his hair. "He asked me not to go. I did, and now he's dead. My parents are dead. Philip's dead. Katie's dead."

"I'm glad you have Luke." Zeke didn't appear shocked at any of her confessions.

"For now." Until Tobias remarried.

"Did I tell you I'm an orphan?"

Eloise shook her head. "When did it happen?"

"Mama died when I was twelve, and I only have vague memories of Papa. He was caught up in the war and never came back."

"Where did you go? Did you have any other family?"

"I do now. In a way. Paul and Beatrice Donnely took me in. I have six brothers and sisters now. It was a good home. Different from what I was used to as an only child. But good."

"But not good enough to stay?"

He shrugged.

Remembering how he'd stormed away from her a few days ago, she felt she'd asked too much. "Excuse me, I shouldn't pry."

"It's not that it isn't or wasn't good enough. It was great, you know? I mean, to have a family take me in like that and make me one of their own. It's not that I'm not grateful, because I am. But, I'm not a farmer. I don't want to be a farmer. There's lots of things I could do—and so much more to see." He set his hat on the ground. Running both hands through his hair before clasping them behind his neck, he sighed. "I don't know, Chipmunk, do you ever feel like everyone's got a plan for your life and forgot to ask how you felt about it first?"

"Why do you call me that?"

He grinned at her. "Wouldn't you like to know."

She pulled a handful of grass and threw it at him. The wind caught most of it. She watched it drift. "I envy you."

"How so?"

"You wanted to go, so you did. To have that kind of freedom. To be brave enough to take a chance."

"Stupid enough, you mean. Did you get a good look at the goober who fell on his face? That man was lonely, dirty, and starving."

Eloise did remember and blushed thinking of it. "At least you kept smiling through it. I think I've forgotten how to have fun."

"I just do what makes me happy. Within reason. Fried chicken? Makes me happy. Catching frogs? Makes me happy. Singing? Makes me happy. What makes you happy?"

What did make her happy? Some things used to make her happy. But she was stumped now as she considered his question. The last time she'd gone out with the sole purpose of having fun, it hadn't ended well.

Zeke prodded. "There isn't anything you do that makes all the bad stuff disappear for a while?"

"I don't know. If there is, I've forgotten."

"How about when you were a child? Before life stepped in and messed it all up? There's got to be something."

Eloise chewed on her lip, thinking. *This question shouldn't be so hard. Surely there is something.* She chuckled, thinking of silly childhood games. "Climbing trees."

"Well, let's climb some trees!"

"Now?" she asked, alarmed.

"Sure, why not?" Zeke shoved his Stetson on his head and scanned the cemetery. He wouldn't find any nearby. Any of the trees here were hardly big enough to hold her weight. "Hey, where's Luke?"

"Ope!" She chided herself for losing track of him. "Luke!"

Climbing on top of the gravestone, she saw his little blond head bobbing behind another stone. Pointing him out, she said, "He's just there." Suddenly, she remembered the note in her pocket and why she had left the house this afternoon. She began to teeter on the top of the stone.

Zeke stepped closer and offered his hand. When she grabbed it to steady her balance, her stomach flipped. It wasn't until Zeke cleared his throat that she realized she'd been staring at their hands. For how long? She didn't know.

"Coming down?" Zeke asked. He winked at her. "Unless you wanted to keep the high ground. By all means, don't let me foil your plans." He dropped her hand and backed up a step. She didn't miss the breath he took, as if he'd been holding it.

Zeke splayed his fingers and shook out his hand. He wrapped his arm around his front and tucked it into his side, trying to rub off the odd way his stomach was feeling. She'd been about to fall. Only a cold-hearted fool would have done less. It was completely appropriate to offer a hand, but his stomach did a weird thing and clogged up his lungs. And then after the way she'd looked at him . . . he was intimately aware of his accelerating heart rate.

He'd wanted to ask her more, before the hand-holding incident, but held his tongue. Not usually a strength of his. *Who was Philip? Who was Katie?*

Eloise jumped to the ground and headed toward Luke. She called over her shoulder, "If you'll excuse me, I do have to run.

We've business to take care of in town."

He scrambled back to his tree and checked to make sure both gloves were still tucked at his waist. "I'll walk with you." He waited for her to fetch Luke from the other side of the cemetery and fell in line next to her on the side of the road.

Preoccupying himself, he tried to identify every tree they passed. And failed. He had more questions now than before. "What's this tree?" he asked.

She followed his gaze and shrugged. "I don't know."

"How about this one?" He pointed to the left.

"That one will have large white flowers for a few days and then foot-long bean bods."

"Fascinating! What's it called?"

"I don't know."

"Tell me about this one," he pestered.

"Zeke!" She laughed. "I don't know anything about trees."

"Then we are of the same mind." *And if it makes you laugh, I'll keep asking.* If only she could see herself. How he loved that laugh. *Not love, Zeke. It's a nice laugh. Let it be.*

A cold gust of wind caught under the brim of his hat. He held it in place to prevent its escape.

Luke ducked his head into her shoulder.

"Uffda." She strained against the wind. Talking was out of the question for the next few minutes as the wind only grew stronger. They turned the corner onto the main street, and the wind immediately let up.

He took his hand from his hat and checked to see if the gloves were still safe.

Luke squirmed to be let down, but she hitched him up on her hip again.

"Let me carry Luke, if he'll come to me," Zeke said.

She stopped walking, and her mouth hung open. Her large eyes darted between him and the toddler, but she didn't argue. Handing him over, Luke settled in Zeke's arms. "He grows heavier by the day. Thank you."

A flash of her surprised face reminded him of when he'd shoved the basket lunch into her arms and left her standing on the hill. "Chip—Eloise, I'm sorry about the other day. I was rude."

She walked with her arms hugging her body against the cold. Her bonnet still hid the side of her face, but she wasn't using it to hide today. She looked at him when she spoke. "Things have a way of working themselves out sometimes."

"How so?"

"Luke and I had a fine picnic."

Zeke tipped his head and laughed. He bumped his shoulder into hers as they walked.

Her blue eyes sparkled with mischief. She raised both hands and shoved his shoulder.

Luke giggled and tried to grab her, and Zeke went along with it. Flipping Luke to face outward, he took the toddler's leg and kicked her shoulder. More laughter from the boy ensued when she feigned surprise. "Shall we get her?" he whispered to Luke.

Eloise skipped ahead, staying just out of Luke's reach. Whenever they were close enough to grab her, she ran away again. Luke was in toddler heaven, squealing with laughter. They were in front of Palmer's in no time.

"You owe me a lunch," he said. *No. What are you doing?* This wasn't just any girl. Why did he keep putting his foot in his mouth? And here he thought he was doing so well in keeping himself from prying about Philip and Katie.

And then she replied. "How about a dinner? Tomorrow night."

He was speechless again. Her expression perplexed him. Her half-smile made him think she was teasing, but he didn't see the joke. Thankfully, he had an out. He snapped his fingers, "Doggone it. I'm already booked for dinner. Boss beat you to it."

She laughed as though he were incredibly funny. Women were confusing.

"I hope I didn't rush you," she said. "Do you think you've stalled long enough for the washroom? I have business with Jessica."

"Never mind. I'll manage."

Eloise found Jessica in the backyard, cutting the first asparagus harvest.

"Well, hello," said Jessica, upon viewing Eloise's light smile. "What's put the bounce in your step today?"

"Simon, ha!" She shook her head. "No, but isn't it sort of wonderful how you can be blazing angry one minute and then God plops someone right in your path to help smooth things over?"

"Uh-oh, what's happened?"

"Simon Oakfield happened, again."

"I'll admit the man is obnoxious," Jessica said, "but essentially harmless."

"He invited me to the dance Friday, among other things."

Jessica laughed. She stood with a handful of asparagus in one hand and the paring knife in the other. "El? The man has a right to ask a single woman to a dance. He's not the first man to show an interest." She punctuated her words by waving the knife around.

Eloise flopped dramatically to the grass. "Oh, I know. And stop pointing that at me. Honestly, if you had only heard the way he spoke to me. It was just like a teacher reprimanding a wayward student. He didn't just ask. He practically told me what to do and implied so much that was not in his right to say."

Jessica tossed the stalks onto Eloise's lap and went to work looking for more. "I'm sorry he was rude."

Eloise took a bite of the smallest one and gathered the rest into a neat pile.

"Those are for dinner, don't eat too many."

"Yes, ma'am."

"What if you did go? Not with him. But with me? You and I could go, and it might be a simple way to break the ice without committing to anything. Anyone. You needn't worry about dancing. Just be there."

"Do you think I've cloistered myself too?"

Jessica sliced another spear and took the bundle of asparagus from Eloise. "I don't expect it will ever be the right time, truly. You will never wake up and not have lost a husband. Your marriage to him and his death will always be a part of who you are. But maybe— and I say this with all my love—maybe it would be enjoyable. Someday. To be with another man." Jessica let out a frustrated laugh. "But who am I to give advice? I'm going to end up an old maid."

Eloise clapped her hands to her cheeks. "Oh! Oh, oh, oh! I forgot. That terrible Simon and his dad-blame fitted suit. Good news and fresh bread should not be hidden away. Here." She dug the note from her pocket and shoved it into Jessica's hand. "Read it aloud."

Jessica smoothed the crumpled paper and read: "Dear Miss Palmer, please, will you go with me Friday? I'll pick you up at seven."

Eloise clapped her hands, "Well?"

"I don't know. This handwriting is atrocious. If I had to answer based on that, then I'm saying no. And there's no signature." She checked the back of the paper and read the front again. "Are we in grammar school passing notes? He's picking me up at seven, but what if I don't want to go? Land sakes, El, stop grinning at me like that. Who is it from?"

"It's from Mr. Swenson."

"Mr. Swe—Roy!"

After a round of squeals and Eloise telling and retelling Jessica the whole story about her conversation with Roy, the girls discussed what Jessica would wear and how she should do her hair. She had been to the Friday social many times, but never with the one man in all the world she pined for.

When the excitement subsided, Jessica looked around the yard. "Hey, where's Luke?"

"Zeke has him. Last I saw, he was playing horsey or something in the parlor." Eloise jumped off the grass, just remembering the beans she'd left on the stove at home. "I have to run, Jess. So sorry. Dinner is either cold or burned. Tobias will wonder what's become of us." She flew back into the house to grab Luke, waving a hand behind her.

Jessica hollered after her. "Tobias knows where to find you."

That was true. The brickyard, the cemetery, the Palmer's, and on occasion, the smithy. She could be found in few other places. When had she become so predictable?

Chapter 10

E loise stared at herself in the bedroom mirror. Friday evening had arrived, and she'd changed from her usual blue dress into a newer day dress—the cream-colored one with the red cuffs and sailor collar. Even though it was new, fashionable, it didn't suit her as well as the blue. She stuck her tongue out at her reflection, unsatisfied.

The table was set, the house tidy, and dinner was in the oven. Chicken and vegetables. Simple. When Tobias had company, she always prepared her easiest, fail-proof recipes. Tonight was no different. She'd arranged the meal earlier in the day, cleaned the kitchen, and only the roaster needed to be put in the oven.

She practiced a smile. The girl in the mirror smiled back. No one would suspect the way her stomach had been forming knots all day. How her throat felt full, and if she stopped for too long, she might just start crying and not even know why. Eloise had already tried her hair in three different styles, finally resorting to her regular twisted bun at the nape of her neck while Luke busied himself, unrolling stockings from her bottom drawer.

This dress would never do. It was too pale. Too breezy. It was better suited for a day trip in the sun. A picnic. She undid the knot at the collar and unbuttoned the bodice front. Tossing it to the bed, she pulled out her second-best dress. The dark purple with a wide band at the trim waist. She held it in front of her. Too formal. She'd only ever worn it to church.

Frustrated, she threw it on the bed with the other cast-offs. She knew she was overthinking it. But she didn't want to look like she'd tried too hard, and yet she wanted to look nice. Wearing only her chemise, corset, and bloomers, she sat on the floor with Luke. He pulled one of her stockings over both of his bare feet, bunching his trousers to his thighs.

"Luke, what am I worried about? This is not the first man Tobias has brought home for dinner."

Luke gave her an unconcerned glance and continued his task.

"You're making a mess of my things, you know."

"Mess," he said. "Big mess." He pointed to the other stockings scattered around.

She groaned. "I know. You put these away, and I'll do my part. Dada will be home soon."

If her blue calico was good enough for dinner with Tobias, it was good enough for Zeke. And regardless of what they shared over the week, she would protect her heart. Falling for a man who was passing through town was no way to heal.

Not that she was falling for him. Zeke was friendly and made her laugh with his silly jokes. He had an easy manner that made conversation enjoyable. That was all. But if that were true, then why did her stomach flip when their hands touched? Why did her heart break up in tiny little pieces to see him wrestling with Luke on Helen's parlor rug?

Digging through the dress pile on her bed, she pulled the blue one back out. Comfort and familiarity was usually best.

It was only dinner. Food and conversation.

That was all.

No need to fret.

Zeke wasn't sure what to think about the evening. Tonight was the night. Dinner with the boss. It could be an honor, a review, or something else? He had worked for the man for less than a week. Interactions with him were minimal. Boss spent most of his time in the office, making rounds to talk with some of the men, often in conference with Dee or the other senior workers. Zeke knew the man had a family but nothing else about him.

Zeke looked himself over in the mirror. He liked what he saw. He wasn't a bad-looking fellow. Scrubbing quickly after work, after fighting the others for the use of the washroom first, he threw on a clean set of clothes and combed his damp hair.

He needed a haircut. It would do for now, though. Zeke winked at the mirror. And then felt stupid. He was having dinner with his boss and family. No need to get all dolled up. Still, no harm in dressing up a little. He hoped the guy wasn't a bore. Some of the boys from work were going to a dance at the town hall, and he planned to drop by after dinner.

Snatching his hat, he sauntered through the hall and down the steps. The other boarders were gathering in the dining room.

George whistled at him. "Where are you off to looking so fine?"

"Wouldn't you like to know," Zeke said.

Thomas thumped him on the back. "Aw, Zeke, don't leave a fellow hanging all night. How'd you meet a dame so quick?"

"It's nothing like that. Boss invited me for dinner." He made a face and pretended to loosen his collar. "Hope I'm not getting the ax."

Simon, already settled at the table, cleared his throat. He snapped a napkin noisily before settling it across his lap.

"What's ruffled your feathers, professor?" Thomas yanked out the chair next to Simon and took his seat. "Miz Helen?" He called loudly toward the kitchen. "Your cooking's been teasing my stomach since I walked in. Shall I come back and help you?"

Helen answered from behind the door. "You wouldn't dare, Thomas. I'll be right out, and you know it."

Zeke waved at the group. "Boys, I'll be seeing you."

Jonas hollered after him. "Save a dance for me."

Catching Simon's eye, Zeke's smile faltered. His smart remark to Jonas died in his throat. Leaving the house with a nod, he pulled the door shut until he heard the click of the latch.

There was something different about Simon today. Usually the man was sophisticated. Annoyingly proper. He had an obnoxious habit of sniffing and raising his nose just enough to appear superior in every way. Zeke caught on quickly, and since no one else in the house paid him any mind, Zeke did not either. Members of the house ignored Simon and sometimes used him for sport.

But tonight was different. There was a darkness in Simon's eyes as he brooded at the table. His parting glance was troublesome. Zeke had done absolutely nothing to Simon, good or bad, to elicit such an emotion.

Eloise sat on the floor with Luke in the front room. They worked together to stack blocks until he decided it was high enough and knocked it down with such force that they scattered in all directions. He ran around in high spirits, gathering them into a pile and began working on the tower again.

Tobias came into the room combing his freshly rinsed hair. "That's what you're wearing?"

"What's wrong with it?" Eloise steadied Luke's tower.

When Tobias joined them on the floor and picked up a block, Luke snatched it from his hand. "I've asked Maribeth to save a dance for me."

"Will you be picking her up?"

"Not this time. Wasn't sure how late dinner would go." He added a block to the top of the tower only moments before Luke used both arms to windmill it like a hurricane against a lighthouse. "El, I'd love to see you in your other one tonight. The blue one with the white stuff on the edge."

"That's a party dress. And that *white stuff* is called lace. It would be silly to wear that for a simple dinner." That was one of the few she hadn't bothered to try on. Eloise caught Luke in her lap before he tripped on the blocks around his feet. "Goodness, this boy is wild."

"Join us tonight, after dinner. I miss having you there. My poor feet are bruised after an evening with those other girls. You know the two of us are the best dancing match in the whole of Nebraska."

"I don't know. It's been so long." She brought over the tin can for the toys and gathered a few. "Roy and Jess are going together. Finally." She raised her arm to prevent Luke from climbing into the can. "All the people." Weighing a block in each hand as if deciding which one would solve her dilemma, she sighed. Luke took them from her and squished them against his cheeks.

Tobias showed him it was time to clean up and tossed a few in the can. "I will stay by your side the whole night."

"Ha! Poor Maribeth. I wouldn't hold you to that."

Luke clanged each block into the can with as much force as he was able.

"Maribeth would understand," Tobias said.

"You're a sweet brother. But I can't. You forgot about your son."

"I didn't. Agnes is coming later to sit at the house." Tobias stood and brushed his suit.

Eloise surveyed her attire. Perhaps it would be appropriate to dress up a little. Tobias was wearing his nice suit, after all. But go out tonight? To a town social? A dance? Going with Tobias wouldn't be terrible. He knew how to have fun, how to relax and enjoy himself, and they did dance well together. They'd had so many evenings practicing as children. Their mother had been a wonderful teacher. It wasn't like Eloise was putting anyone out by going. He had even gone behind her back to arrange for Agnes to watch Luke. And Jessica would be there. Tobias would take her home the moment she asked, she knew.

Rap, Rap, Rap.

The staccato knock startled her. Zeke was waiting outside her home, and Tobias wanted her to go dancing tonight. So much to do yet for one evening.

"He's here," Tobias said. "Right on time." He helped her off the floor and scooted the toy can to the wall with his foot. "Wear the party dress, if that's what you call it. I can stall our company for a few minutes."

"We'll see." Eloise clutched her skirts and hustled upstairs. Would Zeke notice if she dressed up? Did she care? He was a hard one to peg. One minute he was calm, inviting. The next, he obviously wished to be somewhere else. When he sat with her at the cemetery, it was as if he had all the time in the world to listen to her. It took more strength than she was willing to admit not to pour out her heart to him.

Of course, a few easy conversations were not enough to build the kind of trust she was looking for. *What are you looking for, Eloise?* She most definitely was not looking for a so-called adventurer. One minute he was stiff and widening the gap between them by shutting down their conversations, and the next minute, he was offering her his own handkerchief. She was not normally in the habit of crying in front of strangers.

Jessica's words came back to her. *Someday . . . being with another man.*

No.

What she wanted now was freedom. She yearned to really and truly be free. Philip had been the heart of her life since she was fourteen. After they married, life was blissfully happy, except for when it wasn't. Philip often needed her to talk him out of bed in the morning. She grew weary of making excuses for him when he couldn't leave the house.

His death, instead of setting her free, somehow bound her tighter. The self-doubt that used to claw around the edges pounced on her, and she often found herself overwhelmed by it. She was shadowed by a fear that covered any joy that tried to make itself known.

Dare she entertain a hope that she wouldn't always feel stuck? Could she take the night off from being Eloise the Widow? She wasn't sure she knew how to just be Eloise anymore. What would people think? Not many paid attention anymore. *Can I be someone else for a night?*

Zeke didn't know it was her fault Philip was dead. She smiled, remembering how easily Luke went to Zeke. He'd snuggled into his chest, hiding his face from the wind and tucking his arms from the cold. Zeke had held him close, one arm securing the child's legs and the other hand splayed across his back, shielding him. She could imagine Simon's disdain at being asked to hold a toddler; he would have never volunteered for it.

She'd wear the dress for Tobias. Never-mind how the waist accented her trim figure, and the skirts flowed around her like a stream. Surely she was old enough to wear the flattering square neckline without the older generation raising their eyebrows. The pale blue brought attention to her eyes, and inches of elegant lace cuffed the short sleeves and hem that brushed the floor. It used to be her favorite dress. *Can I be Eloise in this dress again? The Eloise from before? The one who knew how to have fun?* Could she keep the memories of Philip without being shrouded by them? Tonight could be a night of new beginnings. Celebrating her survival of the last year and a half. Tonight wasn't about moving on or forgetting or going out or staying in. It was about dressing up and being free.

No strings. No chains.

The warm smell of roast chicken and herbs filled the house when Tobias greeted Zeke at the door. Zeke smiled and offered his hand, promptly pushing away thoughts of Simon. He had other things to worry about. Particularly, dinner with his boss and family.

"Welcome!" Tobias said. "You're just in time. We'll eat as soon as the lady of the house joins us." Tobias picked up a baby blanket and threw it on a pile of toys in the corner before he relaxed on the sofa. "Have a seat."

The lived-in feeling of the place put Zeke at ease. It was tidy, but not the sort of place where he was afraid to sit. He saw three wooden blocks hiding under the chair across the room.

"I admire your plans of going west. Have you any people there?"

"Nope. Making my own way."

"All the stories that find their way back sure paint a pretty picture. And here I thought we were already west. Do you have work lined up? Whereabouts are you landing?"

"You trying to talk me out of it?" Zeke asked. "I'll level with you, and here's the whole of it: I've no family, no real ties anywhere.

There's adventure to be had out there, I'm sure. I've nothing to lose the way I figure it. I've only got myself and my horse to feed, so it's no trouble so far to work a little here and there along the way." He laughed. "I've forgotten your other list of questions. Did I answer them all?"

"Just about. Where's the end point? Where are you going?"

"My sights are set on Northern California, but if something else calls along the way . . ." He shrugged.

"California," said Tobias, as if tasting the word on his tongue.

"Yup."

"You're halfway there, I reckon."

Zeke laughed. "Don't tell anyone. I've only been on this trip for a few weeks. I moved with my adopted family from West Virginia to a farm in Iowa. It's fair to say I've been taking the scenic route. This is my third real stop."

"No harm in that. Maybe in another life I would have joined you. I've never been free of family ties that you speak of, and now with Luke, I like the idea of sticking around and growing strong roots for him."

Zeke must have heard wrong. "Luke?"

"My son, Luke. Eloise tells me you have met? A couple of times, she said. I never did get the full story. Which makes me even more curious. El isn't usually interested in meeting people. Especially men. Nothing personal."

Zeke didn't believe it. It couldn't be. He rubbed the back of his neck. This was Mr. Davidson. His boss. Of all the men and all the jobs he could have found. *It's dinner, Zeke. Food and conversation. No need to fret.* Opening his mouth now would land him in the fire. He could imagine the whole thing. *Yes sir, Boss. I met your wife mostly naked. I found her in the creek. Soaking wet. Her wet shift clung to her body and left little to the imagination. Not only did I see her, but I didn't even avert my eyes. Because I'm a low-down rotten cad. Would you be so kind as to pass the salt?*

"What's so funny?" Tobias asked.

Zeke was saved by Luke's entrance.

The boy ran through the room and climbed into his father's lap. "Dada! Pitty! Big Pitty."

"Pretty? You think I'm pretty?"

Luke gave him a blank stare and tried again. "Big pitty." This time, he pointed to the stairs. Both men looked as Eloise entered with a shy smile.

If Zeke hadn't already been speechless, he sure was now. Along with the confirmation that he needed to guard himself closely.

"Sorry to keep you waiting," she said.

The men stood when she walked into the room. Tobias went to her. He put an arm around her shoulder and whispered in her ear.

She blushed and looked at Zeke. "Welcome to our home, Mr.—" she smiled. "Zeke. Welcome, Zeke."

He returned her smile and had trouble swallowing. He was the one to avert his eyes this time. The way she looked at him just now did things to his gut that he wasn't prepared for. Was it too late to feign a stomachache and leave early? In the week since coming to Ockelbo, being in this home and meeting this family was too much. He felt truly welcomed. He felt at home. At peace. And yet, he was in the wrong home, having the wrong feelings for the wrong girl. His conscience flared. *What am I doing here? All I needed was a shoe for a horse and a few bucks for food. This is turning into a disaster.*

Tobias cleared his throat. "It appears we all know each other. Zeke. Eloise." He nodded to each in turn. "Eloise and Zeke. There. I'm starved. Let's eat." He tossed Luke high over his head to get a squeal from him and led the way to the table.

Chapter 11

⚜

Eloise bit back a smile as she served dinner. The game was working better than she had hoped. Anticipation for her evening experiment of freedom vibrated within her. She felt both shy and daring with Zeke; she didn't have room to worry about her past. The dress helped firmly make up her mind. Tonight, she would be free. Even if just for pretend. Let it be a game. Free of the guilt of being unfaithful to Philip. Free of the chains to the cemetery. Free to smile and dance. Free to be and feel alive in a way she had not in years. Even for one night. She would not be held back by death or fear.

Zeke was oblivious to her extra attentions. His initial reaction when she came down the stairs was strong enough to ensure that he did, indeed, notice her, but he directed most of his conversation to her brother. Throughout dinner, Zeke threw questions at Tobias about everything from the business to town history and politics. He was insatiable with his questions. She was surprised at how interested he was in anything Tobias said. Though Tobias shamelessly directed many of them to Eloise, Zeke rarely looked at her and developed an odd quirk of nodding his head with a vague smile to her answers and then began again, "So tell me, Boss."

The one thing that caught his interest in her was the food. He praised the meal and asked about her recipe for the bread. Embarrassed, she confessed to buying it from Anderson's Bakery. He laughed easily. "I wouldn't go through the trouble either. This is amazing!"

In some ways, it was better he sent so much energy to Tobias. It gave her room to enjoy the evening without pressure. This week had dealt her such a rush of emotions from the nightmares returning and then meeting Zeke. Simon's insults, Jessica's encouraging her to open up, Roy's interest in Jessica, and weaved through it all were constant reminders of Ezekiel James. She didn't know what to do about it all.

Consistent with her cautious nature, it was foolish to think about him as more than a stranger. The feelings she had would amount to nothing because there was nothing to feel. She didn't feel anything for him. Nope, and because he was only passing through, it made him a fantasy. A safe daydream. He had no prior knowledge of Philip. Or her. She could be whoever she wanted to be. And that was enough to crack open a wall of her cell, which allowed a ray of sunshine to blaze inside.

Once the meal was over, Zeke pushed around a few stray rosemary needles with his fork. Eloise stacked the other plates and Tobias wiped clean Luke's hands and face.

"El, I'm going to put him to bed," Tobias said. "I'll be down soon. If you'll excuse me." He manually waved Luke's hand at Zeke, "Say goodnight, Luke."

Eloise followed him to the base of the stairs, cupped Luke's face in her hands, and kissed his forehead. "Goodnight, baby. See you tomorrow."

Tobias leaned in as if to kiss her on the cheek but instead leaned into her ear and whispered, "Be nice."

She glanced at Zeke before whispering back. "I'm always nice."

Tobias's eyebrows shot up. "Always? Always like Luke *always* sleeps through the night? Come on, I mean it. I think he needs a friend."

"What's that got to do with me? Besides, he doesn't want to talk to me. He appears wholly uninterested in speaking to me today."

Tobias chuckled. "Trust me, he's very interested."

Zeke found a smudge on the table to pick at while trying not to appear interested in whatever Tobias was whispering to his wife. He had never witnessed a couple quite like them before. He couldn't nail down what it was, but something was off.

Eloise, gorgeously beautiful Eloise, was happier tonight than he'd ever seen her. Granted, he'd known her for less than a week. But he felt he'd known her much longer. Her eyes shone, and with no ugly bonnet to hide her face, he did his best to keep his attention from constantly staring at her. He felt her eyes constantly burning into him and feared any minute the truth of their meeting would be made known. Sitting across the table from her husband was unnerving. He was paranoid that he would give something away. Therefore, he'd chatted incessantly. *Lord, help me.*

Hearing a gasp from Eloise, he looked up in time to see her slap Tobias on the arm. Her cheeks were a rose-pink, and Tobias laughed aloud before disappearing with the boy upstairs.

Eloise returned to the table and gathered the remaining dishes. "Excuse us, Tobias just remembered a funny story."

"Oh, yeah? What about?"

"Oh, silly toddler things. Honestly, it wouldn't interest you." She bustled around the kitchen, not stopping her flow of words. "How was your first week? I know the pit isn't very exciting. Especially after all your adventuring, you must be used to much more entertainment than swinging a mattock." She tied an apron around her slim waist and loaded the dishpan. "I'm always telling him he ought to do something, switch the rotation, or allow for more breaks. Some of those jobs are incredibly monotonous. I don't know how a body could continue in it day after day. I know I never would. But he has an answer for everything. As always. If I'm lucky he'll give me an answer, that is. If he doesn't have a smart remark, he'll pretend he didn't hear me. You know how men can be."

He watched her dress swish around her ankles as she turned this way and that. She'd paused by the stove to look at him pointedly. As if he were the one to answer for all men on why they were the way they were. When she braced herself to lift the large pot of heated water from the stove, his resolve to keep his distance was forgotten.

He jumped to help her. "Let me." Carefully, he lifted the stockpot and began pouring it over the pan of dishes. "So, you were saying, about men. How is it again, how men can be?"

"You know, having a woman tell you what to do, even if it is, obviously, superior to what you were planning to do—"

"Obviously."

"—would drive you to do the stupidest thing you could have done." She stood too near him, watching the water pour slowly over the dishes.

It was difficult to focus on the task with the feel of her dress touching his calves. He prayed Tobias didn't return in the next minute. "I have heard of this condition before, but in my observation, it inflicts only married men." He stepped back from her and she moved into his place to dunk the rag in the hot water.

Setting the empty pan on the stove, he found a towel and waited to wipe them. "Usually the woman, having all the better ideas, has a snarly, contorted face from years of scowling at a man for not listening to her."

"What kind of face?" Eloise passed him a dripping plate and waited expectantly.

"Like this." He stopped drying for a second, squished one side of his face, and grimaced, looking altogether ridiculous. Whatever the means, the result was worth it.

Eloise burst into laughter, and he couldn't stop himself. He twisted his face again. "Or this."

She flicked water into his face. "Nobody looks like that. You ought to see yourself."

"Should I? And if you're going to be splashing, I need a shield. These are my only dancing clothes. Where can I get one of those fancy aprons?"

She tossed him a pale blue one that was dotted with pink flowers and ruffles along the edge.

After a one-handed catch, he held it up for inspection. "Oh, this color is my favorite. It brings out my eyes, don't you think?" He knew it did nothing for his eyes—they were green. Hers, on the other hand, were a different matter, as he found himself only inches from them when he looked up from the apron he was inspecting. The air hitched in his throat at her nearness. For a moment, he lost track of his thoughts as she studied him. The lace around her neckline clearly accented her, well, her figure. Not that he noticed. Much. Her blue eyes were all the brighter against her flushed cheeks. His eyes flicked to her lips, and he wondered if she had any idea what she did to him. *And how quickly she'd slap you if she knew.* Her lips, that he wasn't watching, turned up at the corners.

"I think green is more your color." She spoke lithely and returned to the sink.

He let out a breath he didn't know he'd been holding. *Dear Jesus, help me.* Where was Tobias? How long did it take to put a toddler to sleep?

He stepped away from her and tied the apron around his waist. Attempting to fill the silence, a tumble of words poured out. "Does Boss always do the bedtime? I don't have much experience with little kids. I just always assumed bedtime was a mama thing." When he looked up, she was staring at him oddly. Land sakes. Her intense glare and pursed lips were not helping him to avoid looking at her mouth. "Get to work. Come on now, you're falling behind. You still have a pile of dishes in your pan. Hustle, Chipmunk." *Eloise.* Or maybe he should go back to calling her Mrs. Davidson. That would keep him in line.

"I'm hustling." With exaggerated finesse, she washed another plate. Zeke stood ready at attention with his towel. He wiped each plate dry, setting it neatly onto the counter, and turned to await the next item. They worked in rhythm until the dishpan was left only with the dirty water.

They tossed light banter between them, but Zeke carefully kept his distance. Rubbing shoulders with her bare arm would not be prudent. Not in his current condition. It shouldn't be this hard to get a hold of himself, but he kept picturing the last time he had seen her bare arm, with white muslin undergarments clinging to her. *Knock it off, Zeke.* The night was turning into more than a simple dinner and conversation, and he needed to get out.

Soon they were finished, and she ran the rag across the counter. "Thank you," she said. "I could get used to having an apprentice. Maybe you should come for dinner more often."

Heavens, no. If she only knew his mind. Zeke offered a smile, nonetheless. "I would like that. But I couldn't. Mrs. Palmer serves wonderful meals, and the boss might have something to say if I showed up here like a beggar. He might wonder why he's paying me."

"He's paying you to swing a stick all day. He is in charge of making bricks. I am in charge of everything else. At least that's what I tell myself." Eloise wiped the table, and Zeke followed behind to dry the wood with his towel. She hung the rag on a peg and removed her apron.

Looking around for something else to keep his hands busy, Zeke asked, "Broom?"

"It's behind the door in the lean-to." She nodded toward the back door as she busied herself with loading the dried dishes into the cupboard. He paused while opening the door. Her back was to him as she lifted the plates to the shelf. This woman. She was so easy to be with, to talk to—when he didn't have his stomach stuck in his throat in the presence of her husband. He ought to leave now before he got into trouble. Nothing good would come of this. Better to set his mind on something safe. Like the West. And the ocean. And how he was going to get there.

He found the broom, but hanging on a nail next to it was a black apron. It was all black, with black ruffles along the bottom and black lace accents decorating the middle. Smiling, Zeke took it inside with him. "Hey! You're pretty funny dressing me up in flowers when you had this extra all along. The ruffles and lace are still there, but a man could—" he stopped as soon as he saw her stricken face.

She stood frozen until one hand fluttered to cover her mouth. Gently removing the apron from his hand, her hands shook, and her cheeks lost their rosy tint. "This one is mine . . . I—I don't wear it . . . anymore . . . sort of a . . . personal."

A gentle knock sounded on the front door before it opened. "Hello?"

Zeke backed away from Eloise; he'd been caught standing too near again. He moved to the other side of the kitchen, folded his towel, and set it to the side, waiting for Eloise to compose herself. He wondered if he should greet the guest.

She ran a hand across her face and tossed the apron on the table, seemingly forgotten. Skipping into the front room, she cried out. "Agnes!"

Agnes and Eloise exchanged hugs, and a hushed conversation began between them with quick glances in his direction. He was either the topic of discussion or meant to be kept from it. Both options rankled him. *What am I even still doing here?* If only he had left before Tobias retreated upstairs.

He came forward. "How do you do, ma'am. Pleasure seeing you again." That promptly shut down the women's chat. Bright smiles flashed between the women like a white-washed facade. Good grief, maybe he should leave and go on alone.

Agnes almost read his mind. "I'm here now. You kids can run along. And you!" She took both of Eloise's hands in her own and held her back to admire her. "Honey, how long it's been since I've seen you dressed up. It suits you beautifully. You will have a grand time." She pulled Eloise in for a long hug. As she released her, both of the women's eyes glistened.

Women were so odd. Zeke could feel that edge of reservation in Eloise again, but her response made as much sense to him as a pig in a prairie.

"I will be fine. I can manage to put it aside for this evening at least. It'll be a practice run. One of many, let's hope? Honestly, I could never make it through without friends like you."

"That reminds me," Agnes said. "I brought a tea ring for your breakfast tomorrow. Baked it fresh this afternoon. My gift."

Zeke had never heard of a tea ring. It was baked and edible. That much was enough to interest him.

"Oh, lovely!" Eloise said. "How you spoil me. If it weren't for you and Helen, my boys wouldn't ever get bread."

Agnes pulled a cloth-wrapped bundle from her basket and

walked into the kitchen to put it on the table.

How Zeke wished to unwrap it himself to determine what a tea ring was. He would just have to order one the next time he ate at her bakery.

Agnes settled on the sofa after removing her coat and gloves. She dug through a basket of sewing things she'd brought with her. Looking up, she clicked her tongue to see them still standing there. "Do I need to say it again? You can go on and play. Luke will be fine."

"Tobias will be down soon," Eloise said. "We'll all walk together."

Together. Zeke smirked. *If only.* He tried not to squirm when Agnes paused and looked between the two of them.

"Very well," she said. She tilted her head as if she truly noticed Zeke for the first time. "You know, dear. I've never seen a man so confident in that apron. Those pink flowers really bring out your eyes." She winked at him before making herself comfortable.

That's when he noticed the broom still in his hand.

Chapter 12

The firm support of the wall calmed Eloise's nerves. Somewhat. Her mother would have reprimanded her for slouching, but the solid wall reassured her. It reminded her that not everything was slipping away. She caught sight of Jessica and Roy spinning on the dance floor. Roy was not a confident dancer, but Jessica was joyful and encouraging. Roy would soon find out what he was in for. Years of waiting for him to make a move had filled a reservoir of pent-up energy in Jessica.

Eloise switched her weight from her right foot to her left. She watched Tobias in the other corner of the room shaking hands with Bob O'Hara, one of his older employees. He nodded to the man's wife and stayed to chat. Tobias was good at that, the smiling and chatting. Everyone had a smile for her brother. They would pat him on the back and share a funny snippet from their week. He would toss his head back with a free and open laugh. The only damper on his evening was her presence, she knew. She didn't know how he kept up the joviality. Smiles weren't forced for him; they came naturally. Unlike her. When she was surrounded by a crowd of people like this, nothing came naturally. Oh, she was plenty happy sometimes, around certain people, when she was unafraid of being asked trivial questions. Nobody really wanted to know what a mess she truly was.

She felt blessed to have Tobias, though she didn't deserve him. Without Tobias, she never would have survived the past five years since losing their parents or the last year and a half without Philip. Her brother refused to give up on her when she closed off the rest of the world. Life had held no meaning after Philip died and then when she took on the daily responsibility of caring for baby Luke . . . well, she hadn't been able to care for the infant and stay in bed all day feeling sorry for herself. Loving Luke was easy. When Katie died only months after Philip, it was the most natural thing for Eloise to assume the role of mother. She and baby Luke, only seven months old, had clung to each other. Tobias clung to them, to his work, and his community. But he wasn't broken like she was. He weathered each storm with a strength she couldn't fathom.

The courage she'd felt in their home with Zeke in her kitchen had faded quickly on the walk over. Zeke walked ahead of her and Tobias, and the wind rushing around her ears made talking difficult. She'd been able to put one foot in front of the other with her arm linked to Tobias's elbow, pretending this was just like any other night, strolling a few blocks across town. She was not going to think about how it was the first time in over a year she had attended a social gathering outside of church. Once she got there, it wasn't anything like she'd imagined.

For the most part, everyone ignored her. She'd spent years ignoring them, after all. The men from the brickyard, who knew her, were respectful. But nobody asked her to dance. Caroline Jenkins, an old friend from school, greeted her with a large smile but was intercepted by Charles before making her way over. She hoped Charles would behave himself. He tended to lean toward impropriety.

Jonas tried talking to her for a while, but even he lost interest, and thank goodness he never asked her for a dance.

She figured Simon would have liked to ask her, but she'd managed to avoid him, though she'd caught him staring at her multiple times. How did the man think he ever had a chance for her heart? She had never given him encouragement, and he'd still pestered her all these years. He was relentless. Philip used to tease him, she knew, by sneaking kisses with her in front of Simon. It was mean of him, but Eloise never minded. She was glad to belong to Philip. To have someone love her and want to show her off.

It was nothing like the way things were now. The only relief of the evening was dancing with Tobias. It felt wonderful to sway with the music and let her mind and body drift together, being led and supported by the safety of the one man she still trusted in all the world. She was not going to think about the last time Philip swept her into his arms across the floor.

Tobias had offered to stay with her while she rested, but she'd set him free, telling him to go on. Maribeth waited for his attention, standing with her other friends or serving at the desserts' table. She was not going to think about how Maribeth and Tobias were happy together. How she'd seen them slip out the side door hand in hand. Her mind was filled to bursting with all the things she didn't want to think about.

She wished all the happiness for Tobias but could not empathize. He'd found love less than a year after Katie's death. Seeing it stung her heart. They used to have their grief in common. But now things were changing.

A sharp memory of Philip invaded her mind. She'd been scheming with Jess when Philip came up behind her. Slipping his hands on her waist, he whispered to her. "Come outside." Her face glowed instantly red; she shook her head and hid a giggle.

He'd sneaked a kiss on her cheek. "I'll meet you by the fountain in five minutes."

She did meet him and ended the night with a ring on her finger and hopes and plans of a storybook future.

Standing here now, her throat grew thick. What felt like a little knife bored a hole into her stomach, and breathing became difficult.

Just be normal.

She closed her eyes and focused on the sound of the music. What would a normal person do? A normal person would have more than one friend and a brother to keep her company. She should go. She would walk out the door and go home. Nobody would miss her, but Tobias would worry when he returned and didn't find her. She could leave a message with Jessica. He would enjoy his evening more without her hanging like a weight to him. He wanted to be alone with Maribeth anyway.

I shouldn't have come. I knew from the beginning I shouldn't have come. Why did she think this was going to work? It was too soon. She wasn't ready. But it was dark outside, and she couldn't go out in the dark. She would never make it home.

Her corset was suddenly restrictive.

A sea of smiling and laughing faces overwhelmed her. Standing apart from the others, Simon stared at her from across the room. His eyes bored into her as if she were a target and he the arrow. She pushed both hands to her stomach to hold in the spreading ache. The thickness in her throat only worsened, and a stinging pain grew behind her eyes.

Keep it together, El. She knew this feeling. The music was too loud. The laughter was hideous to her ears.

Not here. She would not fall apart in front of all these people. Oh, why did she come? Why did she think everything would be okay? She wasn't strong enough and would never be enough. She couldn't even enjoy an evening with friends. What a joke she'd played on herself. Thinking she could pretend her life away. Thinking she could pretend Zeke was interested in being her friend. He didn't want anything to do with her. Since Tobias had joined them after dinner, Zeke hadn't looked her in the eyes, much less spoken to her. One more example of why she should have stayed home. She had nothing to offer. Nothing to offer Zeke and nothing to gain by hanging around Tobias, leaching more of his energy.

Simon raised a hand to wave to her, but she did not have the strength to interact with him.

Zeke watched Eloise on and off throughout the evening. He hadn't found much to do, knowing only the boys from work, and they were busy finding girls to dance with. He'd gone around the dance floor a few times with willing partners—Becky Wisting and Caroline Jenkins—but it fell flat each time. The fact that his eyes kept straying to a certain other someone may have had something to do with it, and then he grew bored of answering the same questions to everyone he met. He sounded like he was convincing himself of his own plan.

What was he doing here? The past weeks of travel were beginning to feel like a fading dream. He'd spent years working odd jobs where he could find them, along with helping on the Donnely's farm. Going west was his plan, plain and simple. He stopped only for a bite to eat and restock supplies. Why did they try to make it complicated? It wasn't a foolproof plan, but he wasn't in a hurry. What he'd originally believed would be a grand cross-country adventure, in reality, felt hollow each time he moved on. And he hadn't even made it through Nebraska. He would never make it to California at this rate.

The Donnelys had sent him off with showers of blessings and words of warning. Though he lived and worked with them for eight years, and though they were as close to family as he would ever have, he'd never seen himself as a farmer. He'd never desired the life of Paul Donnely. Grateful as he was for the family and the love, he was not going to stay on the farm. The move from West Virginia to a farm in Iowa had set a fire under him to see more of the country. Posters encouraging him to launch his western dreams had only kindled his desire until he'd finally set off. So what held him back? What except for a pair of blue eyes and blushing cheeks, and a wedding ring that announced how wrong he was to even think of her.

He was only at the beginning of his journey. True, there was no deadline. As long as he kept his health and was able to work, he could take as long as he wanted to find the Pacific, but being here, in this town, with these people, it made him yearn for something extra. Something like a family. Someone like Eloise.

No, it's Mrs. Davidson to you. Someone *like* her who wanted to be with him and laugh about life together. Someone who wasn't already married. Someone who made adventures worth adventuring. A companion to share in his dreams and a friend to sit and be silent and content with, knowing he wouldn't have to say goodbye. To have someone to wake up with and not be alone. Was that too much to ask for?

Chipmunk was standing alone and had been for some time. And even though Zeke had succeeded in keeping his distance throughout the night, he knew something was wrong. Something was off, and nobody else seemed to notice. He found himself quickly moving toward her. Before he reached her, she suddenly grabbed her skirts as if to run away.

"Eloise." He touched her arm.

She startled at his nearness but paused in her flight when she saw him. A flash of panic in her eyes receded, and she surprised him by leaning into him. With staccato breaths, she pressed her forehead against his chest and took a moment to slow her breathing. Her hands gripped the sides of his shirt.

He stiffened and patted her shoulder gingerly. "You okay? Can I get someone for you?" When he didn't get a reply, he tried again.

"Want to tell me what's wrong?"

She popped up and looked over his shoulder. Scowling at the people behind him, she said, "Ask me to dance with you."

"What?"

"Quickly. He's still watching." She clicked her tongue, and turning her face to him, she gritted her teeth in a smile that looked more like a grimace, "Dance? Oh yes! I would love to. This way." She took his hand and pulled him toward the others on the floor.

He would never understand women. "Chip, I don't think this is a good idea. Why am I asking you to dance?"

She shushed him and fervently looked over his shoulder again.

Obediently, he placed his hand on her side and held her right hand in his. Fingers dug into his shoulder as he attempted to lead her.

Her scowl hadn't improved, and her arms were stiff while the waltz took them into the crowd. She pushed them to the opposite side of the room, trampling his feet repeatedly. Focusing elsewhere, her eyes roamed, and her face was drained of all color—not the tint of pink he was used to seeing.

The fourth time she stumbled over his feet without an apology, he was done. He dropped his arms and took her hand in his, pulling her outside the nearest door. Her hand fit snuggly, and he couldn't have shaken her free with the clasp she had on him. When they were just outside the door he turned her to face him. The lights of the hall spilled out to where they stood. Placing his hands on her arms, he tried to make eye contact. *Careful, Zeke.* The feel of her skin quickened his heart. It was soft and warm to his touch.

"Eloise." He spoke sternly. "Mrs. Davidson. What is it? Who are you looking for?"

She continued drifting her gaze to the edges of the hall, ignoring Zeke.

Zeke ran his hands up to her shoulders. He told himself it was necessary to get her attention, and he cradled her head in his hands. Only because she was ignoring him. Not because he yearned for more. With his thumb pressed gently under her jaw, he felt her rapid heartbeat. What would it take for her to see him? A kiss would do the trick. If he bent his head to hers, would she fight him? Oblivious of the intimate position they were in, she never once looked at him.

Leaning in, he spoke softly in her ear with her face almost touching his. "Look at me."

Her face whipped toward him, and he was forced to jerk away, lest his lips touch hers.

Playing it off with a smirk, he said the first thing that came to mind. "There you are. I've been meaning to talk to you about something, and I wondered when I'd have the pleasure of your company. Now listen, young lady, if you wanted to dance, why didn't you ask?" He softened his voice when her eyes widened. "But I get the feeling you didn't really want to dance, Chipmunk. As a friend, I'm concerned. You're anxious, and it shows."

Eloise locked eyes with him. Her shoulders drooped, and her breathing slowed; she visibly relaxed. Slowly, the panic left her face. "Friend?"

He kept talking, anything to keep her focused. "Friends can dance, can't they? If we're going to dance, you've got to let me lead.

I'm nothing special, but I can hold my own." He should not encourage this. Dancing was a bad idea. A really bad idea. He couldn't keep his heart in line when he *wasn't* touching her, but now that he had his hands on her bare skin, his fingers laced behind her head, his thumbs caressing her jaw . . . well, it wasn't helping matters. Jumping on his horse and continuing his journey west right now, this very minute, was a better plan. And yet, he kept talking, and he didn't move his hands from where they rested against her neck. She didn't move away. "My boots can't take any more abuse."

She cupped her hands over his, closed her eyes, and let out a breath before she gently moved his hands away from her. When she opened her eyes again, she wasn't the same girl from a few minutes ago. This Eloise smiled. She let out a breathless laugh and ducked her head. Almost an apology to his boots. "I'm silly. Forgive me?" She curtsied to him and offered herself—holding her hands out to him.

Zeke cleared his throat and raised his eyebrows. One minute she's dancing with her husband. Smiling, beautiful, graceful. One of the best on the floor. The next, she was standing alone. Antsy, fretful, with panic in her eyes. First, she yanked him around, nervous and stiff. And now, she laughed? What was next?

A waltz, apparently.

"Ready?" he asked. Gently he put pressure on her waist, and joining the other couples, he began the waltz again.

Her eyes remained on his, and she moved with him, following his lead. It was as if part of her had melted into him. The slightest pressure on her waist or hand guided her about the floor. He was lost in her eyes. Swimming in a sea of blue. Her full lashes blinked, and a faint pink grew on her cheeks. It was a good sign that her color had returned. Finally, he noticed that she was grinning at him. "What's so funny?"

"You said you'd been meaning to talk to me about something. Earlier. Remember?"

He grunted. "I don't remember." He couldn't tell her he was sunk. She pulled him in and held him in a way that made him feel like he was home. Safe and secure. He couldn't. He needed to be done with her.

She was dangerous. He wasn't safely home. She was a siren bent on drowning him. She was dangerous for his heart, his job, for his moral standing. *God, help me. I've got to get away from this one.* Dragging his gaze away from hers, he breathed deeply, trying to clear his head. Even breathing deeply around her was a mistake. All he could smell was her floral perfume. "Where is Tobias?"

Eloise laughed. A musical sound that did not help his situation. "Worried?" she asked. "You needn't be. He's as protective as they come, but his mind is elsewhere. I'm sure he's worn out with babysitting me all night long."

How did she smile with those words? It didn't make sense. And it wasn't just his imagination. She had clearly eased her body to his. Zeke had been very careful not to pull her closer, with his hand barely touching her back, but she now pressed lightly against him.

When she and Tobias danced they'd stayed a respectful, chaste, arm's distance apart. Not the intimate position she was assuming with him now.

He wanted to ask her what her previous statement meant—to clarify her meaning, but he couldn't think. He was out of breath from all the concentrating. With her soft face gazing at him and her body against his, what he really wanted to do was gather her into his arms and taste her lips. He licked his own. Thankfully, they were surrounded by witnesses. He was preparing to flee as fast as Joseph from Potiphar's wife. Passages from Proverbs flashed in his mind. This was it! This was the harlot God warned about in the Proverbs. The ones who tempted men and called out to them during the night. He'd never thought they would be as desirable as this one. He'd pictured them wearing red with rouge on their cheeks, low-cut tops that invited a man to investigate. He was prepared to walk away from one of those. But a vision in blue with delicate lace around a neckline that only hinted at supple curves underneath? Shooting his eyes away from her body, he cleared his throat. Why didn't he run away?

"Don't be obvious," she said. "But as we go around, do you notice the man brooding in the corner?"

It gave him something to do with his eyes. That was good. Something else to focus on. He quickly found who she was referring to. "Simon Oakfield. Yes, he lives down the hall from me. Brooding in the corner is one of his favorite pastimes, I've noticed. Before I left tonight, he was more out of sorts than usual."

"Did he know where you were going?"

"I imagine so. The boys teased until I'd announced it. Why? What's his story?"

She huffed. "Serves him right. He has a hard time with, 'No.' I'm desperate to be away from him. Maybe there's more to his story, but I'm not privy to it. What I know is every time we converse, I feel like bashing in his head."

Surprised by her vehemence, Zeke chuckled. "Dear me. What does he say?"

"Everything! Nothing. Oh, honestly. He's infuriating."

Conversation. He could do this. No more thoughts about kissing and harlots and desire. Just conversation and dancing. No need to fret. Keep talking, keep his eyes away from her face, away from her eyes, and especially her lips. "Can't be having that. If there's one thing I've learned, it's to avoid angry females."

"I tell you, Simon is insufferable. Are you making fun of me?"

"Maybe. Does it make you angry? Then, no." He thought she smiled. It sounded like she was. But he refused to look at her. Her face was so close to his now. *For the love of temptation, would this song never end?* He needed to get away from her, to run away, before he did something terrible. Like take another deep breath and catch a whiff of her perfume, or accidentally brush his lips to her temple. "Ease my curiosity. What makes a girl like you angry?" He spoke softly near her ear.

"Honestly?"

They danced in silence a few turns, and Zeke couldn't handle the waiting. He tried another angle. "Tell me more about Simon." That was something that kept her talking.

"He's an incredible bore, among other things." She answered quickly with a good amount of sass.

"Yikes. Better keep it lively. Do not be a bore. Check." Zeke scanned the dance hall for her husband again. "Do you know where Tobias is? I am beginning to worry." He looked at her now as the music ended. *Thank the Lord.* Taking his hand from her waist, he stood what he considered to be an appropriate distance from a lady who was not his wife.

The light went out from the blue sea when she answered. "I'm sure he's with Maribeth. It's hardly a secret."

"I don't understand. Why isn't he with you? And who's Maribeth?" Guiding her off the dance floor, he ducked his head closer to her ear to be heard above the noise of the crowd.

"I'm not very exciting," she said. "I could hardly expect him to stay with me the whole evening." She removed her hand from his arm.

"Pardon?"

"Come with me. I can hardly hear you." She tugged on his sleeve until he followed her outside. Light spilled from the hall into the dark night. The evening air was cool, but it was a relief from the stuffy building.

"Start again," he said. "I'm confused. Who is Maribeth, and what's this drivel about you being unexciting? I thought we established that Simon was boring."

She laughed. "Maribeth is nice. I don't know her very well, but that's my own fault. I've been jealous." Lifting a shoulder, she smiled at Zeke. "Silly, I know. She works at the mercantile on the square. But she didn't go to school with us. She moved here a few years ago with her family. She's nice."

"Nice? Nice! Chipmunk, do you hear yourself? I still don't understand, but you're telling me Tobias is not with you because he's with her, and you're jealous, but she's nice? You are not silly, and I think you're perfectly in your rights to be jealous."

"Honestly, I don't understand why she has you so worked up." Eloise stepped closer and berated him in hushed tones. "If I didn't know better, I'd say you were jealous. I've done my part to stay out of it. After all he has done for me, the least I can do is be happy for him in this." She shrugged again. "If he wants to be with someone else, that is his choice."

A few strands of hair came loose, and she reached to tuck them into their pins. Calmly, as if discussing when the next shipment of coal would be delivered by train, she continued. "The transition may be hard for Luke, but I will be around to help him. And who knows, maybe they are not as serious as we all think. It may amount to nothing. Maybe a spring fling?"

Zeke's stomach dropped like a rock. "How long has this been going on? Are you okay? I know how hard this must be for you."

In one swift move, Eloise stepped to him. Placing her hands on his shoulders, she stood on her toes and kissed him on the cheek.

Jerking his head to the side, he grabbed her hands and pushed them away. "Don't."

Her face was as bright red as he'd ever seen it. She bit her bottom lip but did not look away.

Breaking out in a sweat, he tried to speak carefully, even though he wanted to run. Everything was falling apart. "Mrs. Davidson, I'm sorry. I'm really sorry this is happening to you. It's time you did something. But you, I mean, you can't." His raspy voice betrayed him. "Lord knows how I . . . I can't—I'm not the answer. I hate to see you this way. I can't imagine how you will carry on if he continues. But for you to stand back and take care of his child, and—while he . . . I don't know. Do you need help?"

Her eyes flashed at him, and she brushed off his hands. "Excuse me? You've been in town for, what? Four? Four days? You think you will show up and fix everything? Am I so weak in your eyes? Why don't you mind your own business? Why doesn't everyone mind their own business?" Her hands flew up, palms facing him. "Forget it. I'm going home. I should *not* have come, and I don't know why I bothered. For a moment, I thought that you—that we—that maybe things could be different. Obviously, I misjudged you. And myself."

Her speech fell on him like an avalanche. He was trapped. Buried and immobile.

Turning away, she spoke softly. "I've been a fool."

Before he could even think of a reply, she left. Fleeing from him like a startled bird or a chipmunk on the prairie. Go after her or stay? The latter held no appeal, and rational thought did not dissuade him. His longer legs and lack of skirts caught up to her in seconds. "Let me walk you home; I can do that for you at least." Reaching her side, he put a hand on her elbow.

She suddenly spun to face him, and if he thought there was a fire in her eyes before, it was nothing compared to what she displayed for him now. Jerking her arm away like he had burned her, she spit out her words like acid. "Go away, Zeke. You've done enough for one night. Some things can't be fixed by riding off into the setting sun. We aren't all as free as that. And I don't need your pity." And she was off again, striding down the boardwalk.

If his adopted sister Rachel had taught him nothing, when a girl marched off in tears, she wanted to be followed. He heard his mother's voice quoting more Proverbs. *A soft answer turneth away wrath: but grievous words stir up anger.* He had stirred up something. But it didn't add up. What she displayed was the fire he currently felt for Tobias, and yet, she attacked him for wanting to help her. *She* kissed *him*! He should be the one running from her. There was no reason for her to turn around and jab at him personally. Is that what she really thought about him?

So what if he was running away. He wasn't hurting anyone by doing so. He was free to make his own choices. Good grief, these women of the West and their opinions. What did they know? And why did they insist on beating him up about it incessantly?

His desire to chase after her dwindled. More scripture popped in his mind—this time from the Gospels. *But whosoever shall smite thee on the right cheek, turn to him the other also.*

He answered under his breath. "I hear you, but she kissed me first . . . and now I'm confused. Turning the other cheek isn't the same as running and asking for it." He kicked at a pebble on the street and watched it bounce ahead. If only he had run away when he had the chance. Before things got personal. Before the kissing and the insulting.

Barely making out the sound of her feet on the boardwalk, he let her go. It's what she wanted anyway. He could make amends later for any pain he had unknowingly caused. Or he'd leave town, and she'd heal. Who could understand women anyhow? Not him. They were all irrational. It wasn't his fault.

Going back inside the dance hall held no interest for him. Letting a married woman tangle up his thoughts was a recipe for trouble. Surely, there were some single girls who could have helped take his mind off those blue eyes.

Another time.

Besides, his shoulder ached from swinging a mattock all week.

If he returned to Palmer's early, he could sneak in a hot bath before the other boys arrived.

When he turned to go the other way, Tobias was just coming out and greeted him with a grin that took up his whole face. The man was sure pleased with himself. "I'm looking for El. You seen her? I left her right over—"

"She left." Zeke balled his hands into fists. Knocking the grin from Tobias's face with his own hands would make him happy right now, but he wouldn't make a scene in front of the ladies.

"Left? With whom?" Tobias's grin slipped all on its own.

Drat. Didn't even get a punch in. Zeke gritted his teeth. "No."

"Zeke, I don't have time for games." Tobias grabbed his shoulders. "I need to know where she is."

"I told you, she left." Zeke backed away, shrugging off Tobias's grasp.

"But it's dark."

Her husband put on a good show of pretending he cared.

"She wouldn't leave on her own."

"Well, she did."

Another woman slipped in next to them with two glasses of water.

"Did you find her?" She smiled, looking at the men expectantly.

"Mari, I've got to go. I'll find you later, if I can. Don't wait for me if I'm not back in half an hour." Tobias was all business now, and he didn't even stay to collect his hat. Instead, he bolted out the door and took off at a sprint.

Chapter 13

Putting one foot in front of the other, Eloise walked as quickly as her slippered feet would take her without giving in to running. Ghostly hands reached to grab her between the gaps in every picket fence. Phantom footsteps followed her. Demons lurked behind the bushes. The darkness pressed closer, and she knew she wouldn't make it home.

Berating herself amid the fear, she held the tears back. She was not a child. Walking a few blocks home in the evening should be something she was able to do without falling to pieces. But she couldn't. She had never been comfortable in the dark, but since finding Philip's body, she avoided it completely. Tobias even dumped the wash water out for her if she didn't get to it before night fell.

Philip almost looked like he'd been asleep when she found him. But the moment she walked in, she knew he would never wake. His stillness was unnatural. She had gone to him, drawn by invisible strings and rested her head on his shoulder, curling up against him, and wrapped an arm over his chest. He was still warm. The blood-soaked boards had later been replaced where his head laid.

The tears hadn't come that day. Only an emptiness. She didn't know how long she would have stayed with him if Katie and Tobias hadn't stopped by with Luke, who was only a few weeks old at the time. Tobias immediately took charge of the situation, and Katie took care of Eloise. She didn't remember much of the weeks that followed, except once the tears started, it sometimes felt as if they hadn't stopped in all these months.

And then Zeke happened. He messed with her mind and made her livid. Through her panic, his words echoed. *It's time you did something . . . I hate to see you this way . . . How you will carry on.* If everyone would just leave her alone!

And she'd kissed him. He'd swooped in and rescued her from spiraling. He'd been a friend. He'd taken her from the brink and reminded her that she wasn't alone, that someone cared, that there was goodness to be found, and she acted on a ludicrous whim, and he'd been repulsed by her. She shook her head, wishing she could wipe away the memory of Zeke's face. He had been surprised, yes, but disgusted hadn't been the reaction she'd expected.

She'd enjoyed his hands on her shoulders, cradling her neck. Making a fist, she wished to wash her hands of the feeling of his hand wrapped around hers. His heaving chest, as he caught his breath, had shown an edge of vulnerability. She'd leaned into him, thoroughly enjoying the warmth of Zeke's body. He'd called her a friend, and he'd looked at her with such compassion and heartfelt sincerity.

She must have imagined the whole thing, blinded by her own physical desires. Okay, so she missed her husband. So she wished Philip was there with her. So she thought she could have one measly evening and pretend it all away. She wanted to scream, "I'm sorry! He's dead, and he's not coming back." *Ever.*

If only God had let her help him more. Everything would be different if he were alive. Never once had she dreamed of a future without Philip in it. She didn't know how to be without him. Indefinite grief was her future, and tonight taught her that it wasn't even worth pretending it was otherwise. Slowing her walk, she noticed where she was. Her house. At least, it used to be her house. *Their house.* One tear slipped out and opened the floodgates. Bracing her hands against the maple tree, she cried. She cried for Philip; she cried for her lost future. Sinking to the ground, she hugged her knees. She cried for herself and for being a fool. Pulling handfuls of grass on each side, she grappled for support. But there was none.

She found no comfort in the grass. *From dust to dust . . .* Words from his funeral haunted her. *The* LORD *gave and the* LORD *hath taken away; may the name of the* LORD *be praised.*

No! She would not praise him for this. Philip was goodness and faithfulness, and he should be there with her. Katie should too. Luke was growing up with an aunt as a poor excuse for a mother because God messed up and took the wrong people.

Eloise's thoughts ran in circles with little coherent pattern, and she had no means to stop it. Sobs contorted her breathing, and her face was soon drenched with tears that fell onto her dress as she buried her head between her knees.

"Hey, I'm here."

She startled at the voice. Seeing her brother's face brought on a new wave of tears when he leaned over, hands on his knees, breathing hard. He gave her his handkerchief and said nothing else while he knelt beside her and pulled her close.

She slowly gained control of her breath and balled his now soiled handkerchief in her fist.

"Why didn't you wait for me?" He rubbed her back. "I would have gladly brought you home."

She shrugged, and a hiccup escaped when she swallowed.

"Did something happen?"

She shrugged again and sniffed.

"Did somebody say something?"

She nodded.

"I'm sorry." He kissed the top of her head. "Want me to go rough 'em up a bit?"

She nodded.

"Sure thing, sis. You just say the word. Any chance you want to tell your big brother what happened?"

She shook her head. But he waited quietly until she whispered, "Zeke happened."

After Tobias sprinted after his angry wife, Maribeth attempted polite small talk. The strumpet even offered him a glass of water.

As if he would take a drink from the likes of her. Zeke made poor excuses to get away, and when she tried to keep him talking, he brushed her off and walked away, leaving her pretending to be confused on the boardwalk.

Dancing with Mrs. Davidson was a mistake. He should have refused her. Regardless of how she twisted his arm and his heart. He knew better. The answer was, "No." *No and No.* And yet, even now, visions of her played constantly through his mind. Her sadness. Her smile. Her anger. Her rounded cheeks and full pink lips. He wanted to crush her to him and tell her he would fix everything. Rubbing the memory of her kiss from his face, he grew more frustrated with himself and Tobias.

Her husband's behavior fueled his anger, and the faster he walked, trying to push the couple from his mind, the more sullen he became. His mother's voice continued to play in his head, reminding him of the scriptures she'd forced him to memorize as a young child. *Thou shall not covet . . . Thou shall not commit adultery . . .*

He pushed against it. *How about, thou shall not treat your wife like one among many? Thou shall not flaunt your attractions to other women when you're at a social with your wife? Where was, 'Thou shall not be a rake?'*

No wonder Eloise was heartbroken. It was obvious now. She wasn't cherished as she should be. The kiss should never have happened. He should never have been standing alone with her. She was reaching for comfort, and he must have given her the wrong impression. But how brave of her to show her face in town at all.

He held his hands together behind his neck and looked to the sky. If only he could squeeze out the growing frustration. This was not his problem. Eloise was not his. Jealousy flared, and he knew he was far more emotionally invested than he should be. *Thou shall not covet . . . Even when it's desirable.*

Go to work. Get paid. Leave. He did not need to be involved in anyone's problems. Good riddance.

Looking around, he realized he had angry-walked half a mile down the road out of town. Abruptly, he turned and stalked the other way. The ten minutes back into town did not cool his anger. He rolled around the idea of approaching Tobias on Monday morning and slugging him in front of his crew.

He was playing through the whole scene when a girlish laugh broke through his angry rants.

"Tobias, really!"

Low murmurs answered her, and Zeke saw the pair down the alley.

"Mari, I've been waiting all week to be alone with you."

"I'm sure." She laughed again. "Is Eloise going to be alright?"

"I think so. She had a good time, for a while. She's resting at home." He kissed her forehead. "Can we talk about us now?"

"Have you told her yet? About us?"

Zeke froze. Walking away would be best. This was not his problem, and he wanted nothing to do with this vile man, yet his feet didn't move. He watched the silhouettes of the two between the dark outlines of the buildings.

Tobias pressed his body against Maribeth, pushing her back to the wall and moved his hands to her face. He leaned his head down and whispered to her before he planted a kiss on her cheek, her jaw, and moved to her lips.

Clenching his fists, Zeke boiled. He was not aware of having moved until suddenly he was yanking Tobias off Maribeth. Grasping the man's shoulder with one hand, he made contact with Tobias's face with the other.

Maribeth screamed, running wildly into the streets crying. "Help! Help!"

Zeke barely registered her cry as the adrenaline coursed through him. With both hands, he violently shook Tobias. "How could you?"

Once the initial shock passed through Tobias, he took hold of himself. He easily pulled free from Zeke and slammed him against the brick wall. "Zeke?!"

Warning bells were ringing through his head, but Zeke ignored them. He'd gone too far to back down now. Hardly a match for Tobias, he struggled to stand. Ramming the top of his head into Tobias's face, he aimed a fist at his ribs.

Tobias stumbled, holding his side. "Zeke! Are you drunk?"

"Don't play dumb." Zeke launched himself from the wall and charged Tobias. He struck at air as Tobias dodged his swing. Grabbing Zeke's hand and twisting it behind his back, Tobias forced him to the ground.

"You want to stop swinging at me?" Tobias released him, stepping back and breathing hard.

But Zeke wasn't listening to reason; he surged to his feet and shouldered Tobias in his midsection, using as much strength as he had to knock him into the wall. "You're disgusting," Zeke grunted when Tobias shoved him again.

"Quit it." Tobias spun Zeke and shoved him face-first into the wall, pinning him there. "You don't want to pick a fight with me. I'm taller, stronger, and outweigh you. Now knock it off. Something's gotten into you, and you're acting insane."

"Take your hands off me." Zeke gritted his teeth as he struggled against Tobias's weight.

"And let you attack me again? I don't think so."

Running feet came down the boardwalk and skidded to a stop next to him. "I'll take it from here, Boss."

"Thanks, Sheriff."

Rough hands grabbed Zeke from behind, and cold metal handcuffs slipped onto his wrists.

The fight went out of him then. He relaxed and hung his head. *Lord, what have I done?*

"You're under arrest on the charge of aggravated assault, disturbin' the peace, and probably drunkenness. I'm inviting you to stay the night at my place until we get this straightened out."

Chapter 14

Lying in a musty jail cell worked wonderfully at calming his rage. The back of his head throbbed where a goose egg had formed when he'd made contact with the wall. He flexed his fingers, testing the joints. He had swelling there too. Lying still for an hour or more, he'd let his mind drift and his body relax. Every now and then, he heard voices, small groups or couples walking outside, leaving the event. The lamp in the jail illuminated the clock on the wall, and the second hand kept a steady beat with his fingers drumming the side of the cot.

Not that anyone had asked, but he had no words in his defense, and the sheriff did not return that night. After a few hours, the lamp sputtered out, and night closed in on his cell. The clock kept its perfect rhythm and, therefore, kept Zeke from sleep. The cold crept into the building, and the thin wool blanket did little to counter it. Eventually, he dozed and spent the night shivering.

Early Saturday morning, Zeke woke to the crunching of tiny teeth. The gray morning light streaked across the floor where he spied a mouse gnawing on a crust in the corner. Zeke lay on his side and watched the furry animal until it scuttled off, afraid of Zeke's movement.

He should feel some level of guilt for what he had done. The fire under his skin cooled enough for him to think clearly, but regret was not one of the emotions that currently plagued him. Men like Tobias were of the lowest kind. Zeke pushed the palms of his hands into his eyes, and visions of her face pained him. What could he do to be rid of thoughts of her?

Eloise was not his problem. Someone needed to save her, but it wasn't him. A pain in his chest ached. He wondered what excuse Tobias used when he came home bruised. Did she tend his wound and sleep next to him, still living with the shame of her husband's behavior? His stomach rolled at the image of her tenderly wiping his face and talking softly to him.

Zeke determined he needed to get out of this despicable town before he did something else he couldn't simply walk—or ride—away from. Was there no one to stand for justice? He grabbed the thin pillow and covered his face. Calculating his earnings for the week, he barely had enough to square with Palmer's, including the fees for laundry and meals. That left him enough for Suzy Girl's shoe and nothing else. When he ran out of air, he threw the pillow across the cell. It rattled the lock and dropped to the ground. It was another reminder of the mess he was in. Pulling his knees in, he rolled to the side that faced the wall.

The front door opened, and he didn't bother to move. But the voice he heard was not the sheriff's.

"Well. What a picture you make. This is what comes of sticking your head where it is not wanted." Simon Oakfield stood in the middle of the room. His voice put on a show that his posture betrayed. His nose pinched against some invisible odor, and he absently wiped his hands as if to remove the filth they'd acquired by entering such an establishment.

Zeke stretched out on his back, crossing his hands behind his head. Too bad he'd thrown the pillow. Gazing at the spider webs that filled the corners of the rafters gathering dust, he waited. When he was ready, he drawled out, "Hello, Simon. Nice of you to stop by."

"Boy, sit up when I am talking to you." Simon tugged at his vest. "I am here to help, after all. Not that you deserve it after a stunt like that." He edged a step closer to the cell.

"I'm listening." Zeke clenched fists of hair behind his head to keep from doing something impulsive. Putting on a front of disinterest, he succeeded in irking Simon further. *Good.* Simon was the last person he'd wanted to see, after Tobias that is, and the last he had expected to come calling.

"I could not help but notice your . . . predicament. And if my observations are correct, you may be lacking the required funds necessary for the near future. I thought to myself, how inconvenient to be in a new town with no job, no money, and now, no place to sleep outside of a jail. I was up half the night pondering how I could aid this poor soul.

"Of course, at first, I was inclined to let the chips fall where they may, seeing as you did certainly bring about your own demise, as it were. But the Christian in me felt it necessary to help a brother in need. As Jesus specifically commanded us dutifully to visit those in prison, did he not? I do not wish to be found wanting. As he says, and I quote, 'Inasmuch as ye have done it unto one of the least of these my brethren, ye have done it unto me.' Well, then. Here we are. You in prison. And I, visiting."

The pain of Zeke pulling out his own hair wasn't enough to keep him from surging toward the bars. The iron was sturdy, and only the bolt in the lock made noise when Zeke shook it. "I am not your brother. Or your *brethren*. You may leave now."

"Oh, no, no, no. I have not told you why I have come."

Zeke's stomach growled, and he realized his lack of breakfast was adding to his annoyance. "Get on with it."

Simon sniffed absently. Removing his wallet, he counted out five bills. Holding them toward Zeke as if he would bite, he offered the cash.

Zeke's gaze hardened. "What are you doing?"

"What does it look like?" Simon shook his hand with the money. "I am helping you. Take the money. Pay your debts. Get out of town."

"Or what?" The clock's ticking hand continued its path, shouting its presence into the uncomfortable room.

"I need not stoop to threats. But if I were you, I would not be fain to stay in a town where I clearly was not wanted. If you know what is good for you, you would say, 'Thank you.'"

Tick. Tick. Tick. Tick.

Simon sighed when Zeke didn't move or acknowledge him. "Yes, well. I will leave this here." He rolled the money, and reaching through the bars, tucked it into Zeke's vest pocket. Wiping his hands on his side, his polished shoes clicked their way to the door. He turned back to smile and tipped his hat. "You are most welcome. I wish you well on your journey."

Pacing the tiny room was worse than sitting. Three steps one way, two another, and back again. Only three circuits later, he lay back on the cot and covered his ears to block out the incessant clock.

"Rise and shine, man. Breakfast." The sheriff slammed a tray on the desk and whipped off the napkin. A simple plate of eggs—enough for two men—and one biscuit. Good to know he wouldn't starve. "Let's go." Keys jingled, and the door squeaked open.

"You're letting me go? Thank you, sir."

"We're still working on your situation. It'll take some time to get to the bottom of this. You've got a mess on your hands, and I don't put up with your type, even if Boss isn't pressing charges."

The sheriff escorted Zeke to the outhouse and back to his cell for cold eggs. The sheriff was not forthcoming with any new information, and he stood with his arms crossed, watching Zeke eat.

Fear of making his situation worse, Zeke didn't speak. Perhaps it was best to wait it out. He didn't have anything to say in his defense. He had, in all fairness, attacked Tobias, unprovoked, in the presence of a witness and a woman.

The sheriff took his plate, fork, and empty cup and left, leaving

Zeke with the dry biscuit to nibble.

He spent the next hour watching the clock. It had been fourteen hours. He wondered what specific laws he had broken to warrant a situation, as the sheriff implied. The front door opened again. Zeke made sure to wipe his face of stray crumbs until he saw who it was.

Simon Oakfield again. This time loaded with Zeke's bags.

Keeping an air of disinterest wasn't possible this time. "What are you doing with my things?" Everything he owned in the world was in those bags, though it wasn't much, including his mother's jewelry, his Bible, and other keepsakes. "You had no right to go in my room." Zeke stood close to the bars.

Simon only laughed. "It is not your room anymore. Not after Mrs. Palmer heard the news. You can imagine my hesitation to share the gritty details, but when you did not return last night, one thing led to another, and I was unable to remain silent. She is loath to let you return. Naturally, I offered my assistance. Anything I could do to help her during this stressful time. This has the possibility to leave quite a black mark on her establishment. She is usually more insightful in the type of men she accepts to board with her. Rooms do not remain empty for long; therefore, she is relieved to be through with you. Oh well. Glad to see I did not miss you. I was afraid you might have skipped town already. Perhaps this evening for your release? I expected a simple overnight incarceration to be sufficient. I surmise the sheriff has his reasons. I am never one to question those in authority—"

"Are you finished?" Zeke eyed his bags. The picture of Simon rifling through his things was not a pleasant one.

Simon sniffed. And somehow managed to look down his nose,

even though he was the one required to look up when Zeke stood to his full height. "Again, you are welcome. I have saved you from quite an unsavory meeting with Mrs. Palmer."

"I'm not thanking you, and I'm formally requesting you cease all other forms of help you may be inclined to provide." He retained the spit he wanted to shoot at Simon's feet to punctuate his words. What a mouthful of words. He found simplicity worked better. He tried again. "Go away."

"Very well. I can see when I am not appreciated. You should be so lucky as to have a friend like me looking out for your best interests." Simon dusted off his suit. "You have breakfast on your shirt. What a sight you are."

"Get. Out." Zeke did not watch to see Simon leave. He listened to the footsteps and the door shut behind him. Absently, he brushed the crumbs from his shirt and buried his face in the musty pillow, throwing the blanket over his head. The waiting and not knowing was difficult enough without Simon popping in to pester him and rekindle his anger.

It was too bad about Helen. He hadn't meant to hurt her too. Losing his board wasn't something he'd considered when he'd gone after Tobias. He hadn't considered much of anything, or he wouldn't have let his temper run amok in the first place. He'd like to pretend his cause was purely for justice and not jealousy. If he couldn't be with Eloise, then at least her husband should treat her right. Even now, though he lay still, he felt coiled—ready to burst. Dreaming of ways to get back at Simon was not helping. With the roll of money pressed into his side, he made plans to spend it on something nice for Helen before he left town. Perhaps a new serving platter or a washbasin. He'd see what types of things the mercantile stocked.

The front door squeaked open on its hinges, and Zeke tucked the blanket tightly around him. "Go away, Simon, and let a fellow rest in peace."

"Mr. James," a timid voice said.

Eloise? Zeke jumped off the cot. The blanket came with him and tangled around his legs. Arms flailing, he tripped over his boots on the floor and stumbled to his hands and knees. A quick twist, a few kicks at the boots in his way, and he was on his feet again. He tossed the blanket on the bed and turned to face her. Carefully. He combed his hair around his ears and tugged at his untucked shirt. He cleared this throat.

She stood midway between the front door and his cell. Her eyes were wide, and her lips were parted.

He grasped the bars, waiting for her to speak. Imploring her to stay. To understand. His hair fell into his eyes, and he brushed it back. It fell down into his eyes again.

Eloise's eyes were red-rimmed and swollen from crying. Her hair was in a haphazard braid down her back. Loose strands framed her face. Her appearance gave the impression she had been the one to spend a cold night on a hard cot with a musty pillow.

Reaching a hand through the bars, he didn't expect her to take it, but the gesture came naturally. Desperately, he wished to be on the other side.

"Eloise, can I explain? I'm—"

"Mr. James." Moving away from him and taking a deep breath, she raised a hand to silence him. Her shoulders were stiff, and her chin jutted out determinedly. "Listen carefully." She swallowed.

He ached to listen. He waited quietly, waited for her to begin.

She swallowed again and pointed a finger at his chest. "You will stay away from me. And you will stay away from my brother."

With skirts twisting around her feet, she turned and was out the door before he could respond.

Zeke remained standing long enough that his feet grew cold on the stone ground.

Her brother?

Did he know her brother? He didn't know her brother. He ran through the list of men he'd been in contact with the past week. George, Jonas, Thomas, Charles. Not Simon, obviously. Roy? Maybe. As far as he could recollect, he did not know, nor had ever met her brother. He and Eloise had conversed plenty of times, and she had never mentioned a brother.

Still standing and staring at the far wall, he didn't move when the front door opened, letting in a blast of sunshine and warmer air. It was his foreman, Dee Williams. Clearly, it wasn't possible to land in jail and be left in peace. Did the whole town know of his foolishness? Maybe he should thank Simon for bringing his things and giving him the means to slink out without another word.

"There you are." Dee removed his hat and shook out his straight blond hair, squinting in the low light of the room. "I almost didn't believe it. I didn't take you for a fool. Clumsy, yeah. Easily distracted, sure. But not a fool. What possessed you? His strength outmatches you by a—I just don't get it. I knew you had eyes for Miss Davidson, but this is a strange situation."

Zeke wasn't listening. "Who is her brother?"

Dee stared at him.

"Mrs. Eloise Davidson." Zeke's volume rose. "Who is her brother?"

Dee tapped his hat against his other hand. "Eloise? She only has one." Motioning toward Zeke with his hat, he said, "Don't change the subject. I'm here to officially discharge you from the brickyard. Though you really would be a tenderfoot if you showed your face there again. As uncomfortable as it is here, it would be worse not to take care of this now."

"Answer the question," Zeke said. "Who is he?"

"Who is who? Zeke. Who knocked whose head? From what I heard, Boss didn't even take a punch."

"The brother. Tell me who her brother is."

Dee looked at him as if he had sprouted feathers on his head. "Are you foolin' me? My wife was worried about you being here. She felt you might have been falsely accused. I'm going to call in the doctor."

Zeke shook the bars, or tried to, but they didn't budge. "Williams! So help me, if you don't give me a name. Eloise Davidson has one brother. Tell me who it is."

Dee shook his head. "Tobias Franklin. Boss. The man you attacked. I'm going for the doctor now. The wife might be right about you. How does your head feel?"

Zeke melted. He sank slowly to the floor, running his hands down the bars and relaxed into a sitting position on the hard floor.

Crossing his legs, he rested his forehead against a bar. "Who does Luke belong to?" he whispered.

"Boss."

Zeke scrubbed his face. "You're telling me Eloise isn't married."

"She's a widow."

A widow! *A widow?* Eloise Davidson was a widow. Chipmunk was not married. Eloise Davidson was not married. *Not married.* She was single. She was beautiful. She was the most lovely thing he'd ever seen. She didn't have a kid, and she was not Boss's wife. He was not jealous or coveting Boss's wife. She was living with her brother.

Her brother. Her brother! He had punched her brother. Twice at least. He had ruthlessly attacked her brother in front of another woman out of sheer jealousy, which didn't make any sense because he was her brother. Not her husband.

"Hey!" said Dee getting his attention, startling Zeke. "Don't hang up your fiddle, man. You have got to pay attention. Listen to me. And get up off that floor. You look ridiculous. And put your shoes on."

"Yes sir." Zeke obeyed. First one boot and then the other. All the while attempting to process this new information. Tobias Franklin . . . Franklin . . . Mr. Franklin. Eloise was not married, and he was a fool. Tobias was not her husband. And Simon . . . Simon? He brushed Simon away. He would deal with Simon later.

He looked up to find Dee waiting expectantly for the answer to another question he hadn't heard. "Pardon?"

Dee shook his head. "That's it. I'm fetching Doc to have your head checked."

"No! No, don't. I'm alright. Just. Stay. I didn't know he wasn't, you know, seeing other women. Hear me out." Zeke finished with his boots and walked back to Dee. "Please."

"Alright, start talking. I have somewhere to be. I don't get paid to guard prisoners."

"She was married to Philip." It wasn't a question. All the pieces began clicking together.

"Yes."

"I didn't know he wasn't cheating on her. Eloise deserves more, and she just took it. It's not right, you know, for a man to treat his wife like that. When she talked about the situation, you could just see in her face how hard it is for her. I mean, no man should be allowed to carry on like that."

"Stop," Dee said. "You're not making any sense."

"Tobias is her brother!" Zeke said.

"Yes. We've established that."

"I didn't know she had a brother. She spoke of a husband and a father-in-law. She cares for his son. They live in the same house. She wears a gold ring on her left hand!" Zeke faltered, sinking down on the cot; he held his head between his hands. "And now I'm in here for defending the honor of a woman who didn't need my help. I've betrayed her trust. She'll never forgive me."

The laugh lines around Dee's eyes creased. "Snö ock vrede smälta med tiden."

"Is that supposed to make me feel better?"

"Both snow and anger melt with time." Dee laughed as he adjusted his hat and turned to leave. "You're alright, Zeke. You're still fired. But you're alright."

Chapter 15

The last strains of *Amazing Grace* drifted through the opened windows of the church house and into the bars of Zeke's cell. He sang along with the bits of music he could hear, matching his tenor harmony to that of the congregation. Two nights in the cell was more than enough time for Zeke to cool from the events of Friday. He was still reeling from the newest information.

Thank God there was enough grace for all. Boy, did he need it. He knew it was freely given by the Lord Almighty if only Tobias Franklin would be as generous.

Such a small piece of family information, yet how vital.

Eloise Davidson. A widow. He laughed at the irony but sobered quickly. She might be unmarried, but that didn't mean she was available. Her heart was an open wound, unable to heal. Yes, she'd filled his thoughts since their first meeting. He wanted to make everything better, and he felt oddly responsible for her well-being. Especially now that all he had done was cause her more pain. Yes, they'd had some great moments and a growing friendship. But judging by the daggers she shot at him, she wouldn't be leaning on his arm anytime soon. He'd made a mess of things alright. Zeke had assaulted the one man in her life she loved more than anyone. That she depended on. And what an impression he'd made on Maribeth! Sam Hill, take it all, he had a lot of fixing to do.

He thought of all the things he'd muddled over the past week. From their first vulnerable encounter at the creek to the angry sparks after the dance, her flushed cheeks and blue eyes were prominently featured in each memory. Marveling at how a few days could change everything, Zeke put in order what he needed to do when he got out.

Rachel once threatened that he'd meet someone whose opinion would matter more than his dreams and derail all his plans. He hadn't believed her. Yet here he was in jail. For the honor of a girl. A girl that he'd just met. A girl who didn't want anything to do with him. *Oh, boy. Rachel was right.*

It was time to move to another town. And quickly. He had the new shoe on Suzy Girl and enough cash to feed himself for a few miles. Too bad he liked this place so much. He would be more careful next time. Stick to himself. At the next stop, he would work enough for a train ticket straight to the ocean. He'd learned that traveling by foot was too painful. Making friends only to leave them after a few days wasn't the life he wanted.

The front door squeak set his heart racing. It was Tobias. His left eye was swollen shut with dark bruising around it.

"Oh," Zeke said. "Oh, Boss. I mean, did I do that?"

Tobias shut the door painfully slow and stood there and stared at Zeke. The silence grew more uncomfortable by the second—as the blasted clock on the wall wouldn't let him forget. Tobias sighed and pulled his shirttails up. "And this." He lifted the side of his shirt to show more bruising on the taut muscles below his ribs. "I've not looked this bad since school. I got into it with an older boy about a girl. You should have seen the other guy."

Zeke shook his head.

Grabbing the arm of the one available chair, Tobias scraped it across the floor. The screeching didn't seem to faze Tobias, but to Zeke, it was akin to the judgment trumpets. Tobias sat facing Zeke. Even sitting there with a wrecked face and his elbows on his knees, he had the presence of authority. Tobias was a well-liked man. That was a given. But there was a reason he did well running a company with multiple men working under him. He had a way about him that invited others to pay attention.

"Ezekiel James," he said.

Zeke swallowed. "Yes sir."

"Sit down. You're hurting my neck."

Zeke dropped to the edge of the cot. This slow dialogue ate him up. His stomach growled, reminding him of Sunday lunch and how he hadn't had any yet. To fill in the terrible silence, he started talking. "I'm sorry. I don't know what came over me. I can make it up to you. I mean, I'll try. I know you probably don't want to ever see me again, but if there's anything I can do to show you how dreadfully sorry I am. Maybe you'd rather I just leave. I can skip town as soon as you say the word. I mean, as soon as I get out of here. The sheriff has told me nothing." He knew he was doing the babbling thing again. *Shut up, Zeke.* But the floodgates had been opened. "I know better than to fight with my hands. I was taught better than that. And doing what I did in front of a woman. Good grief, and my boss. I guess you could say I shot myself in the foot on all accounts."

Tobias waved his hand in front of his face and made a fist, silencing Zeke. Leaning forward, Tobias looked him in the eyes, and a smile spread across his mouth. "Dee came by yesterday."

"Yeah, but I still shouldn't have—"

"I'm honored," Tobias interrupted. "I'm honored to have seen the fire come out in you for a just cause."

"But—"

Tobias stopped him again. "Oh! Believe me. I would rather you carry out your sense of justice without fists and after you've checked your facts. You've got a mighty left hook. I'm proof of that. But if I understand what's going on here, I name you as a friend through and through. I'm dropping all charges . . . and insisting that all other charges be dropped. Sheriff is always butting in, but we'll have you cleared as far as the law is concerned. Sheriff is dragging his feet for political reasons, trying to make an example out of you, but he's played long enough."

"Really?" Zeke sat up straight. For the first time in days, a glimmer of hope spread through him.

"Yep, Sheriff will be here soon. I asked him to give me a minute first."

Relief flooded Zeke. Grace upon grace upon grace. He didn't deserve it, but there it was.

Tobias wasn't done. "I can't believe you would think so low of me that I would marry my sister . . ."

"What? No! I didn't think that. I was—"

Laughter filled the room, and then Tobias winced and held his side. A groan escaped as he tried to hold in further laughter. "You should see your face. It's going to be a long time before I let you forget about this."

A long time. That wouldn't be a problem. Zeke never stayed anywhere for a long time. No reason Ockelbo would be any different.

"About that." Zeke rubbed the back of his neck, scrambling for the right words. "How is Eloise?" Not what he'd meant to say.

Tobias's laughter stopped, and he stared hard at Zeke, then he sighed and looked down at his hands, picking at the skin around his thumbnail. Just when Zeke thought he couldn't take the silence anymore, Tobias answered. "She's hurting."

"Because of me?"

"Some. Some because of you. And because of other things. She's been hurting for a long time. Years. I'd like to ask you to leave her alone. But," he offered a half-smile and shrugged, "I haven't seen El smile so much in one day as I saw on Friday. I haven't seen her get so worked up about a dinner guest in, well, ever. She's been different this week, and the only thing new in her life is you."

The blood drained from Zeke's face. What had he gotten himself into? He didn't mean to tangle with a girl. He had plans. He was going west! A girl wasn't going to distract him from that. He barely knew her. Okay, so he thought she was cute and funny, but he didn't have feelings for her. Not the kind of feelings to keep him from leaving. *Just the kind of feelings to keep you in jail for three days after attacking a man out of jealousy?* That was different, he lied to himself.

He knew the way she avoided eye contact when she was sad. He knew how she blinked her eyes low when she was nervous. He knew how she pursed her lips just so when she was angry. He knew she had a banked fire inside, just waiting to come alive again. He'd seen glimpses of it and wanted to fuel it. He wanted to kindle the spark. He wanted her to share her dreams, fears, and excitements. He wanted to make her laugh and tease her until she smiled at him again. He knew that if she looked at him too long, he would drown in her sea-blue eyes.

"I didn't mean to hurt anybody," Zeke said to Tobias, feeling defeated.

Tobias guffawed. "I'd say I'm a walking contradiction to that. Listen. For what it's worth, I think she really did like you. For whatever reason, she came out of that shell of hers this week for the first time in over a year. Do you know how long it's been since she's attended an event besides church?"

Zeke shook his head.

"Too long. More than fourteen months. But after what happened," he pointed to Zeke, "she doesn't trust herself. She's angry. She's hurt. I don't know what was said between the two of you on Friday, but she was a mess. And then I came back looking like this because of you?" He whistled low. "It's a lot to process."

"She kissed me," Zeke whispered.

Tobias cocked his head. "She what now?"

"On the cheek. Sort of friendly like." He swallowed. "But I shoved her away. Thinking she was married and all. It was complicated after that. I'm not sure what happened."

Tobias stared until Zeke squirmed under the scrutiny, then shook his head. "Dee came by last night to talk to us. The man could hardly tell the story because he was laughing so hard."

"She knows, then?"

"Heck, yes, she knows. You think I could keep a joke like that quiet? Land sakes, everybody knows." Tobias started his wheezing laughter again.

Perfect. Does the jail have a back door? He would make a straight shot from here to the livery and nary a goodbye to anyone. *God bless Simon.*

"Don't fret," Tobias said. "Helen may take longer to find forgiveness. She's got a reputation to uphold, but we'll find you a place. In the meantime, you'll come for lunch today, and I'll help get things sorted out." Tobias moved to the door. Stopping with his hand on the frame, he turned back. "Do me a favor and give me a heads up the next time you want to start a brawl. So I've got a fighting chance."

"Tobias."

Tobias cocked his head and waited.

"She blames herself. For Philip. She thinks it's her fault."

Tobias stared at him with his one unswollen eye, his face unreadable. His shoulders seemed to take on another burden before he pivoted through the door and pulled it shut behind him.

"You did what?" Eloise resisted the urge to kick her brother. A sleeping Luke in her arms prevented further violence. If his one bruised eye wasn't so pathetic, she might have blackened it all over again. Well, not really. No matter how many times she took a swing at him, he rarely allowed her to make contact. Zeke must have thoroughly taken him by surprise in order to do such damage. She settled for a foot stomp. *Very ladylike. If Mother could see me now. Get over yourself, Eloise.*

"Stop worrying so much. It will be fine." Tobias rubbed her shoulder, but she jerked away. Tobias opened and held the door for her to enter first.

She would not be coddled. She strutted inside. "What do you expect me to feed him? Maybe I'll sound the trumpet and announce to the whole town we've invited the man who assaulted you. Let's bring Maribeth over, too, and they can have tea."

"El, I don't care what you feed him, and if you have something against Mari, too, out with it already." Tobias quietly shut the door, careful not to let it slam and wake Luke. "You should have seen him. He looks terrible. I can't believe Sheriff held him so long, especially when nothing happened. I could have cleared up the whole thing if he'd let us be. It's unfortunate he was nearby."

"That's your takeaway? Oh, honestly. Tobias, it's *unfortunate* your eye is so swollen that you can't see out of it. It's *unfortunate* that Zeke has a temper. And it's *unfortunate* that you invited the man over to our house without asking me first." She shifted Luke. Her angry whispers hadn't affected him in the least.

"We've been over this." Tobias gently removed Luke's shoes and set them on the floor near the door. "It was a misunderstanding. I can't say that I wouldn't have done the same thing under the circumstances." Easing out of his jacket, he draped his and Eloise's shawl over the chair. "I think he's got grit."

Eloise ran out of steam, and she huffed. "Maybe the next time he can misunderstand without slugging anyone." She eyed Tobias. "*Don't* leave those on the chair, please," she said, adding an eye-roll out of habit. "I still don't know what you expect me to feed him. All I have is last night's soup to warm up. And some dry bread. I hope you're pleased."

"Sounds great." He moved his jacket and her shawl from the chair and dumped them at the foot of the stairs. "If it's good enough for us, it's good enough for him."

"Pick those up." Sitting straight-backed on the edge of the sofa, she glared at him. "Doesn't seem right feeding a guest leftover soup."

"Then don't think of him as a guest." Tobias pulled his tie over his head and tossed it on the discarded pile he had no intention of picking up.

Eloise smoothed the tuft of hair on the top of Luke's head. "Would you rather I think of him as a released convict?" she asked sweetly.

"El." He gave her a pointed look. "Be nice." He nodded toward the window. "He's here."

Her big talk evaporated when she saw Zeke out the window with his head down. She unceremoniously transferred Luke to his father and fled to the kitchen. Clanking the dishes and utensils loudly, she stomped about the kitchen in her preparations. As she busied herself in setting the table for the four of them, she ignored the men's conversation in the other room. Soon, she had nothing else to do. Unable to hide any longer, she steeled herself for the awkward, terrible, and unappetizing meal to come. Was it too late to run and hide in her room? She wiped the sweat from her palms on her apron again and smoothed her hair one last time before calling out. "Boys! Dinner!"

Hanging her apron on its peg, she left the kitchen. The men ignored her. They were deep in conversation. About what, she didn't know. *And I don't care.* At least, that's what she tried to convince herself. Luke squirmed out of Tobias's lap to run to the table. At least one of them was hungry.

Eloise stood, waiting, and tapped her foot. They paid her no mind. They had their heads together, talking over something of great importance. She spun on her heels, making a show of her departure. Finding Luke on the table, she caught him stirring the pot with the long-handled spoon.

"Oh no you don't!" Clicking her tongue at him, she plopped him in his chair. He was growing and learning new tricks every day. He couldn't be left alone for one second. "You hungry? You can wait just like the rest of us. Dada will be in soon."

The men sauntered in just as she took her place. Tobias ignored her glares, and Zeke ignored her entirely. The feeling was mutual. Tobias sat opposite her with Zeke on the corner across from Luke.

Offering Zeke a tight-lipped smile, she added a slight nod of acknowledgment in his direction. "Welcome."

"Thanks for having me." He didn't quite look her in the eyes either.

What a day this was turning out to be. How should she treat a man who heroically defended her honor by accidentally attacking her brother? Not forgetting how he shoved her away after kissing him on a whim. These situations were not covered in the etiquette books her mother made her read.

Tobias held Luke's little hand and offered a blessing over the meal before serving.

She had never felt so out of place in her own home before. The air was thick with tension between Zeke and her. Eloise only picked at her bread and stirred her stew absentmindedly.

"Smells great," Zeke said.

Luke clapped his hands on the table, anticipating food.

Eloise shrugged. A biting remark remained on the tip of her tongue. "It's quite simple. I wasn't expecting company."

Tobias shot daggers at her, admonishing her to remember her manners and *be nice*. He was forever the older brother. She sighed, turned to Zeke with a false smile plastered to her face, "How *unfortunate* for . . ."

Zeke gagged. Spitting a large mouthful of soup back into his bowl and covering his mouth with his napkin, his eyes were wide as he stared back at her. His shock was mirrored by Eloise. He fumbled for words. "I'm sorry. I—have you"—he pointed to his bowl—"There . . . seems to be something." He stared at his soup.

Looking down at her own bowl, she tried a sip of broth. It was awful. Quite possibly the worst soup she'd ever eaten. Inedibly salty. "Tobias, did you?"

He shook his head.

That's when she noticed the large salt shaker on the table. Completely empty. Groaning, she showed it to the toddler. "Luke? Did you put this in the soup?"

Luke bounced in his chair. He was busy pulling his bread apart into tiny crumbs and sprinkling them on the floor.

She surveyed the room. Luke with his breadcrumbs. Tobias eyeing a large chunk of beef on his spoon, and Zeke looking all manner of meek and guilty. It was too much. Her laughter bubbled quietly. Covering her face, her shoulders shook with laughter.

"El . . . don't cry. It's just food." Tobias stood, but before he could make his way around, she waved him off. The two men shared a concerned look; both were afraid to move. But before long, all three of them were laughing. As one would catch his breath, another would start again, and round and round it went.

"Zeke," she managed between breaths, "your face! What you must think of my cooking." Tears from laughter streamed down her cheeks. Standing, she dumped her bowl back in the pot and did the same with the others.

"My face?" Zeke slumped in his chair, holding his stomach. "You should have seen yours." He tossed his napkin at her face and Luke joined in the excitement, banging his spoon and squealing at everyone, inciting another round of laughter from the adults.

"Her cooking is bad," Tobias said. "But it's not that bad."

"Hey!" Eloise shot Zeke's napkin at her brother. "Oh dear," she said when the laughter simmered. "What are we doing to do now?"

"You have flour?" Zeke wiped his eyes with the palm of his hand and shoved his too-long hair off his forehead.

"Yes," she answered.

"Salt, sugar?"

"Yes, of course."

"Butter?"

"Yes, we have all those things. What are you getting at?"

"I'll take care of this, if you'll let me. Just fit me with one of those fancy aprons with the ruffles and flower buds."

The good humor lingered in the air, thankfully, melting through all remaining tension. She became his assistant in the small kitchen, bringing him the items he asked about. A bowl. Spoon. A frying pan.

He wouldn't share his plans but made a big show of the preparations.

Tobias pulled Luke into his lap, and the two of them enjoyed watching while talking and playing together.

Eloise almost forgot who she was. She could almost pretend that she was any other girl at any other house having a fine dinner party with friends and family. *I could be this girl again.* But caution prevailed, even when Zeke smiled and teased.

Just as had been the case so many times the past week, banter flowed easily between them. Except this time, she noticed an extra charge between them. An energy that grew and made her want to find out where it led. The same pull that brought an impromptu kiss out of her the other night. Could she really be this girl who wanted to be with this guy? Even after everything? When he smiled at her, she smiled back without thought.

"Hold still," he said. "If you insist on playing with flour, you need this." Zeke held her apron he'd found on the hook. Standing behind her, he efficiently wrapped it around her waist and knotted the back.

Butterflies flipped through her middle when his hands touched her waist, even though they didn't linger. "Thank you." Turning around, she met his gaze with a bright smile. She didn't back up, and he didn't either.

Luke and Tobias interrupted the moment. "More food!" they chanted, startling Eloise.

Before long, pancakes were frying in the butter, and she busied herself clearing the table.

"Order's up," Zeke said. He elaborately presented the first plate to the starving toddler. A drizzle of honey completed the meal.

"Catch!" Zeke cried to Eloise.

A flying pancake was heading her way, and she grabbed the corners of her apron to cradle it, calling out in surprise.

"Well-caught. Have another?" He waited expectantly, and his eyes twinkled.

"Yes! One moment." This time she held a plate at the ready.

Tobias mimicked Luke's toddler speech. "More food!"

Eloise smiled and offered him the next loaded plate, ruffling Luke's hair who still sat on his dad's lap, enjoying the meal, the show, and the extra attention.

Zeke continued pouring the batter, flipping and tossing. "That's the last one. Take your seat Chipmunk, and hold up your plate."

Soon, they were full to bursting, and there was a lull at the table. Luke had long since left Tobias's lap and was off playing in the other room.

"Where did you learn to cook so well?" Eloise asked. "These might be the best I've ever had."

"A gentleman never tells." He wiggled his eyebrows at her.

"You. You can't fool us," Tobias said. "You're no gentleman."

Zeke saluted with his fork and smirked at Tobias. "Mama

taught me everything she knew, but I picked up this particular recipe while working in the kitchen in a boarding house in Iowa last summer." One of his many employment endeavors, no doubt.

Tobias pushed back his plate, feeling satisfied. "Which reminds me. You can't stay at Palmer's. Even if Helen agreed to it, your room filled up yesterday. A salesman for some nonsense is passing through."

Licking a drop of honey from the side of his thumb, Zeke thought about it for a few seconds. Finally, he spoke. "I don't need to stay." He sighed. "I will be leaving as—"

"Agnes!" Eloise jumped from her chair, startling the men. "The Andersons will take you. They have that extra room in the back and . . . and . . ." She turned quickly to Tobias. "I'm sure they will keep him."

"It's more than I deserve." Zeke shook his head. "But I can't go back to the brickyard. He can't rehire a man who behaved the way I did." He rubbed his neck. "No, I need to go. No reason to stay with no job."

Tobias nodded. "He's right, El. Dee agrees with me. It just doesn't look right."

Eloise dropped her face into a pout. She wanted to argue. It was their company! They could do with it as they pleased. Still standing, she stacked her plate with Luke's and reached for Zeke's. He intercepted and caught her hand. She froze and looked him in the eyes—his forest green eyes that warmed her to her toes.

"Thank you," he said. "Thank you for . . . dinner."

Rational thought fled. He held her hand, and it didn't feel wrong. As she stood looking at him, his gaze captured and welcomed her.

Invited her to settle in, accepting her and all her brokenness. It was more than his words that kept her frozen. Her eyes flickered to his mouth. *What would it be like to be kissed by those lips?*

Heat rushed into her face. *Be reasonable, El.* She yanked her hand free, absently wiping it on her skirt as she walked to the dry sink, forgetting what she was doing. She stood there, staring at the plates in her hands.

Tobias held his plate for her, but she did not take it.

Zeke looked at his hand that rested on the table. It burned from her touch. Was it possible she felt the same current between them? He liked her, yes. Had been jealous of a fictitious husband and wanted to protect her, yes. But he wasn't worthy of her attention. He wasn't the kind of man she needed. She needed a reliable man. One who would stay put. One she could depend on. And that wasn't him.

Tobias stared at him.

"What?" Zeke asked.

Glancing from Zeke's hand to Eloise and back again, Tobias raised an eyebrow.

Zeke grabbed the plate Tobias still held up. "I don't know what you're talking about." His mind was overtaxed. This wasn't a part of the plan. Meeting a girl who did funny things to his stomach and made his skin tingle wasn't part of the plan. Making friends was natural, sure. Everywhere he'd been, he was well-liked. He liked people and knew how to engage with them, and in turn, they welcomed him. He'd made stops in almost every town along the line. Getting people to welcome him had never been the problem. That's what made this trek fun. He met new people and saw new things, and it was all part of his grand adventure westward. Until lately. The effort of saying goodbye was getting harder. He was tired and yearning for something more than superficial acquaintances. That was all. What he felt, or thought he felt, for Eloise was only his loneliness speaking. It wasn't real. He'd move on and promptly forget about her, and she'd forget about him. All would be well.

He'd thought he'd wanted freedom. What he truly wanted was a home that was all his.

Tobias leaned in to whisper. "I might only have one good eye, but I'm not blind."

Eloise hung her apron. "I'm going out."

"Tell Jess I said hi," Tobias said.

Without a glance, she was out the door.

Zeke wasn't sure if he was relieved or disappointed. Either way, breathing came easier with her out of the room. "She usually run out like that?"

A smile lit Tobias's face. He mimicked Zeke. "I don't know what you're talking about." He slapped Zeke's shoulder. "Not that you care. But yeah, she has her moments. She'll be back before night-fall. Don't worry."

"I'm not worried."

"Of course you're not."

Trying and failing to put her from his mind, Zeke spoke of practical things. "I need to find a room in town for tonight. I'll square things with Mrs. Palmer before I take off tomorrow."

A loud crash came from the front room.

"Luke?" Tobias jumped up. A large can was over Luke's head and he crashed into the wall again.

Zeke laughed.

Tobias leaped across the room and was only a second too late to catch the boy who tripped and fell over a pile of wooden blocks. Seeing the fatherly side of his boss, former boss, was funny. He watched the two play on the rug. Luke used Tobias as his personal climbing station.

Finding a comfortable seat on the sofa, Zeke settled in to enjoy a relaxing afternoon. His neck ached. His wrist was sore. His face was scratched from the wall Tobias had shoved him into. He was exhausted from two nights of huddling in the cold cell. Propping a pillow behind his head, he stretched out. Vaguely, he thought about looking at a map, planning out his next route. If he was leaving in the morning, there were things that needed to be done.

Tobias, who had Luke on his back, spoke up. "You don't have to go, you know."

"I almost don't want to." Zeke found a more comfortable position on the sofa. "This place is starting to feel homey. I've been here too long. But you knew from the start I wasn't staying. I just needed a shoe for my horse."

Luke slipped off his back when Tobias sat up on his knees, resting on his heels. "I still don't see what's so great about California. I doubt they have anything better than we do."

Zeke snorted. "Oceans?"

"Ostkaka?" Tobias said.

"Bless you."

"No, it's a Swedish dish." Tobias pulled Luke from where he was trying to climb on his back, then gently tossed him to the ground in front and tickled his chest. "That settles it. You can't leave until you've enjoyed ostkaka."

Zeke smiled and added that to the list of things he needed to do before he left. He wondered if it was something he could order for breakfast from the bakery in the morning with his tea ring. Spending all of Simon's five bucks in town would be more fun than giving it back.

"El likes you, you know," Tobias said.

Zeke rubbed his face and rested his eyes. His eyelids were too heavy. He spoke the truth in his answer. "I like her too. But I'm not staying." He yawned. "She doesn't need someone like me."

"Best you leave soon then," Tobias said. "But there's no reason you should stay at the hotel. We have space for you, at least for tonight. The sofa is all yours. It's nothing fancy, but it's better than a cot. And warmer." Tobias stood. Luke dangled from one arm. "Zeke?"

Zeke grunted. The weight of his eyelids proved too heavy to pry open any longer. He closed them for a minute. The tension in his face released a fraction with each breath he exhaled. His frame slumped into the corner of the sofa with a pillow tucked beneath his head. Luke's giggles faded from Zeke's consciousness as sleep overtook him.

Chapter 16

E loise burst through the door. "It's all set!"

Tobias held his finger up and motioned to Zeke on the sofa.

"Ope!" She covered her mouth and pushed the door until the latch clicked. "Is he sick?"

Tobias draped Luke over his shoulder. "Tired."

"He doesn't look well." She squatted near his face. "Zeke?" She poked his shoulder.

He opened his eyes, but they drooped closed again without acknowledging her. His slow breathing didn't change.

"Leave the man alone," Tobias said. "He needs to rest."

"Fine." She took Luke when he reached for her, flinging his body away from Tobias, trusting that she would catch him.

"How was Jessica?" he asked.

"I was with Agnes. They have the back room fixed, and he can stay there tonight and start work tomorrow." She squeezed Luke in a tight hug and rocked him back and forth until he squirmed out of her hold.

"Impressive," Tobias said. "You forget something?" He jerked his head at Zeke's sleeping form. "What if he doesn't want to work at a bakery. And I remember a girl last night ranting about how she never wanted to see a certain someone ever again. How does that fit into this?"

"I don't know. Seems like the right thing to do." She peered at Zeke and whispered, "Are you sure he's okay? He didn't even flinch when I came inside."

"Leave him alone," he said. "I'm taking this rascal out to play. He's crazy as a loon. I need him to run it off before the evening service."

After Tobias left, she knelt on the rug near Zeke. On impulse, she put her hand to his forehead. It wasn't hot. *Good.* One could never be too careful about fevers.

His skin was smooth under her hand and pale on his forehead where his hat offered shade. She ran a finger gently along the pink line of the new scar above his eye, remembering how it bled the day they'd met. Brushing back a lock of hair that fell over his eyes, she took the liberty of running her fingers through it and tucking it behind his ear.

He sucked in a breath and turned his head.

She froze, waiting until he stilled. She imagined a world where she could be so much at peace to let herself fall asleep on a sofa in someone else's home. Chuckling under her breath, she shook her head. *Impossible.* But here he lay, breathing softly, completely unaware. Completely at peace.

Tobias said he had grit. *He has more than grit. He is innocent somehow, trusting.* He saw wrongs to be righted and took action. It was sweet. Almost.

She wouldn't quickly forget how she'd found Tobias the night of the fight, stumbling around in the dark kitchen trying to rinse his face with cool water.

He'd tried not to let her see. Wouldn't even tell her what happened until she'd accused him of starting fights and holding secrets from her. Tobias turned on her in anger then. Spilled the whole story in exasperation. He said, "And don't you ever accuse me of lying to you. You know me better than that."

And she did. Tobias could always be trusted. He'd proved his worth to her time and time again. Philip was the one who used to pull her strings. How she'd loved him and how it hurt when he didn't trust her. He told her daily how much she meant to him and begged her never to leave. She grew frustrated with his pleading. Of course she wasn't going to leave. He was her life, but he was oddly frantic and secretive and moody. He often woke her during the night, worried about things she couldn't help him with. Did he properly bank the fire in the forge? Was the chicken coop secure? Did Mr. Anderson short-change him at breakfast last week?

Finding the words to console him wearied her, though she would never tell anyone about those moments. Rarely did she acknowledge them herself. He worked himself up; she quieted him. He said she was his light. His anchor. Though in the end, even she wasn't enough, and every bit of love she'd given to him was now buried.

Was it possible to find love again?

Zeke was something else. He was like a tree. He lent strength. When she was with him, she felt secure, making her want to stay near him. Perhaps she could find shelter in him. Even when he found her in the creek, his presence shamed her because of her immodest attire, but he did not frighten her. Not really.

Why does he pull me in yet build a wall against me? Realization came like a gust of wind in the winter, sucking the air from her lungs. The cold shoulder he'd given her a number of times now made sense.

He'd thought she was married.

She looked down at her left hand, where the gold band mocked her. Slipping it off her finger, she cradled it in her palm. Taking it off felt like a betrayal. But she was very much not married. And having Zeke here, sleeping on her sofa, it felt like when she rested beneath the shade of the large oak near the creek when the sky was blue and scattered with white puffs of clouds with miles and miles of uninterrupted sky. She could breathe in his presence. *What if he stayed?* Could there be a future for her that connected her to him?

Guilt stabbed her. Even the mere thought of comparing Zeke to Philip was wrong. They were different, that's all. "Oh God," she whispered, "forgive me." But the window that had opened and let in a wave of peace that flowed through her did not close. She put the ring into her skirt pocket to deal with later.

"Zeke," she said, and he did not move. She whispered oh-so-softly, barely letting the words out. "Ezekiel James. Will you stay? For me?" She shook his shoulder, speaking louder, "Zeke, wake up. I have good news."

He grunted and opened his eyes. Surprised at seeing her in front of him, he sat up. "Hey, Chipmunk." He swiped his face with the back of his hand. "Sorry. Guess I dozed off." He looked around, almost as if he'd forgotten where he was.

"Are you feeling okay?" She didn't ask about the nickname, secretly pleased that he still used it.

"Never better." He smiled at her, warming her all the way to her toes. Patting the seat next to him, he invited her to join him. "Get off the floor. I'll scootch over." He rubbed his face and stretched his arms up, arching his back like a cat. Or a toddler. Bringing his arms down, he left one on the back of the sofa behind her.

She leaned back a little, testing the feeling of his arm along her shoulders. Disappointment hit her when he slid his arm away and leaned forward on his knees.

"I'll get a move on," he said, stifling another yawn. "Thank you, I mean, well, for everything. It's been an interesting week."

She smiled at his sleepiness. *Interesting* was one word. "It's not over yet. We'd like you to join us for the evening service in half an hour, and I have a surprise." Excitement bubbled through her, and she clasped both hands in her lap, anxious for his reaction.

He raised his eyebrows. "Should I be worried? You look pleased, but I feel I should be worried. I don't know if I like surprises anymore."

"You'll like this one."

"Hmm." He offered her a small smile. It almost felt like he was teasing her. "Okay, let's have it."

"I found you another job. With the Andersons. Anderson Bakery? You've met them, right? They need extra help, and you obviously know at least a little something about baking. Anyhow. I set it up for you. They have a room behind the shop for you, and you start tomorrow. They agreed to a trial run at first to see if it's a good fit. But I can't imagine why it wouldn't be. The Andersons are wonderful, and you, well, you are . . . nice, and I know you will get along beautifully."

But he didn't react as she'd expected. Then again, did he ever do what she expected? He neither smiled nor frowned. He just sat there. Sat and stared at her.

"Ostkaka," he said.

"The prophet Isaiah shares with us promises of new blessings. 'Behold, I will do a new thing; now it shall spring forth; shall ye not know it? I will even make a way in the wilderness and rivers in the desert.'" The preacher's voice droned through the crowded church.

Zeke sat on the hard bench, squeezed in with Eloise on one side and the large dark-haired blacksmith and his wife on the other. Tobias held Luke, who flipped through the pages of a picture book, mooing and being shushed whenever he found a picture of a farm animal.

They had found seats in plenty of time. Zeke felt out of place to be sitting in a family row, and he'd left plenty of space between him and Eloise. Enough space that Luke had scrambled between them and tried to pull the pins from Eloise's hair. But just before the service began, the man motioned for Zeke to make room for him and his wife on the pew. There was not enough room to be made, even with Luke on Tobias's lap. So here he sat, shoulder, hip, and leg pressing intimately against Eloise, and it was too much for him to handle. He was mindful of every move he made and breath he took, as he, in turn, felt every one of hers.

He leaned forward, elbows on his knees, attempting to give himself room to breathe, but that put his face only inches from the necks of the couple in front. That was no good. Slowly he sat up and wiggled back into place. Eloise appeared not to notice. She sat calmly with her hands folded in her lap and her eyes trained on the pulpit.

He focused again on the message, but the gentle rhythm of Eloise's breathing stole his concentration, and his mind wandered. Therefore, he missed the invitation, and suddenly the congregation stood for the benediction. The preacher said something about freedom in Christ, and then people were turning and shaking hands, filling the aisles. He heard a shout of "Yay!" from Luke.

The blacksmith on Zeke's end introduced himself as Jacob Davidson. "Pleasure to see you again. Gave us quite a scare the other night. Glad to see you're still hanging around. I know it can't be for Eloise's cooking."

"Pa!" Eloise said.

"Grab him!" said Tobias, as Luke pushed by Zeke and ran down the center aisle.

Zeke wasn't quick enough. "I'll watch him," he said to Tobias and excused himself from the crowded pew. He weaved his way around the people, keeping an eye on the child's blond head until they both made their way out the front door. He caught up with him on the front steps. "Hey, you."

Luke crawled backward down the steps, giggling at being chased and led Zeke around in silly circles on the lawn, making as if to run away, and then turning to run back to Zeke.

Zeke was greeted by many of the church-goers as they trickled out the door. Some offered a smile and nod, others introduced themselves, and a handful he'd met previously. He smiled at the train of children behind Dee Williams, with his expecting wife bringing up the end of the line. The kids piled into the back of the wagon except for one little boy who ran over to him and Luke.

"Hi! I know 'bout you. I'm David. You're Zekiel. Pa says you have a cloud head."

"A head in the clouds?" Zeke squatted in front of the boy, with Luke propped on a knee.

"Yeah, and when I ask, 'What that?' Pa says when you was workin', you was not always workin', an I'm should mind my own business and yeave him alone. But Ma says to yet you be. D'ya know Ma's gonna have a new baby. Sally always wanna girl baby. But I wanna boy baby. Last time God gived us Fwed, an he's a boy baby, Fwed. Pa says Fwed will be a pal, but it's takin' a yong time for Fwed to go up. Now he's always takin' my stuff, and I says, 'No, Fwed!' alla time, but he don't yisten."

"I can imagine. How old are you, anyway?"

David held up three fingers and then ran away to his pa. Williams loaded him in the back of the wagon and returned Zeke's wave.

Tobias thumped Zeke on the back and took Luke into his arms. "He keeps us hopping, doesn't he?" Leaning closer to Zeke, he pointed to his black eye. "Check this out." The swelling had receded, and his eye could open again. "All's well that ends well."

Zeke grimaced.

"I've got to get this kid home," Tobias said. "Would you do me a favor and wait for El? I'll get this guy to bed, and I can help move your bags over to the Anderson's place in a bit."

"Sure thing, Boss."

The sky displayed its brightest variety of colors. Blues streaked with oranges, pinks, purples—lavenders—and touches of yellow. The cotton puffs provided a magnificent tapestry for the light to play upon.

Zeke walked side by side with Eloise. Neither of them was in a hurry to end the evening. Physically, he wanted to be near her. That had never been in question. It would be a simple thing to reach over and take her hand. But he wasn't ready to take her heart.

He had plans that didn't have a place for her, and she had a history with another man—a man she still grieved. Pressing down those thoughts and tamping them hard, he envisioned a sunset just like this one over the Pacific Ocean.

"What's that sigh for?" she asked.

"Oceans," he said. "I've seen a lot of things, but not an ocean. You think it could be any more impressive than your prairie?" He waited for her response. When it didn't come, he kept talking. "Interesting to think how the grass ripples like waves, but I read somewhere that these prairies are a sort of desert. Hard to imagine this place as a desert."

"It feels like a desert sometimes," she said, chiming in with a somber voice.

Eloise gazed at the painted sky with her hands clasped behind her back as they strolled through the square.

If only she could see herself. Nothing about her made him think of a desert, but rather a vibrant life yet to be lived. "How about dry bones coming to life?"

Her steps faltered when she looked at him, eyes wide. "Pardon?"

He stopped in front of a park bench in the square and motioned to it. "Want to sit?"

"No."

Zeke took a seat anyway and rested both arms along the back of the bench. "You never heard about the dry bones?"

"Zeke . . ." she said slowly, appearing to be confused.

"It's from the book of Ezekiel. There's some loony stuff in there, but God showed him a vision of all these bones, not just any bones, but dried out bones. Piles of them. And they came together to form a skeleton that grew sinews, muscles, skin, hair, fingernails." He sat up straight, excited to share his favorite story. "The bones turned into a full flesh-and-blood army with breath in their lungs."

Eloise *tsked* her tongue at him. "But they didn't! Not really. He saw a vision. It's not the same."

"No, those bones didn't come to life. But it was a sign to him that something just as wonderful was going to happen. Israel was dead! They'd been conquered multiple times. Babylon, Syria, and I don't even know, but the point is there was no nation left. Like those piles of bones. And God was still there, showing them how he was going to bring them back together and save them. That's the whole thing, right? God saving his people. That's Jesus. That's been the story from the beginning. Bringing them back. He's been trying to bring us back since we left the garden.

"Just think of Lamentations. The prophet Jeremiah is in agony over the destruction. His city was destroyed, and he describes the rubble, starvation, and all sorts of terrible things. And get this, the best part," Zeke gestured with both arms, "after all, and I mean, *all* of this crying, Jeremiah says, 'It is of the Lord's *mercies*, his love and charity, that we are not consumed.'"

Zeke relaxed onto the bench and stretched out his legs, crossing his ankles. "How wonderful is that? Every time I read it, I get fired up. How was Jeremiah able to look at all that mess and say that it was the Lord's *mercy* that kept them alive? All they could see was a pile of dry bones."

Eloise stood silently before him with her arms crossed against the evening chill.

Zeke continued. "I don't know, Chipmunk. When this life seems to be more than we can take, somehow we still wake up again the next morning."

She scoffed at him and kicked at the ground. "But what about those who don't?"

"What do you mean?" He made room for her on the bench, and she sat, staring across the lawn.

"What about those who don't wake up the next morning."

"You mean, dying in your sleep?" He was confused. He placed a hand on her back. Any less contact would have seemed uncharitable.

"Something like that," she said.

"Not everything makes sense," he said quietly. "But believe me when I tell you, I know he is continually working for our good." His hand moved up her back, and she sighed, leaning into him.

"It doesn't feel that way." She turned to him. "I've never met anyone like you."

"What, chatty? Dashing? Sophisticated?"

She elbowed him. "No, getting so passionate about the Bible. You make it sound a lot more interesting than it is." Taking a deep breath, she stood up. "Come on; it's getting dark."

He roused himself, looking wistfully at the sky and offered his arm this time, pleased when she took it.

She clung to him, surprisingly, pulling in close. "Tobias's wife Katie and my Philip. My parents. Your family. All taken from us. How do you keep from being discouraged? Death is always hovering."

He squeezed her hand. "Chip, did you feel afraid when you were little, and your parents were with you?"

She shook her head.

"The way I figure it, we are His children. You ever think of that? The maker of the sunset each night loves us as his kids. I think he'd rather dump a heap of blessings on us, but sin is here, too, and working its consequences throughout everything. He knows we hurt. But he also knows how many hairs are on your head and how the sunlight shines through your eyes when you smile."

Eloise didn't speak for a long time. He was afraid he'd said too much, went preacher on her and killed the moment. They'd paused in front of her house, but the sunset blazed across the sky with such a display of colors that neither of them looked away.

Hesitantly, she let her hand drop from his arm. "No one has ever talked to me so candidly about God like that before. Like he was your friend."

If only he could wrap her in his arms and heal the brokenness of her heart. Show her the exciting truth of the gospel, how he understood it. But he settled for draping a hand across her shoulders and watched the last colors fade in the sky. Sneaking a look at her, he noticed a silent tear dripping down her cheek. On impulse, he wiped it with his thumb.

She leaned into him. "Thank you for your stories. We'll march you up to the pulpit next week. Maybe you can keep more of us awake on Sunday. But you've made me cry five times this week. I'm beginning to think I'm allergic to you."

Zeke laughed, but it didn't last long. "My stories are all well and good, but I have my own heart issues I'm working through. Your sheriff might raise a fuss if he saw me up front. I'll be out of your hair soon enough." And he meant it. He was only staying for a day or two. Just long enough to set things right with Mrs. Palmer. Maybe he could stay a few weeks at best and earn enough for the train ticket to take him the rest of the way in one shot.

He resolved to stay out of Eloise's path until he left. He didn't want her as a friend. He wanted all of her. Saying goodbye to a friend was hard enough. Messing with someone's heart was cruel.

Except there was nobody else he would rather be standing with and watching a sunset. He shouldn't be with her when he had other plans. He stiffened when she rested her head against him. Removing his arm from her shoulders, he edged away and cleared his throat. "I'd best be getting my things."

Chapter 17

꧁ ❦ ꧂

Clutching her shawl against the wind, Eloise hustled Luke to the bakery Tuesday morning. It was well before nine o'clock, and though she'd fed Luke hours ago, she was hungry. And not just for breakfast. She'd made herself wait at least a day before going over there. She didn't want to give him the impression that she was checking in on him. She was just stopping in for breakfast.

Her blush betrayed her, though, she knew. Pausing a moment outside to compose herself, she saw Zeke through the large store windows, and her heart skipped. When she entered the bakery, his head whipped around at the sound of the bell, and his face lit up with a smile. It set her blush climbing her cheeks all over again.

He looked the part of a baker, and it suited him. He had a white apron wrapped around his waist with the strings long enough to tie in front. The sleeves of his shirt were cuffed to show off his fore-arms, and they were smudged with flour. Loading a tray with used dishes, he balanced it on one hand and ran a rag across the table with the other to clear it of stray crumbs. He worked energetically, but his puffy eyes betrayed his tiredness. *Poor man has probably been awake since three or four in the morning to prepare the morning's menu.*

His smile at her entrance warmed her middle, but he didn't look her direction again. He was busy with other customers. For a moment, she doubted he even wanted her there.

Eloise! The man lingered to watch a sunset with his arm around your shoulder. A man wouldn't do that if he didn't want to see you. He'd made it clear on Sunday how he felt. Why would he hide now?

Agnes Anderson greeted her with an embrace. As usual, she knelt to offer a handshake to Luke. "Hello, big guy." But he ignored her hand and fell into her for a hug. Agnes held him, and he rested his head on her shoulder with one thumb in his mouth and the other wrapped around her neck. The corner table she led them to was perfect. Eloise would be able to watch the whole room without being obvious, and Luke was less likely to bother anyone from the out-of-the-way table.

"Order will be right up, kids," Agnes said.

"But I haven't ordered anything!" Eloise adjusted her chair and moved the place setting away from Luke.

"You'll want today's special. Our new baker outdid himself this morning." Soon she returned with a tray of the largest cinnamon rolls Eloise had ever seen.

"Goodness! Agnes, I don't know if I could eat one of those on my own."

"You'll have to give it a go with your little helper then. See what you can do with it." She served one to Eloise and transferred a portion to Luke's plate. "He offered to make these, and we let him. So far, they've been a crowd favorite. Much different than our usual style. Says it's some secret recipe. Now he's thinking he wants to try it out when he gets a place in California. He's something else; got more ideas than a grasshopper in July."

Eloise agreed. Pulling off sections of the soft bread, she observed him working. It was fun to get a chance to see another side of him. Zeke was especially friendly with the children, and he didn't rush orders with the elderly. Waiting for him to come over, she rehearsed her invitation to dinner tomorrow, hoping it came across naturally. She'd planned to work it into the conversation easily. Like it was a passing thought and not give away the undercurrent of nerves she felt at having him in her home again.

The boy, Samuel Forsberg, came in; she recognized him from church. Zeke chatted with him as if they were old pals and sent him on his way with a brown paper sack. Zeke looked her way as Sam was leaving, and she signaled for Zeke to come over, but he never did, offering her a half-smile instead and nodding at a table that needed to be cleared. A steady drip of orders came through, but the shop was not crowded. Both Agnes and Oscar each found time to sit and rest by the counter, but Zeke kept moving. He topped coffee cups, wiped tables, and even sat and spoke with the customers at their tables. But he still did not find time to acknowledge her.

Eloise fiddled with her fork, taking small bites. She had to constantly remind Luke to stay seated. Eventually, Zeke disappeared into the kitchen, and business in the shop slowed. When the nine o'clock bell rang clearly through the town, signaling time for school, she sighed. "Come, Luke. Time to go."

He stood in his chair and the crumbs scattered from him onto the floor. The mess embarrassed her, and she left an extra coin on the table. Embracing Luke against her, she escaped, wincing at the sound of the bell announcing her exit. It seemed to shout, "Here goes Eloise the fool! What a silly girl."

Wind fought at her skirts, and she held her bonnet to keep it in place. It was another brisk April morning. The sky was white and low, colder than she'd been prepared for after the warm spell of last week. "Let's get home, little man."

Walking past the church, she was greeted by the sheriff. "Mrs. Davidson, I heard everything's patched up with Boss? All appeared friendly-like at church Sunday. I found Mr. James's coat under the cot. I need to get it off my hands. I was taking it to him now, but I need to see Frank first. You wouldn't mind?"

"Luke and I must—"

"Good, good!" He pushed the coat into her arms. "Much obliged." Tipping his hat, he went the other way toward the livery.

Luke wanted to be put down, and she let him. The overcoat was awkward enough to hold without a wiggling toddler in her arms. She held the dark wool open for inspection. It was his, alright. He'd been wearing it the night of the dance, though the night had been too warm to need it. She folded it over her arm and changed course to return to the bakery. The wind pushed at her back, asking her to *hurry, hurry*. She didn't want to return, but the wind didn't listen. What it did was tease the hair around her face and grab her skirts. It flapped at the coat she carried, and a folded page fell from a pocket and fluttered ahead of her.

The paper flew against the wall and got itself stuck in the corner. She wasn't required to chase after it, thankfully. Running through town, even to catch a wayward paper, would be a sight—one directly forbidden in certain etiquette books. "Keep up!" she called to Luke and then stepped on the paper to keep it from floating away. A quick look showed the page was filled with a flowing script. Well-worn creases in the folds showed frequent handling. Scanning the document, her heart fell like a brick. She didn't mean to intrude on his personal affairs, but a few phrases burst out at her, "*Dearest Zeke . . . Will you not stay? . . . How you will be missed . . .*" She dropped her eyes to the signature. "*All my love goes with you, Rachel*"

She jerked her eyes away and refolded the letter, hiding the words. The all too familiar ache in her chest throbbed. Shoving the letter into her pocket, she took off for home. Tobias could return the coat. If she never saw Zeke again, it would be fine with her.

Whatever she'd thought was special about him, she'd made up in her head. He didn't even want to be in this town. Why was she kidding herself? He was leaving. Going west. Ockelbo wouldn't miss him, and he could keep Rachel's love and take it all the way to the Pacific while he was at it.

West, west, west! *Ockelbo doesn't want you here anyway. Only a glutton could eat a cinnamon roll that big.* He could take his big ideas and his food to California.

"Luke." She snapped at the toddler. "You cannot sit in the middle of the walk. We are going home." She didn't wait for him to decide when he was ready to get up. Her back already ached from carrying him. Why did little boys insist on running when they should sit, and sit when they could run? He fussed when she pulled on his arm. But she didn't relent. "If you want to play, we can play at home. Now walk. Please." He turned into a limp doll, sinking to the ground. "Get up."

He cried.

Bending over, she snatched him from the ground. Bundling him and the oversized coat together, she marched through the square with Luke's screams echoing over her shoulder.

Chapter 18

*E*loise inspected the pie while red syrup oozed from the edges to drip on the floor.

Was there anything more lovely than this cherry pie? At this moment, nothing came close. If only it tasted as good as it looked. She had her doubts—from previous experience—and therefore, proceeded carefully. This was her third attempt at making pie just this week, and she hadn't met with success yet. Neither of the previous two pies was worthy of presentation. She must have gotten a few things right this time.

Helen suggested she practice her baking skills with pies. They were harder to mess up, she'd said. Eloise wondered how this could be true. The past week of a smoke-filled house told a different story.

The overcast skies brought the night earlier than she'd expected. She'd rushed home from the mercantile, enjoying the leaves that had turned vibrant shades of yellow and were beginning to fall. There was a nip in the air most nights, but she looked forward to the evenings snuggled close to the fire.

Taking a quick glance out the window, she went back to the table and flaked a bit of pie crust off the edge. Philip should have been home by now.

The crust was crisp and rich with the taste of butter. So far, it was a success. She waited to cut a slice until she had the chance to show it off. Where was he? Still giddy over the pie, she pumped cold water to fill a pan. "It's perfect," she spoke to the dishpan, watching the clear water splash into it.

"Miss me?" said Philip, circling her with his arms. She hadn't heard him enter over the sound of the water pump. Embracing her, he kissed the side of her neck, just under her ear, taking her breath away.

She turned in his arms, and as he leaned down for another kiss, she was already up on her toes to give him one. Their lips brushed, and he pulled her close, hands on her hips, pressing her body against the counter. His hands trailed around behind her, tucking her body against his.

"Phil," she mumbled between kisses. "Philip, stop."

"Mm?" he asked, drawing a breath.

"You're covered in soot. You know you're supposed to wash before coming home. You've ruined my apron. Again."

Philip smiled. A slow grin that made her shiver and showed his disinterest in her apron. She had black marks on her face, her hands, and one obvious handprint on her hip where he'd first held her.

"Then take it off," he said.

"Philip!" she said, blushing.

"I think all wives of blacksmiths should have black aprons." He brushed his lips across her cheekbone and whispered, "Black dresses, black hair. . ." And he took her into his arms again, kissing her like he'd been gone a week, not just the few hours since lunch.

She giggled. Blocking his mouth with her hand, she wiggled away. "I've made another pie!"

His face gave away his lack of confidence in her abilities. "Oh?"

"It's beautiful. Come see." He laughed at her enthusiasm. Eloise turned and pushed him toward her latest attempt. It sat displayed in the center of a well-set table with a crisply ironed cloth.

"Mmm." He breathed it in, seemingly surprised. "It does look amazing! Ellie, honey, I think this is the winner. We should preserve it for the fair next year." Now he teased, pulling her close to his side. "Minimal overspill, no charred edges . . . I trust the sugar to salt ratio was put to order?"

She smacked his chest. "Oh stop it! Honestly, you needn't remind me. Let's just eat it first. Before dinner?"

"Let me wash up and we'll eat." He kissed the top of her head.

"I'll help." Trying and failing to control her expression, she unbuttoned his shirt that was covered in dry sweat from working in a sweltering forge all day. One. Two. Three. She made it four buttons down before he grabbed both of her hands in his.

"Ellie, honey. We could skip dinner?"

A giggle escaped, and she turned bright red before spinning away. "No! We eat." She took the knife and cut into the pie. "I have been waiting and waiting to show off this lovely, delightful, gorgeous, delecti—No! No, no, no!" Struggling to lift the first slice from the pan, she stomped her foot. The bottom half was black and stuck tightly to the pan. It was burned into a solid black mess.

Roars of laughter erupted behind her. Philip rested a hand on her back, his shoulders shaking as he observed the ruined pie from behind her. He gasped between laughs and crushed her into a bear hug. "Oh, Mrs. Davidson, my light. I love you so very much. So very much."

She sank into his hug, breathing in the strong smell of iron and smoke. "Chickens will eat burnt cherries again?" She mumbled against his chest.

Placing another kiss on the top of her head, he grabbed the warm pan with one hand and walked out the back door. "Consider it done."

Eloise did not waste time on self-pity. What was one pie? Or three. She had other talents that were yet to be discovered, she was sure. She couldn't suppress a laugh of her own as she sliced bread from Anderson's Bakery. Serving scoops of mashed squash on their plates, she sprinkled a touch of sugar on each. Still smiling, she moved around her kitchen and hummed. "Can She Bake a Cherry Pie, Billy Boy, Billy Boy?"

Bang!

The unmistakable sound of a gunshot froze her mid-step, and a sickly black liquid spilled from the sides of the pot she carried. She dropped it, and it crashed to the floor. The liquid splashed on her skirts. The rest seeped into the wooden boards and stretched across the cracks in the floor. She reached to cover her eyes from the horror but could not as her hands were covered in the blood from the pot.

A new burnt-red puddle oozed toward her from under the stove. She stayed rooted to the floor, knowing there was nowhere to run. She had been here before.

She knew this place.

If she turned, the darkness would be making its way to her from the window and under the door.

Drip . . . Drip . . . Drip. Drops of red splattered on her arm, falling from the ceiling. Covering her face with the skirt of her apron, she cried.

"Yea though I walk through the valley of the shadow of death, I will fear no evil for thou art with me," she whispered. Hunching her shoulders and keeling back and forth, she chanted the words, "I will fear no evil for thou art with me . . . I will fear no evil for thou art with me . . . I will fear no evil for thou art with me . . ."

The red pools advanced from all directions, closing her in. Someone or something held her heart and squeezed the life from it. Any moment, death would claim her too.

"El, wake up!" Tobias stood over her bed. "I'm here." He found her hand and held it tightly, sitting on the edge of her bed. "Hush, now. I'm here. You're okay. You're safe."

"Tobias?" She sat up and leaned into his warmth. Cold sweat beaded on her forehead.

He held her and lent his strength. Familiar. Safe.

Slowly the vice on her heart released, and she could breathe again. "If I had stayed with him that day, instead of going to play on the ice with Jessica, he would still be alive."

"Hush," Tobias said. "You don't know that. Nothing that happened is your fault. I don't want to ever hear you speak like that again."

She shook her head, a lump in her throat preventing her from speaking.

Tobias sat her up, away from him and his hands gripped her shoulders. His big-brother expression had never been stronger. He gave her a little shake when she didn't look him in the eye. "Listen to me. Philip made his own choices that day that had nothing to do with you. Nothing. You are not to hold yourself responsible for what happened." He released a hand and tipped her chin until she was forced to look at him. "You hear me?"

She nodded and something cracked inside of her. It was as if the chains that bound her had been unshackled. The release was painful, and it brought a new flood of grief. She blinked as her vision blurred and streams of tears ran from both eyes.

Tobias pulled her to his chest and held her until she stopped crying.

A lamp burned low on her dresser, and she noticed her brother was still fully dressed.

"Were you going somewhere? What time is it?"

"Late," he said. "Not yet midnight. Mari and I—I walked her home." He chuckled. "Her father was waiting up. We'd lost track of time. I was just coming to bed and heard you thrashing about again."

Eloise moved over and pulled the covers up, allowing room for him to stretch his legs.

Keeping his arm around her, he relaxed against the headboard.

Resting her head on his shoulder, she asked, "Do you love her?"

"I . . ." Tobias stared across her room. The curtain covered the window, and the moonlight cast a few streaks on the floor wherever it found a way in. He sighed. "I love how I feel when she's with me. I love her smile. When she knows I've had a long day, and I'm tired, she will sit with me and let me hold her hand. She doesn't talk or pester. She serves her parents, working at the mercantile. I love how she brightens when I walk into the store and how she brushes my hand with hers when she thinks no one's looking." Tobias pulled Eloise in for a hug. "My men are on to me. I've been running my own errands to the mercantile long enough. Dee has joshed about it often enough."

"I'm sorry," Eloise said.

"For what?"

"For being in the way."

"Stop that. You're not in the way. You're my sister, and I've loved you from the moment my four-year-old arms held you for the first time and your pink face screamed at me."

Eloise elbowed him, and he released her. "I mean it, though. You don't need to try to hide from me anymore. I know I've been less than hospitable toward her, and I'm sorry about that. I shouldn't bring my mess into your life. You can invite her over whenever you want to. I will be fine."

"She would like that." Tobias scooted lower on her bed, crossing his arms together. "She is pretty amazing if you get to know her."

"She'd better be. I'd expect no less for you." Eloise turned to Tobias and gently brushed her fingers around his eye. "Has she forgiven Zeke?" A week had passed since the fight, and the purple bruising had subsided, leaving only a smudge of yellow and green that didn't show in the dimly lit room.

He jerked his head away. "Stop." He snatched her pillow and

shoved it behind his head. "We could have them both over—one grand dinner party. You and Zeke, me and Maribeth. It'll be great."

Eloise pulled at the pillow, but he grabbed her hands and held them between his, his strength outmatching hers ten to one. "Stop putting Zeke and me together. He's got plans that don't include me. I'm not so desperate to chase after an *adventurer* who doesn't even know what he wants with his life."

"Who says anything about life plans? I like him, and you can't tell me you don't enjoy his company. I say we invite them over, and they can make amends, and then Mari will take me into her arms, and kiss me sweetly, and all will be forgiven. In the meantime, you have something to do and won't be lonesome while I sneak out back to look at the flowers or whatever nonsense I use to lure her outside."

Eloise twisted her hands away from him and attempted to shove him out of her bed. He wouldn't budge. "Get your muddy shoes off my bed. I'm tired."

"Sure thing, sis." He rolled off but took her pillow and blankets with him.

"Tobias! Would you knock it off?" She grabbed at her bedding, and he let her take them.

"Quiet now; you're going to wake the baby." He poured himself a drink of water from the pitcher on her dresser. "So we'll have a dinner party tomorrow?"

"No." She spread the quilt back over her bed and ducked just as Tobias tossed the pillow at her head. She glared at him before picking it off the floor. "I don't want to host a dinner with Zeke."

Tobias frowned. "I thought you two were friendly."

"Well, you thought wrong."

"He asked about you when I picked up the order for the boys this week," he said.

Now that her bed was made again, she folded back the blankets and slipped between the sheets.

Tobias swirled the water in his cup. "I told him he should come by and see for himself."

"You didn't!" She jerked her face back to him. "Tobias." She smacked her hands down on the bed. "Would you quit meddling in my life? I told you, you could see Maribeth without sneaking around. I didn't say I wanted to see anybody."

Tobias grunted. "Okay, suit yourself. I like Zeke just fine. I'll have him over, and you can do as you please."

"Go away." She pointed to the door. "I'm tired."

He smiled, probably thinking he'd won. "Goodnight."

Chapter 19

Eloise went about her days as usual, except for when she couldn't. They were out of bread, and she refused to return to the bakery. Baking it herself didn't present itself as a viable option, but she was reluctant to place an order. Surely, Zeke would be gone by the end of the week, and things would go back to normal. Surely, once he was out of town, she could stop thinking about how comfortable it was to stand with his arm around her and how natural it had been to have him in her kitchen. Surely, she hadn't pretended so far that her heart was bothered by broken promises that hadn't been made. She'd gone and found him a job and a place to stay, and because of it, she wasn't allowed to eat bread. Thankfully, Tobias was busy with a crack in one of the kilns at work and hadn't mentioned the notion of a dinner party again.

On Sunday, she sat in her regular seat in church with Tobias on one side and Philip's parents on the other. Luke was not content to sit with any of them. Though he was quiet, he scrambled from Tobias, over to Ma Davidson and back again. Eventually, Eloise had enough of the distraction. Tucking him into her lap, she attempted to make him be still. With her mouth at his ear, she shushed him when he squirmed. That lasted all of twenty seconds. He whacked his hands against her arms, kicked his feet in protest, and without warning, let out a high-pitched screech. Eloise clamped her hand over his mouth. When it was clear that the noise was only going to escalate, she shoved him at Tobias at the end of the row, who promptly left the assembly with Luke.

Luke screamed the entire walk down the aisle, reaching over Tobias's shoulder for Eloise and calling her name. "Annie Ellie!"

The screams were so loud that Pastor Bernas stopped his sermon, waiting until Tobias left the building with Luke before starting up again. But Eloise kept her eyes trained on the pulpit. Her shoulders stiff. The front door closed behind Tobias, and the noise cut off immediately. Evidently, Luke was pleased to be outside, as the screaming would have only carried through the open windows.

The congregation laughed at Pastor Bernas, but Eloise hadn't heard the joke. She hadn't been able to focus on the message from the beginning of the service, blaming her distraction on Luke's unrest. Now that he was gone, her thoughts still wouldn't be tamed.

Flashes from dreams and memories of Philip kept her mind busy. She pushed down the nightmares and thought instead of the beautiful times they'd shared. The times when he smiled at her when she came into a room. The times he teased her with his black, soot-covered hands. The times his parents welcomed her as a daughter after her parents died. Philip's parents had treated Luke as a grandson and continued to do so now. She wondered what might change in their relationship if she were to marry again. Would Jacob and Florence welcome an addition to their odd family, or would it push them away? Before she could dwell on the hypothetical, it was time to rise for the benediction.

Later, standing on the top steps leading out of the church, she spotted Tobias in the yard, enjoying himself in a group that included a handful of men from work as well as Isaac Sage, the new blacksmith, and Zeke. She scanned the crowd and was not surprised to find Luke with Helen Palmer. Flitting her eyes back to the men, she watched as Maribeth and her friend Caroline edged their way into the circle.

She and Caroline were never close friends in school, since Jessica and Eloise had been enough for each other, but Caroline was kind. Her red hair stood out, always brightening a room. Her smile was contagious, and she'd never had anything bad to say about anyone.

Tobias rested his hand on Maribeth's back and motioned to Isaac and Zeke, formally introducing them to Caroline. Zeke stepped one foot forward and offered his hand to Caroline. She laughed at something he said and shook his hand in greeting. Then it was Isaac's turn to meet the ladies. But Eloise found it difficult to take her eyes off Zeke when Caroline took a couple of steps toward him. Tobias and Maribeth split off with Isaac. Jonas and Charles sauntered away from the yard, and Zeke and Caroline were left together.

Zeke seemed to be enjoying himself. He was pleased with Caroline's attention, and from what Eloise could see by the way his hands elaborated, he was in the middle of an exciting story. When the wind took a feather from Caroline's hat, Zeke jumped and caught the escaped embellishment, returning it to her with an exaggerated sense of achievement. Eloise rolled her eyes. Working at a dress shop, Caroline should have taken care to secure the feathers properly. She had probably orchestrated the whole thing, vying for a man's attention.

"Mrs. Davidson," the pastor said.

Eloise startled at his nearness and blushed for having been caught thinking undeserved ill thoughts toward Caroline. "Good morning, Pastor Bernas. Wonderful message today. Thank you for sharing it with us." Though she couldn't have repeated any of his main points.

"It's always a joy to share from the book of Isaiah. I plan to continue the series throughout the spring season."

"Wonderful." Eloise pasted on a smile.

Pastor Bernas followed Eloise's gaze in the direction of Zeke and Caroline. "Be sure to let Mr. James know we expect him at the church picnic this afternoon."

"He isn't staying," Eloise blurted. She must have completely missed the announcements about the picnic too. "Remind me again who's hosting?"

"We're gathering at the Jenkins's orchard. Four o'clock."

"Of course," she said. The orchard would be beautiful. It wasn't a large production, but an array of plum, apple, and pear trees supplied the produce market with an abundance of fruit each fall.

Since she and Tobias didn't grow much of their own food, it was wonderful to be able to purchase so many things locally.

"Surely Mr. James wouldn't turn down a church picnic with you?" His eyes twinkled at her.

Why did Pastor Bernas put them together? She had not had any interaction with the man since he snubbed her last Tuesday at Anderson's Bakery and her discovery of Rachel's letter. "I'm surprised to see Zeke today. Assumed he would be long gone by now. The way he talks, he will likely be on his way tomorrow. He will have many things to prepare." If Pastor Bernas wanted Zeke at a picnic, he'd have to invite him himself.

"Is that so? Oscar was telling me he planned to keep him on, long-term. By all accounts, Mr. James's work at the bakery has exceeded their expectations. I suppose we have you to thank for the new menu items." He rubbed his stomach and then leaned in, as if sharing a secret. "They told me all about the unfortunate misunderstanding with your brother." Pastor Bernas laughed, shaking his head. "Such an interesting turn of events. It will all work out in the end; it usually does."

Unless it didn't. Eloise was inclined to believe in things not working out. The disappointment didn't sting so badly when you'd been expecting it all along. Was it possible that Zeke had changed his mind since she'd spoken to him last Sunday? Not that it mattered. He could stay or go, regardless. A man receiving love letters from another woman did not hold her interest.

Caroline took Zeke's arm, and they walked out of the churchyard together.

Eloise straightened her shoulders and turned her head away.

Pastor Bernas could rest easy; Zeke was surely invited to the picnic now. *Best of luck to Caroline.* Zeke was a waste of time, anyway. The sooner he left town, the better. Once he was gone, she'd be able to think clearly again. She couldn't put two thoughts together with him always underfoot. And she still needed to buy bread.

"Ready to go?" Tobias was at her elbow with Luke on his shoulders.

"More than ready," Eloise mumbled.

While descending the stairs, she took one last look at Zeke walking away with Caroline. Eloise almost fell off the last step when she found Zeke watching her. He smiled and started to wave, but she turned away, pretending she hadn't noticed. Home awaited. They had leftovers to eat and potato salad to prepare for a picnic that she'd completely forgotten about.

The sooner Zeke left town, the sooner she could stop being bothered by him.

Caroline Jenkins was a fun distraction. She laughed easily, smiled at Zeke's jokes, and was extremely pleasant to be around. There was no reason for his mind to keep straying to Eloise. He had done well in avoiding Eloise throughout the week. At first, he was afraid she had read too much into their walk together, but when she hadn't approached him, save the one day at the bakery, he had been able to relax. He was not what Eloise needed, and the sooner he was out of her life, the better.

"Pardon?" he asked for the third time since he and Caroline had left the churchyard.

Caroline stopped and removed her arm from his and smiled, she said, "I think I will hurry back home now. I wager you have other things on your mind."

The bakery was en route to her home, and he could see her parents and siblings walking ahead.

"I'm sorry," he said. "I must be tired. Thank you for the company." He laughed and gestured to the back door of the bakery. "And for escorting me home."

"My pleasure. We'll see you this afternoon?"

"Absolutely."

Her red hair reflected the sunlight as she turned her face to her family. "Follow this road out of town and turn left at the large cottonwood near the creek. You can't miss our place. It's the one that will have all the people gathered around the food with the horses and wagons hitched by the barn."

"I'll follow my nose."

She giggled. "Bye, then."

Letting himself into the living quarters of the bakery behind the shop, he was welcomed with the ever-present smell of caramelized sugar, cardamom, and freshly baked bread. Even on a Sunday when the ovens rested, the smell lingered, making it a nice place to sleep for a few days. Or weeks. The fifty-pound bags of flour Oscar had him rearranging and the combined hours of kneading dough throughout the week had kept his middle from growing, even with extra taste tests.

The Andersons had a plate waiting for him at their table and a lunch that included Swedish *knäckebröd*—hard bread—spread with soft cheese, boiled eggs, and pickles. It was no fried chicken, but it satisfied, nonetheless.

"Those pies you made on Thursday? I have two leftover for you to bring to the Jenkins's picnic," said Agnes once the meal was over.

"You're not going?" Zeke asked.

Oscar chuckled. "You'll not catch me awake past five o'clock with work waiting the next day. We're too old for such goings-on."

Three o'clock in the morning did arrive much too soon for Zeke's preference. But with an entire display to refill after a day of rest, the early rise was necessary.

"You go and have fun, kid," Agnes said. "You've got the rest of your life to sleep."

Zeke crunched a bite of the knäckebröd, and crumbs spilled over his plate. He still hadn't gotten the hang of this dry food. "I really ought to think about moving on. Suzy Girl is ready to go. An afternoon jog for exercise might be enough for her, but it's time to put her new shoe to the test."

Agnes and Oscar shared a look. It didn't mean much to him, but he recognized from the way they shared a smile that the look was significant.

"Okay," Zeke said. "Out with it." He put his bread down and brushed the excess crumbs from his chest. "What have I done this time?" He drummed his fingers on either side of his plate. "I didn't let mice in the flour bin again, did I? If I did, you need to take it out of my wages. I ought to know better than to repeat an offense like that."

Oscar waved a hand at him. "No, no, no. The mice have nothing to do with anything." He looked again at Agnes. "We've been talking, Agnes and I, and we're ready to offer you a full-time position here, if you're inclined. You know your way around a kitchen, and whatever your thoughts on the matter, you have a gift. We'd hate to see it go to waste. You can stay here, renting the room for as long as you want, and if you decide to get your own place later, then that's something we can talk about. Agnes and I have been running this bakery, just the two of us since we started, and having another pair of hands has been more helpful than you know. It's been a real blessing. Besides, with the extra menu items, and you being new and all, we've had a surge of customers that have more than covered your wages."

Zeke wanted to interject. He was going west. To the ocean. He had plans. Plans to keep following the sun. So that he could . . . what? So that he could say he went west? Followed his dreams of seeing the ocean? Because he wanted to do something with his life? Because he didn't want to be a farmer?

Did he want to be a baker?

Oscar was still talking. "There are a few specials I'd like to add to our menu that take more time to prepare but could be offered with our regular items now that you're here. You can continue your training on the traditional Swedish offerings, but so far, our customers have had nothing but good things to say about your work. Those cinnamon rolls were a hit right out of the gate."

"Close your mouth, Zeke dear," Agnes said. "It's not becoming."

He clamped his mouth shut as thoughts bounced around in his mind.

Agnes leaned forward. "You don't have to answer right off. You can take another week, or however long you need to decide. Just understand that you are welcome here. We enjoy having you

underfoot, even if you let mice into the flour bin on occasion."
She smiled. "We've enjoyed having you as a part of our family and
we're glad to have known you, whether or not you decide to make
Ockelbo your home."

He nodded. His mouth was suddenly dry. *Family . . . home.* Two
words that he yearned for, and for the first time, he realized he was
scared.

Family and home meant commitment. It meant sticking around
for someone else and being responsible for them, as they were for
him. It meant people caring if he stayed or left. Home was a place
of safety, where he could let his guard down. Family loved each
other through thick and thin, and then died. Opening himself up
to that kind of pain was dangerous.

It would be much easier to be the one leaving instead of the one
being left. He'd had a home and family with the Donnelys. They
had loved him as their own, but he'd managed to protect his heart
from feeling the kind of love he'd only had with his mother. Except
for Rachel. A better sister didn't exist. She'd taken him under her
wing from the first day he showed up, hungry, with holes in the
knees of his pants. He loved Rachel deeply, as he could imagine
one loved an older sister. But when she and Daniel Rhys had set
a date for their wedding, it was past time for Zeke to find his own
adventure. She didn't need him anymore.

She was fourteen and he twelve when he joined their family, and
she'd never left him alone a day in his life since. She'd taught him
everything there was to know about what it meant to be a part of
a family. It meant loving each other on the hard days and the good
days. And it meant forgiveness after uncalled for anger, laughing

so hard his sides ached, and crying so the tears poured like rain. She'd been there through all those hard years, and he wasn't about to sit back and watch the family break off one by one while he was stuck plowing fields. The West dangled in front of him, teasing him with stories of adventure and feats of heroism.

He furrowed his brows, deep in thought. But being a baker? Where was the adventure in that?

He watched Oscar take Agnes's hand and raise it to his lips. They smiled at each other, seeming to read the other's mind again.

"Come on, old boy," Agnes said to Oscar. "Let's have a walk." She winked at Zeke. "Zeke is happy to clear the table."

Chapter 20

The April afternoon was as beautiful as it had ever been. Eloise was glad to be among her church family and soak in the blessed sunshine. She'd fallen asleep after lunch while Luke napped and woke up in a better frame of mind. Her attitude toward Zeke could use a slice of forgiveness. And she could use a slice of minding her own business. Following Luke around at the orchard picnic was work enough for her to make excuses or steer clear of unwanted conversations.

The short leaves on the fruit trees whispered of the long winter they'd made it through. Tiny green buds covered the trees, anticipating the sunny days to come when they would grow into fragrant pink and white flowers. Eloise could already imagine the branches laden with fruit. Fall picking would be more fun with Luke this year. She looked forward to watching him experience a fresh plum for the first time. Her mouth watered, dreaming of the sweet juices.

The creek ran just beyond where they had their meal, lending its voice to the fellowship. The only thing that would make the afternoon perfect was if she could turn off her Zeke compass. He arrived late to the meal and was not his usual chipper self. He'd found company with Helen and Jeffrey Palmer. They were together for the weekend when Jeffrey stayed in town instead of their homestead, but from Eloise's vantage point, she saw Zeke wasn't participating in the conversation. His spark was missing. His hands stayed in his lap, and that was a sure sign that something wasn't right.

"Afternoon." Jessica blocked Eloise's view of Zeke, joining her and Luke on their blanket.

Eloise smiled at her friend and made room for her. "Keep an eye on your plate," she cautioned Jessica. "Luke will take anything that doesn't belong to him."

"Hello, cutie." Jessica pulled the boy into her lap. "You're in luck. Auntie Jess will share anything with you that you want." But she squealed when Luke stuck his whole hand into her mashed potatoes. "Oh, help!" she said to Eloise, laughing.

"I warned you." Eloise tried to take Luke from Jessica, but he fought against her.

"Leave him be. He's already made a mess of it. He may as well eat it."

Eloise shook her head. "You'll spoil him."

Jessica angled the plate off her lap and let Luke feed himself, though he did more playing than eating, squishing the potatoes between his fingers.

"I'll send Tobias over with a rag. Sit tight." Eloise dusted her skirts and went hunting for him.

She found him at the dessert table, surrounded by friends, balancing a full plate on one hand and storytelling with the other.

He raised his eyebrows at Eloise, asking if she needed something.

She nodded to where Luke sat with Jessica, still intent on squishing the mashed potatoes.

Luke brought a hand to Jessica's face, offering her a bite. "Jessica's going to need help. I'm handing him over to you." She reached for Tobias's plate. "What did you find? Anything good?"

"See for yourself." He handed it to her, pulled a bandanna from his pocket, and shook it out.

"You'll need another one of those," Eloise said.

Tobias smiled and flourished a red one from his other pocket. "Got it covered."

Eloise's focus flitted behind Tobias to where Zeke made his way toward the creek with his hands shoved in his pockets and his head down.

Tobias followed her gaze. "What do you think is going on with him?"

"Beats me," she said.

"Why don't you ask him?"

She looked back at Tobias. "Why don't *you* ask him?"

"I'm not as cute. He may not want to talk to me."

"Stop it." She swatted his arm.

Tobias whipped her with the end of a bandanna and went to save Jessica.

Eloise watched Zeke until he sat on the edge of the bank and jumped down, disappearing. She set the plate of food on the table, and her feet moved toward him. One in front of the other, she walked the hundred yards to the creek. Looking over her shoulder, she saw that nobody watched her. Tobias sat next to Jessica and fed Luke with a spoon. Helen and Jeffrey were caught up in each other. Other family groups intermingled around the tables and blankets. Caroline and Maribeth joined a group playing bag toss.

She came to the edge of the bank, a four-foot drop, and saw Zeke standing on the dry sand, watching the water run by, inches from the toes of his boots. Tree roots held the sand and dirt in place where she stood, waiting for another flood to be useful.

Zeke toed the ground and bent to pick up a palm-sized stone. He held it in his hand a moment before flinging it into the water.

"Hello," she called to him.

He turned at her voice. His eyes were wide, and he looked behind her.

"It's just me," she said. "Mind if I come down?" She sat and dangled her feet over the edge, resting a foot on a root. "How are you liking the bakery?"

"You ought to come by and see for yourself." He looked up at her, smiling in that easy way of his.

"I did. Once." She broke contact, and her gaze followed the movement of the water. That was safer than whatever she might find in his eyes. Or revealing too much from her own. The water wasn't vulnerable.

Zeke scooped a handful of sand from the ground, sifting through it to find the pebbles. He tossed one into the water and then another.

"Chipmunk—"

"Zeke—"

They spoke at the same time.

She waited for him to go on, but he looked at her expectantly. "I watched you leave the picnic. You looked . . . not yourself."

He shrugged and threw a few more pebbles, listening to the individual *plink* as they broke the surface of the water. His eyes lingered at the spot where the water swallowed his pebbles.

"I'd better see if Tobias needs help with Luke," Eloise said.

"Wait." Zeke brushed the sand from his hands and turned to her. "Thank you for coming over. I would like the company."

"Okay." She looked at him, waiting for him to say something else, but he only locked eyes with her until she looked away, blushing.

"Want to throw a rock?" he asked.

"Okay." She laughed. "Help me down."

He put his hands on her waist and lowered her to the ground. He smelled like a baker, with hints of a smokey bread oven soaked into his shirt.

"Did you just smell me?" Zeke laughed, and his hands lingered on her waist.

"You smell delicious! Like I've walked into Anderson's Bakery, hungry for breakfast. How can I resist." She stepped back. "You'd drive a woman looney coming home with that scent every day."

Zeke pushed his hands into his pockets and ducked his head.

"Th-the bread," Eloise stammered. "On your shirt. It smells good. That's all."

He squatted and picked out a handful of stones. "Here."

"Thank you." She was thankful for the distraction. This

conversation was not going well. She tossed her pebbles one at a time and bent to find more.

After a few minutes of quiet pebble tossing, Zeke threw a handful in one go and let a breath of air out, frustrated.

She took a chance and prodded. "Do you want to tell me about it?"

He turned from her, watching the creek downstream. "Why is California so far away?"

"It doesn't have to be," she said.

He turned to look at her over his shoulder, offering a half-smile. "A couple of weeks ago, Boss asked what was so great about California." He swiped his boot over the ground, kicking sand into the current. "I had a hundred and one answers for him."

She took a step and reached to place a hand on his shoulder.

He whirled to face her, and she caught a glimpse of his shining eyes. "Want to climb a tree?"

Eloise startled at his nearness and covered her heart with both hands. "I cannot keep up with you."

"Come on." He grabbed her hand and pulled her along. "I saw a good one over here."

"Zeke, stop."

He turned back to her, gripping her hand.

"Throwing rocks and climbing trees isn't going to fix this."

"How do you know?" He displayed that cheeky grin of his.

"Because I know." She ignored the heat coming from his hand. *Settle yourself, Eloise.*

"Have you tried it?" He played at pulling her along, bracing both feet and leaning back, as if she were livestock stuck in the mud and her arm the rope.

She stood her ground and cocked her head. "Avoiding? Absolutely."

He wasn't deterred. "Come on." He squeezed her hand. "Who says I'm avoiding anything?"

She gave in to his whims, though she couldn't have answered why. Same as she didn't have an answer for following him to the creek in the first place. Was *want* reason enough? Longing? Connection? Yearning? She wanted to be near him. Perhaps nothing more was required; no other reason was necessary. She wanted to be with Zeke like Luke wanted to squish mashed potatoes. She suppressed a giggle at the comparison.

Ahead, she saw the tree in question. A sturdy willow with a branch reaching far out into the creek begged to be climbed. She let go of Zeke's hand and placed it on the shoulder-high branch. "It's been ten years since I've been in a tree."

"You tell the saddest stories." Zeke laced his fingers and offered a step for her. "Up you get."

"You're really going to make me do this?"

"I'm not making you do anything. You'll do it because you're up for a bit of fun. Luke is safe, and everyone is busy, so why not?" He moved closer. "Give me a good reason that doesn't have to do with you being a fuddy-duddy for why you won't get up in this tree?"

He was close enough for her to smell the bakery again. She fought against the urge to bury her face in his shirt and breathe it in.

His finger trailed the side of her face and caused her breath to hitch. "Your face is turning red," he said.

No surprise there; she could feel the heat rising quicker than any yeast dough on a hot day. "I'm ready." Eloise lifted her skirts out of the way and placed her foot on his linked fingers. With her hands on the trunk and Zeke's strength taking her higher, she stepped easily onto the branch with her other foot. Hugging the trunk, she looked around, searching for the next step higher. Hearing a scrape and grunt, she turned her head to find Zeke pulling himself onto the branch. "Zeke, wait a moment; I'll go higher."

"Too late," he said with his voice in her ear and his arms wrapped around her, pinning her to the trunk.

She gasped, and she elbowed him in the ribs.

"Watch it!" He gave her an inch more room. "If I fall, you're coming with me."

A lightness blossomed in her middle, and she let it grow, enjoying the comfort of his arms. Fleeting or not, she would take it for what it was. The aroma of baked bread surrounded her, and she had another urge to breathe in more. The joy started in her chest, and she couldn't hold it back. It began with a silent laugh that shook her shoulders, but a giggle escaped and led the way to a full laugh. The ridiculousness of her behavior tickled her, and the laughter kept coming. The more she tried to stop it, the harder it was to control.

Zeke missed whatever prompted Eloise's fit of giggles, but he wasn't about to interrupt. Her laugh was sweeter than any music. The only thing that would make the moment sweeter was to be in on the joke.

Climbing onto the branch behind her was a bold thing for him to do; he knew what her presence did to him and how it meddled with his self-control. With his arms on either side of her, he felt her warmth, and with her laughter filling the air, he forgot why he wasn't interested in pursuing her.

A warm breeze came from the south, picking up the smells of the picnic, reminding him of the others who were enjoying themselves in small groups. Children running, grandparents resting, families laughing together . . . *Why shouldn't I stay? This could be home.* He would bake and court Eloise. A job, roots, family. Community. Isn't that what he wanted? He didn't have to go farther.

She said California didn't have to be so far away. Like she'd read his mind. *Home* didn't have to be so far away. He could make his home wherever he wanted. Oh, but he wanted a home. He wanted to dig in deep and grow the kind of roots that great-grandchildren could talk about.

Right now, he wasn't interested in anything but the girl between his arms. Her shoulders still shook with laughter. "Do I want to know what that's about?"

Carefully, she turned in his arms. With her backside resting against the tree, her hands grabbed the trunk from behind. Her eyes were wet, and her smile—her beautiful, beautiful smile— begged to be kissed.

She looked at him with mischief shining in her eyes. "Don't move. You brought this on yourself." Transferring her hands to his chest, she looked at him for a moment. His eyes moved to her lips, but before he could do anything else, she gathered his shirt and buried her face in it, breathing deeply.

Now it was his turn to laugh.

She tipped her head to look at him, holding fistfuls of his shirt. "You finished?" he asked.

"Yes." Delight showed in her bright eyes.

But she didn't release him. Though it wouldn't have mattered if she did. He'd been caught from the moment her voice pulled him from the prairie.

"I've been wanting to do that." She sighed, and her smile never left her face. "My mother's etiquette books have nothing to say about enjoying the smell of bakers in a tree."

Leaving one hand on the trunk behind her, he brushed his hand along the side of her face, caressing from her temple to her chin and back again. "Lucky for me, I never read any of those books." He kept his hand against her skin, and his fingers eased into her hair, cupping her cheek. His heart sprung from his chest when she leaned into his hand and closed her eyes.

"Eloise!" Boss called his sister, and she pulled away from Zeke, shrinking into the tree.

Zeke sent her a wink and, in two seconds, dropped to the ground. "We're over here!"

The leftover grass from last fall crunched under Boss's boots. He peered at Zeke below him by the creek. "Where's El? Luke's done for the night."

"I'm here." She leaned around the trunk to wave at her brother.

Luke wiggled in his dad's arms, reaching for Eloise.

Boss's slight grin contradicted his serious stance. He shook his head. "If mother could see you now."

"I'll be right down," she said, turning to Zeke.

"Don't bother. You know the way home." Boss gave Zeke a

pointed look, which Zeke hoped Eloise missed from behind the tree.

"Ope! But I—"

Boss turned, and taking long strides, was out of earshot, or at least pretended not to hear.

"Zeke!" She raised her voice, drawing out his name. A sense of desperation flickered across her face. But it was hard to take her seriously when her lip came out in a pout that reminded him of Luke about to throw a fit.

He could save her, ease her fears, run to her, and tell her he would never leave her. But his visceral response to her call frightened him. He had almost gone too far with her. Almost fallen off a cliff into a situation he wouldn't be able to talk his way around.

The sunset over the ocean still called to him, though dimmer. It was hidden by the promise of a steady income doing what he loved, a community that had opened its arms to him, and a woman who trusted him.

"Zeke." Her sharp tone brought his focus back to her. "Are you going to help me out of this tree?"

He sauntered back to her. "I might." He put his hand on her shoe, the height of his shoulder. "And I might not."

She gasped, pretending to be shocked.

"I'm safer down here," he said. "Less chance of any etiquette rules being broken."

"You're a funny man. But it doesn't matter. I can do it on my own." She flapped her hand at him. "Move. I'm going to jump."

He backed up slowly. "You wouldn't."

"You leave me no choice." She bent at the waist, making to leap from the branch.

"No!" He rushed to her, fearing she would twist an ankle at impact.

She burst into another fit of giggles, hugging the tree for support.

"Sit down, Chipmunk, before you fall and Boss blames me for your broken neck."

Still smiling, she eased herself into a sitting position with her legs dangling off the branch.

Leaning against the trunk, he crossed his arms, letting his shoulder brush her knee. "You wouldn't have jumped."

"You goose." She knocked him with her foot. "Not from standing. Besides, this is my favorite dress. I wouldn't risk mucking it in the dirt."

"Blue looks nice on you."

"Think so?"

"You're beautiful in anything, but this shade of blue does something to your eyes."

Turning her face from him, she picked at her skirt. "You don't mean that," she said softly.

"So what if I do? You need me to say it again?" He weaved his face in front of hers, trying to make her look at him. "You're beautiful."

"Please don't," she whispered.

He couldn't be blamed for speaking truth, could he? Just because he confessed that she was beautiful didn't mean he was spilling out his undying love. Did it? Where was Rachel and her advice when he needed her?

"Alright." He pushed himself away from the tree and stalked a few feet away. To pursue or not to pursue. Stay or go. Take the job or leave.

"What are you looking for out west?" Her voice cracked.

"Home," he said immediately, turning back to her.

"What does it look like?"

"A place that I've built that is only dependent on me, where I'm not beholden to anyone." He turned back to look at the water; his hands rested on his hips. It sounded crass coming from him so firmly. Is that what this was about? Making a name for himself. Proving to the world—himself—that he didn't need help?

"Home is a place where you're loved." Her voice drifted to him, almost too quiet to hear. "Being with and creating a future with those who love you."

Letting out a breath, he kicked the ground, sending a spray of sand and pebbles into the water. "People are unreliable." *And they die.*

"Maybe so, but it's better than being alone."

"No one is ever alone," he said. "Wherever I go, God will love me as fiercely."

"You have more faith in him than I do."

"What do you mean?" Zeke returned to her side, reaching for her. He raised his eyebrows, asking if she'd like to come down.

Putting her hands on his shoulders, she allowed him to bring her out of the tree. And into his arms. Wrapping her into a hug, he held her, relishing the feel of her arms around him.

She didn't pull away. Instead, she sank into him, holding onto him as he to her. She pressed her cheek against the hollow of his shoulder. "How are you so sure He's with you?"

"I just know."

She released him, and he let her step away.

A coldness filled the place where she'd been. It was a struggle not to pull her back. "Tobias loves you unconditionally, yes?"

She nodded.

"Is there anything you could do, anywhere you could go, that would keep him from loving you?"

"I guess not," she said. "But if God is like that, why doesn't he show it? If he loves as deeply as you say but doesn't do anything about it, it changes nothing."

"Oh, but it changes everything!" Excitement spilled from him as he launched into his favorite subject. "Remember Jeremiah? *It is only because of his mercy that we are not consumed.* God loves with a passion I can't fathom. Maybe he cares whether I go or stay, or maybe he simply wants me to bring glory to him wherever I end up. I don't know. But what I do know, undoubtedly, is that his love is real. Incredibly real."

She offered a tight-lipped smile. "Tangible love is easier to believe in. Love you can see. Touch." Was she tempting him on purpose? "Love you write in a letter, perhaps?"

"I wouldn't be opposed to it."

She turned from him, shading her eyes against the glare of the westward sun. "I'd like to go home now. It's getting dark."

"Of course." He'd said too much. Pushed too hard. He'd do well to remember her grief was different than his. He'd lost a mother— she, a husband. He'd clung to the promises found in scripture. What had she clung to?

The yearning to put down roots filled him to the brim. The

Pacific was no longer a tangible dream, but was Eloise? He knew infatuation, like waves that crested ashore and receded, and this wasn't it. If he didn't walk away tomorrow, he didn't know if he ever would. Because whether or not she was ready to accept it, what he felt for her, undoubtedly, was incredibly tangible.

Chapter 21

⁂

Avoiding the bakery wouldn't last much longer. Her meager baking skills needed more training than Eloise could devote at the time. She'd grown far too used to depending on Agnes for all her baking needs. Everyone had to grow up sometime. She would attempt biscuits for dinner. How hard could it be?

She hadn't seen Zeke since the Sunday picnic. Four days. Four regular days filled with toddler chatter, singing, rocking, washing dishes, laundry, ironing, walking about town, exploring and watching the prairie come to life—and avoiding accidental meet-ups with a certain man that made her heart skip on sight.

She'd dropped in on the Palmers and rejoiced when she learned Jess and Roy were officially sparking. The news came as no surprise, but the confirmation was good to hear. Once Roy implied that he was interested in courting, Jessica gladly showed her approval of the situation.

Luke spent Tuesday morning fishing with Ma and Pa Davidson, and today, Tobias picked him up after naptime to give Eloise a few hours to complete extra spring chores unencumbered. The housework hadn't gotten any easier with Luke's increased mobility. Climbing was his specialty, along with pulling things down upon his head, putting all manner of objects into his mouth, and only growing more adorable through it all. It was a good thing he was cute; he was everything an eighteen-month-old boy could be.

Tobias wouldn't get anything done at the brickyard if Luke were with him. She smiled, thinking of the trouble the boy could find in Tobias's office. Stacks of paper, pens and ink, ledgers . . . she'd have to wait and see if Tobias ever made an offer like this again.

In the meantime, she rolled up the rugs from their bedrooms and dragged them outside one by one. Tobias usually helped hang them, but she was determined to do something on her own for once. After a struggle, she had the largest situated on the sturdy clothesline.

The dust from the rugs billowed around her and stuck to the perspiration on her face. The amount of dirt she removed was satisfying, and she enjoyed the exercise. Despite how her hands turned red and rubbed a few spots raw, the energy she expended reaped an immediate and welcome reward. If only her circumstances could be cleaned up like a rug. There was pain in the process, but afterward, it was free of the excess grime and fresh again to fulfill its purpose—to collect more dirt. Okay, so it wasn't the best comparison. Still, the energy required to remove the dirt seemed fitting.

Nothing worth having was without its struggle.

She watched the dust blow away with the wind, forgotten. And that's where the relationship between the rug and her ended. No matter how much she wanted to forget something, or someone, they wouldn't be forgotten.

She kept her hands busy to combat the war taking place between her heart and her mind. She had prayed fervently over the past year for God to take away her pain. He had not, and she had only begun to heal before Zeke arrived. She didn't need another loss, but she reminded herself that Zeke never promised her anything. His going or leaving did not involve her, and Zeke and Rachel . . . that situation did not involve her either. Whatever almost happened on Sunday, should not have happened.

Swinging the beater again and again became cathartic. The puffs of dust eventually grew smaller, but she continued until she couldn't see even the slightest bit of dust.

Leaning against the post, her chest heaved against her corset. She inspected her raw hands.

"Miss Eloise?" a young voice called from the street.

"Here!" she answered.

Samuel waved at her from the stone sidewalk.

Tucking wayward strands of hair into her head covering, thankful that only Sam saw her in such disarray, she met him in the front yard.

"I tried to run." He bent over and put his hands on his knees, "But Felicity." He paused again, breathing hard. "She thought I was playing chase, and then I has to tell her I was on an errand. And now—now she's waiting by the mercantile, but I says I was coming back." He straightened again. "Here." Sam shoved a square page into her hands, folded on itself multiple times. "He says to give you this, and then I forget, and now it's yesterday, but better late than never, right? So anyway, here it is, and I'm sorry it's late." He scratched a spot on his arm. "What I was thinking is, he could've walked it over here hisself and saved his penny."

"Who could've?"

"Mr. James. He gives this to me affer breakfast yesterday, but then it was school, and then I found it in my pocket during lunch and remembered today that I'd forgot. You won't tell? Will ya? Cause I already spent the penny."

"Run along with you," she said, waving the note at him.

The boy ran down the block. His arms pumped at his sides. Felicity wouldn't have long to wait at his current speed.

Eloise stared at the folded page with her name scrawled across the front: *Eloise.* Meandering to the backyard, she sat against the side of the house in the shade before unfolding the crumpled page.

My little chipmunk, it began. Why did he keep calling her that? She wasn't little. She was completely average in every way. Except for her embarrassing ability to blush at a moment's notice. The only nickname she'd ever gone by was El or Ellie. "Chipmunk." She practiced the word aloud, enunciating the consonants.

Did I ever thank you for the return of my overcoat? If I didn't. Thank you!

I confess, I miss you and Boss's company. After our frequent run-ins when I arrived in town, I got used to it. Two weeks with only one conversation hardly suffices. Regarding Sunday, I find I have things on my mind that I'd like to share with you. I hope you don't find me too brash in writing them down.

For example, do you have any idea how many cookies the Ladies' Sewing Bee can put down? I had no idea women were so voracious.

For fear of using too many words in honor of our dearest Mr. Oakfield, will you spare a minute?

Foremost, I served the ladies coffee and treats yesterday and commented on Mrs. Delia's lavender ensemble. She found my comment most delightful, so I have you to thank for educating me on the proper color terminology.

I'm rambling.

I hadn't planned to stay in Ockelbo for so long, but things have fallen into place at the bakery. The Andersons have been teaching me the most wonderful things about the business. I've been learning more than I thought possible when I took this job.

The next line was scratched out. Squinting at the blotted ink, it resembled a chicken scratching in the dust. She discovered no hint at the original meaning. She read on.

You've been in the front of my thoughts, and I've compiled a list of scriptures that I find comforting. They've brought me through many trials, and I hope you find shelter in them too. I'd enjoy going over them together, but for now, these will remind you how much God is a father, a brother, a friend, and a shield.

He does love you, somehow even more than an earthly brother ever could.

Jesus once said he wished to be a mother hen and gather the people like chicks under his wing. I'd like to be a chick sometimes. I feel like one often enough. Want to be a little chick with me?

Yours,

Zeke

P.S. Oh! Or "ope," as you people say, I forgot to mention that I have the afternoon free tomorrow. It would be fun to show you a recipe of my mother's. I'll stop over if it's all the same to you. Tell Luke I said, "Hi."

On the bottom of the page, she found hastily scribbled scripture references, many of them from books of the Bible she had never read. He'd scrawled below: *I have more! But this will get you started.*

Eloise didn't know what to do with this man. Zeke didn't fit anywhere she tried to put him. Why did he torment her so? The tug of war he played with her in the middle needed to stop. Surely, he didn't know the angst he created in her. Regardless of Rachel, his stories of the West should have been enough warning to her from the beginning.

She huffed and let out a mirthless laugh. If not for her meddling, he would have left two weeks ago, and she wouldn't be in the position she was in now—staring at his unique handwriting that had been passed to her from a nine-year-old child with smudges of school-yard dirt on his face.

She blushed, thinking of Zeke sitting near her, thumbing through her mother's Bible, reading to her as her father used to read aloud.

Well, honestly. How was she to resist her heart when it painted such intimate pictures? What burned her about this letter is that Zeke considered her a friend. He felt companionable toward her. Friendly enough that he would suggest such a thing. Underneath the small talk and the laughter lay the sparks and the energy that coursed between them, charging her heart to keep near him, and at the same time, raising the alarm for her to stay away. He must be blind to what he did to her. Was he so naive to think he could grow a friendship so easily and then run all the way to the ocean a week later, as if nothing were between them?

Finding the rug beater, she wrapped a handkerchief around the handle to cushion her throbbing hands—the navy blue one he'd given her upon his arrival. It had somehow made it through the wash weeks ago and stayed in her apron pocket, as she had planned for Tobias to return it to Zeke. She should have thrown it away. For now, it served a purpose, and she wasn't going in the house to fetch another.

Heaving the second rug over the line, she stood upwind and took a wide swing at the rug.

Whop.

The dust flew out of the rug in clouds, and it was oddly satisfying to see the large amounts of dirt blowing away.

Whop.

The wind changed, and it flew into her face. Shielding her eyes, she beat the rug again and again.

Before Zeke arrived in town, her grief had become comfortable. Familiar. She knew what to expect and how to go about her days. The grief was safe in its own way. Staying in that place was easier than moving forward into a new happiness and being yanked back into grief suddenly, like each time she woke from a nightmare.

Instead of moving forward, she was now breaking in half. Half of her was still wandering around a graveyard. The other half was singing like a bluebird in spring, hopping about in the wide-open prairie and calling to all the other birds to join her in a dance. This was new territory, and it was exciting. But it frightened the other half of her. *Be careful*, it said to her. *Run away*, it cautioned. And then there was Rachel. Finding love again was one thing, but Eloise refused to play games with a man who was in love with someone else. Or even one preoccupied with a fictitious image of a perfect California.

Eloise put her hands on her hips and arched her back. Her shoulders ached, and her hands burned from the repercussions of the wooden handle—despite the aide of the handkerchief. She'd finished the second rug, and two more remained. She was ready to attack the smaller one from Luke's room. Dragging the one off the line, she rolled it up, stacking it near the first, and filled the space on the line with Luke's.

Suddenly, she remembered Sam's words. "And now it's yesterday," and the significance of that statement. The realization hit her like a blizzard. If yesterday was today, that meant Zeke was preparing to visit today. She didn't even have the choice to refuse his company. Now it was too late, and he could be here any minute, yet here she stood, covered in dust and sweating through all of it. "Dad-blame it!"

She did not want to see him. Rather, she wanted to see him too much. She hadn't had enough time to figure out what was going on inside her, much less did she want him to see her in a dust mop. Inviting Zeke in would only waste her afternoon. She would just have to tell him he wasn't welcome. She spoke aloud to the rugs. "He's an enigma."

"Who's an enigma?"

She screamed, whirling around toward the voice behind her.

Zeke stood in the yard, resting his hands on his hips with his Stetson shading his eyes from the late afternoon sun. He smiled, as content as her imagined bird on the prairie.

Honestly, a man shouldn't be allowed to be so good-looking.

Chapter 22

He watched Eloise beat the rug like a dragon that needed to be slain before he announced his presence. While kneading the dough at four o'clock in the morning, he'd been thinking of her flushed cheeks. While serving coffee to the Ladies' Sewing Bee, he'd imagined Eloise laughing at one of his jokes. And while lugging the wooden crate across town to her house, he'd seen her in a clean apron snuggly tied around her trim waist. Never in any of those daydreams had he seen her covered in dust and cursing at a rug.

Half expecting her to skitter up the tree like a chipmunk after the way she'd jumped at his voice, he waved his hand at her. "Afternoon."

"You frightened me," she said.

"Sorry, I knocked on the front door, but you weren't there." He swung his hands to the front and clapped them once, then swung them around behind his back, and he clasped them together. "I poked my head around and saw you attacking these rugs." Striding forward, he reached for the beater. "May I?" Taking it before she answered, he raised an eyebrow at the handkerchief wrapped around the handle. "I had something else in mind for the afternoon, but this is good too." He'd planned for standing side by side, working closely, hands brushing, with her face turning pink when he whispered in her ear. Days of not seeing her had messed with his mind.

Zeke raised the beater and took a baseball stance that could rival any of the players from the Red Stockings. He swung it with twice the force of Eloise and made quick work of the job. Soon, the wind finished the task by blowing the dirt out of the yard.

Squinting against the dust, he pulled the rug from the line and took the next one that Eloise proffered. He continued hitting it until he felt her hand on his shoulder. It sent shivers down his spine, and his heart thumped a betrayal of his intentions for the afternoon.

"That's fine," she said. "Thank you." She took the beater from him and sheepishly handed him his handkerchief she'd unwrapped from the handle. "I believe this belongs to you."

He grinned. "I believe it does."

She watched him fold it in half and fold again but froze when he reached over and wiped it across her forehead. "What are you doing?"

"Relax," he said. "You've made mud on your face."

"I'm a mess." She dropped her gaze to the grass.

A beautiful mess. He took in all of her from her hair tied back with a scarf to her worn work dress, and noticed her bare feet peeking from below. He put a hand on her elbow until she looked at him. "I've never seen a more industrious chipmunk."

She *tsked* at him. "Honestly, enough with the chipmunk. Why do you call me that?"

"Maybe I'll tell you after dinner," he teased. "What're we having?" And he laughed when her face turned white.

Her blue eyes widened. She opened her mouth, but no words came out.

"I'm kidding!" He laughed like nothing could take his joy away. Ironically, Eloise was not encouraging him today. If she would open up to the idea of him and their growing friendship, he'd have more to work with. He missed the Eloise from Sunday.

When she'd come to the bakery last week, he hadn't meant to be rude but had firmly decided not to stay in this town. He'd wanted no distractions. That meant he wasn't going to build a friendship with a woman who made him daydream about grandchildren. He'd planned to take the week's pay and ride out of town in a few days. But when Eloise left the shop without speaking to him, it tore his heart in a way he hadn't known was possible. He hadn't expected to feel that kind of rejection. Especially when he had been the one avoiding her. The following week, he'd not had one glimpse of her outside of church—and only the back of her head at that.

More than two weeks had passed since she'd walked out, and he still hadn't left town. He served the community breakfast, poured coffee, and wished them a good day, good morning, happy weekend, good afternoon. And he meant it. In small ways, the people had welcomed him. The regulars invited him into their conversations, asking him to sit and share his thoughts. The Andersons taught him about business and taking orders, planning menus, and running the books. They asked and listened to his ideas for new products and encouraged him to experiment with recipes and new-to-him ingredients. They'd taught him how to make Swedish tea rings, dry rusks, knäckebröd, and kardemummabullar. In turn, they had let him make cinnamon rolls as large as his face and soft as a feather pillow.

Rachel's predictions were coming true. She'd said he would meet a woman that made all the pieces fit together—someone who would be more important than any singular plan of his own. From the way he'd found himself watching for Eloise through the store windows all week, he knew he'd found the girl Rachel told him about. He'd fallen. And it didn't even hurt. If Eloise would only be there to catch him, he needn't worry about the rest of it. He'd share his good news with her. Soon.

"Come on," he said, "I have something to show you." He took her hand and stepped to the house, but she didn't move.

She looked at his hand that was holding hers, almost as if it were poisonous.

"Hey, you okay?" he asked.

When she took her hand back, his heart dropped. If she wouldn't hold his hand, he needed to crush the daydream of her in his arms and his lips tasting hers. What would she do if he kissed the scowl off her face right now? Hit him with the rug beater? He tried a more direct route. "Can I teach you my mother's bread recipe?" A grin spread over his face when she nodded.

She hadn't shut him out. Not completely. He knew she needed

space and time to heal, to get used to the idea of him being around. He could give her that. Trust took time to build, and she had been wounded too many times. Even by him. "Well, come on then," he said. "I'm pretty good at what I do, but we're not baking bread in the backyard."

She followed him around to the front of the house where he'd left the wooden box of things he'd brought from the bakery.

"What is all this?" she asked.

"I brought everything we'll need, provided you have a pan, bowl, and a pot? Oh, and you do have a stove and water, right?"

That pulled a smirk from her, at least.

She led the way into the house, and he deposited the box on the table.

"Luke sleeping?" Zeke asked.

"He's with Tobias for the afternoon." She handed him an apron.

"Nice try." He snatched it from her and tossed it on her head. It flopped over her face, and he detected a smile as she pulled it down. "I won't be caught in florals again. I brought my own." Feeling self-conscious now, knowing they were alone, he wondered what her etiquette books had to say about it. He knew it wasn't proper for him to be in her house unchaperoned. With the toddler running around, the situation would have been entirely different—more friendly, light-hearted.

He double wrapped the plain white apron around his waist, dressing up, playing the part of a baker, and wondered if he should cancel the afternoon and go back outside where it was safer. He'd be less tempted. But he wanted to stay with her. To get to know her better. To hear her laugh again.

She was deep in thought, and it didn't bode well for the way he'd imagined their afternoon. Inviting himself over wasn't turning out like he'd thought it would. Did she need more time? He'd waited four days from their flirtations on Sunday; had he waited too long? He'd expected her to show up at the bakery, but when she didn't, it was time for action. Agnes said Eloise was a regular for bread orders, yet he hadn't made one loaf for her. Yesterday, a lesson in bread baking had been the perfect idea.

Maybe he should have opted to buy her breakfast first. Or dropped off a bag of candy and invited her for a stroll. Boss had given him the go-ahead. Should he have asked Agnes too? Jessica would have known what to do. Round and round he went in his mind, second-guessing every interaction with her, from the past to the projected future. He'd never courted a girl. Was it always this complicated?

"I'll be right back. I'm a mess," she said. "Let me freshen up. I'm covered in dust."

Again, he inwardly corrected her, a *beautiful mess.* "The wind has a way of tossing as much back on our faces as it takes from the rugs. I'll get things set up. Hurry back."

With renewed hope, he got to work. While she was gone, he scrubbed his own hands and splashed water on his face. Once he'd rubbed himself dry, he took his time in emptying the box of the ingredients he'd brought: flour, milk, butter, and the rest. Whistling a hymn that was stuck in his head from church on Sunday, he rifled through her kitchen until he found a couple of bowls and spoons.

"What shall I do?" she asked, catching him with his head deep in the lower cabinet.

He found her standing in the doorway, cheeks flushed and bright from a scrub. She was dressed in one of her blue skirts with a white top. He was disappointed that she was now wearing shoes.

"Salt," he said.

"Salt?"

He cleared his throat, deliberately not thinking of her bare feet and what she wore underneath and how her skin showed through her chemise when it was soaking wet. "We need some salt."

"Oh, of course. It's here." She moved him out of the way, lifted on her toes, and brought the small crock from the top shelf. "We're more careful where we store things now that Luke is into everything. I catch him standing on the table every time I turn around."

"Maybe he wants me to come teach him how to cook." Zeke added the salt to the assortment of items on the table. He tapped his finger on the recipe card he'd brought and rubbed the fingers of his other hand across his forehead a few times, attempting to refocus. He cleared his throat again. "Here's the recipe I've adapted for you to try." While he explained the process to her, she was unusually quiet.

Instead of looking at him, she fiddled with the apron in her hands that she'd yet to put on.

"You ready?" he asked.

She nodded.

"You okay?"

She nodded.

He knew she wasn't okay but wanted her to trust him enough that he didn't need to ask. They'd had a number of brutally honest conversations, so he knew she was willing to confide if she felt like it. "After tonight, Boss will have the best bread in town. Rather, second best next to the bakery, of course. The student is not greater than the master."

The corner of her mouth twitched. "You're the master?"

"Better believe it, but you can be the judge when we're done."

She sighed. "Very well."

"Enough chit chat. Measure the flour listed on the card, and we'll see if you pass the first test."

He couldn't bear to watch her struggle with the measuring cup, packing the flour in—like she'd spent too many years watching her brother make bricks—and clumsily spilling it over the edge of the bowl. "Oh, Chip." He clicked his tongue. "Has nobody ever showed you how to measure flour?"

She laughed. "No. That's why I don't do it. I can get by, but that's what bakeries are for." She elbowed him when he tried to take the measuring cup from her hand. "Why do you think I'm such good friends with Agnes?"

"If you're such good friends, why haven't we seen you more often?" Moving behind her, he circled his arms around and placed his hands over hers. At her sharp intake of breath, he considered backing up due to their lack of a chaperon. Clearly, she had feelings for him too, and it only encouraged his imprudent behavior. Remembering how she'd closed her eyes and leaned into his hand in the tree, he took her stillness as a good sign.

Covering her hands with his, his conscience was clean, unlike at the dance when he'd been torn in half, searching for a way out. He closed the gap between them, grateful he wasn't breaking any matrimonial vows this time. He wouldn't mind making vows, but that could wait.

With his face against hers, he softly talked her through the proper way to ladle the flour into the cup with the spoon, keeping it airy and light. "Just like this, one more scoop until it overflows the cup." He took the flat edge of the spoon's handle and scraped the mound off the top into the jar, and then dumped the contents into the measuring bowl.

"Now you try." He removed his arms from around her but left a hand on her back. His boot touched hers.

She added three cups on her own but fumbled with the last and dropped it outside the bowl. Her hands shook. "Ope!" She laughed nervously. "I have trouble concentrating with you staring at me."

"Am I too close?"

She worked at scooping the flour off the table into the bowl, but only blushed in response.

"How about this?" He brushed his hands on the back of her shoulders, trailing them down to rest on either side of her waist. He gripped her sides and turned her to face him. "Or this?" Zeke inched closer, took the measuring cup from her hands, and dropped it into the bowl behind her.

Wisps of her hair curled at the edges of her face, still damp from the wash. He ran his hands along her arms and turned his lips to her temple. He watched her close her eyes, and those pesky alarm bells went off in his head, but he ignored them. Instead, he listened to her breath near his ear.

She relaxed her arms to her sides, and her chest rose and fell, out of breath, as if she'd been working. "Zeke." Her voice was soft. "Please . . ." She lifted her face, and her eyes darted from him to the door behind him. Looking for an escape? *Please, yes, or please, no?*

Did she want this as badly as he did? The edge was an exhilarating place to be, but the spark before the flame could still burn. If she could feel the fire burning in him, she would surely run. With his hand behind her neck, he kissed her temple and rested his head against hers, drinking in her temptation.

Pulling her head away, she looked at him, pleading. "Don't play with me. You have plans that don't include me. I'll not be a toy along your way."

He took her hand and pressed it against his chest. "Do you feel my heart?"

Her hand trembled under his, but she nodded.

"It's trying to beat its way out of my chest. When I'm with you, you make me feel like I've been found. The pull of the ocean has nothing on Ockelbo. I know we've only known each other for a few weeks." He chuckled. "But I've been falling for you from the moment we met. If you'll have me, I'd like to keep falling."

Before he could babble any longer, she pulled her hand away. Her eyes avoided his.

She was a blank chalkboard; he couldn't read her at all. She wasn't saying yes; he knew that much.

His mouth went dry, but he had to take a chance. Gently, he held her face between his hands, still rough from the brickyard. A couple of weeks in the kitchen had not decreased his callouses. Slowly bending his neck, he looked into her eyes, asking for a yes, for permission, for a kiss that would start his heart beating again.

"Do you love Rachel?" she whispered.

"Rachel?" He dropped his hands and scrubbed the back of his neck. "Of course I do. Rachel, she's . . ." *Rachel was family—a sister, mother, friend, and confidant all rolled into one.* "Have I told you about Rachel? She's amazing. But what does she have to do with us?"

"Please leave," said Eloise, the mood broken.

Clearly, there would be no kissing today.

She pulled the wooden crate across the table and clunked the jars back into it.

"Chip, I don't understand—"

"Stop calling me that!" She stomped her foot.

The front door opened, and Luke rushed across the house in a flurry of childhood excitement.

"We're home!" Tobias said. "Hey Zeke, how are you?" He closed the door and shrugged out of his jacket, dumping it on the sofa. "Guess what this little guy found. Tell her, buddy. Tell her about the big bunny we saw."

Eloise scooped Luke into a bear hug. Her accusing eyes never left Zeke's.

When Zeke didn't move to leave, instead meeting her glare for glare, she left the kitchen, discarded the child into Tobias's arms, and fled up the stairs.

"What's with her?" Tobias said.

Zeke shook his head. "Maybe she'll tell you." He tossed the rest of the items in the box and picked it up. "I was just leaving. We'll have to catch up later."

Rejection. Something he'd managed to avoid until now. Being vulnerable had its disadvantages. All the facades he'd built around himself of the West and the ocean beckoned. His words from Sunday mocked him. *Home is a place where I'm not beholden to anyone.* What a laugh. If only he'd been strong enough to walk away, he'd be three weeks closer to his dream and three weeks away from a broken heart.

Chapter 23

When he returned to his room, Zeke stood in the middle of it with his hands on his hips and stared at his unmade bed. He scratched the side of his neck. *What now?* Just when he thought he'd had things figured out, he was as lost as ever.

The quilt hung haphazardly from his bed, and discarded clothes lay in a heap in the corner. He'd become a royal slob. Determined to be in control of something, he straightened his small space, all the time hearing her desperate command. *Please leave.*

He tucked the sheet around the edges of the bed, shook out the quilt, and let it fall. *Good enough.* Shoving the loose items into his pack, he found the bills from Simon.

If there was one person in this town he could do without, it was Mr. Oakfield.

He flopped onto his bed, weary and confused. *God, help me.* Striking out on his own wasn't hard. Packing his bags and loading Suzy Girl hadn't been difficult. The weeks on horseback had been lonely, but nothing he couldn't handle. And now he was trapped. Growling out his frustration, he reached under his pillow for his Bible. Thumbing through it, he turned to Romans for one of his favorite passages. *For I am persuaded that neither death nor life . . . nor anything else in all creation will be able to separate us from the love of God.*

The words calmed his mind enough for him to think again. He would post the letter to Rachel, take Suzy Girl for a walk, and get some fresh air. Feeling antsy, he wanted to be going and doing something, now that sitting cozy next to Eloise was out of the question. He shoved the bills in his pocket and marched out of the room with his letter to Rachel in hand.

Agnes was there mopping the floor in the kitchen when he came from the adjoining room. Looking over at him, she smiled. "I thought I heard you." Focusing on her mopping, she said, "Didn't expect you back so soon. I don't have anything on for dinner, honey, but there are things in the display that you may have your pick from."

"Thank you, but I have business across town. I'll pick something up if I get hungry." Which wasn't likely to happen in his current mood.

"Eloise wasn't home?" The smile she tried to hide came through her words. She was perceptive; he'd not told anyone of his plans.

He stuttered. "She was busy. Spring cleaning and the like."

Agnes gave him a knowing look that stung.

He didn't like to be pitied.

"Another time, hon," she said.

He grunted. That's what he'd tried to tell himself. It took time to grow the kind of relationship he was after. No matter the desire he felt for her, he hadn't meant to bare his soul today, and the reality of her response cut him deeper than he would admit. He chided himself that he hadn't even told Eloise the main reason for his visit. It would have been better if he'd just spit it out. But he was always on the wrong side with the women in his life. Even if he told them what he planned, step by step, they disagreed with him. But if he didn't tell them, they falsely accused him of hiding something.

Rachel always pointed out the fault in his logic. He'd learned it was better for him to barrel on ahead and finish and then pay for the results, rather than be nitpicked along the way. Less chance of failure if he didn't tell anyone. And then, of course, he was free to change his mind. He resented the presence of self-doubt that wedged its way in.

He was a grown man, after all. Going or staying was still his choice. All the better if he was able to enjoy himself in the process, but he would never intentionally lead a girl on for his own carnal pleasures.

Eloise's words had bitten him. She'd accused him of using her. *Pshaw.* Did she not know him at all? He'd just told her he loved her, hadn't he? Maybe not in so many words, but he'd used plenty of other words that practically meant the same thing. He'd been leaning in for a kiss to seal the deal when she felt the need to ask arbitrary questions. What did loving a sister have to do with anything? Women were always griping about their men for not picking up on minuscule hints, yet, he didn't have an inkling of what he'd done wrong this time. Did she not care one iota he was in the middle of telling her he wanted to stick around? By sugar coating his desires, he'd tried to let her warm up to the idea of his intentions. He'd thought women usually liked those kinds of sappy words.

The gusts whipped his clothes as he made his way to the livery for Suzy Girl. He ought to go back for his overcoat but was afraid Agnes would see right through him again. It was colder than before. Gray clouds loomed in the north, contrasting with the bright sun in the crystal blue sky of the south.

Muffled shouts grabbed his attention from the alley between Abigail's Dress Shop and the Mercantile. Three boys were scrapping in the dirt, and from the looks of it, it was two against one. Samuel Forsberg was the one on the ground.

Zeke marched into the alley. "Boys!" His command startled the group and the two on top took off running behind the shops.

Sam jumped up and would have run the other way if Zeke hadn't snagged his suspenders from behind.

"Not so fast," Zeke said. "You want to tell me what's going on here?"

"No." Sam swiped the back of his hand across his nose, smearing dirt on his face in the process. "They started it."

"How?"

"After I slugged Willie, they jumped me together, and what's I s'posed to do then? I's fightin' for my life. You seen 'em, both of 'em on me. Vicious like."

"Hold everything. You started it." Zeke pulled Sam by his elbow and took him to the walkway, back into the daylight.

"You haven't heard the half of it!" Sam said. "Willie said my trousers were short, and I had legs like a flamingo, and I don't even know what a flamingo is."

Zeke stepped back and raked his eyes over Sam's legs. "Your trousers are too short, but that's no reason to go slugging anybody. And you don't look like a flamingo. Did you hear what happened to me the last time I punched a man?"

Sam's eyes grew wide, and he jerked his head to the Sheriff's office.

"Two nights, Sam." Zeke put his face level with the boy's and pointed to the jail. "I spent two nights locked in a cell. With mice. Don't be a dunce. You can't always slug a guy when you feel like it." Zeke straightened and stalked toward the livery. He called to Sam, who wasn't following. "Keep up. I have a job for you. You have too much time on your hands." He'd pay a penny a day to have Sam exercise Suzy Girl. "You know anything about horses?"

Sam jogged to keep up with Zeke's long strides. "Yeah, an' my pa's horses are big. Sometimes he lets me ride them, but mostly they're working."

"Good. Suzy Girl isn't big. And she's not for working." Zeke nodded to Frank at the door and found his horse with her eyes half-closed. "Wake up, girl. Meet your new friend, Sam."

After he'd sent Sam on his way with instructions to be back in half an hour, Zeke walked through the mercantile, looking for ways to spend Mr. Oakfield's money. A pair of boy's trousers caught his eye, but he changed his mind. Sam would be alright for now.

Simon Oakfield was someone Zeke wished he could slug. Zeke

crossed his arms and looked through the shelf of school supplies. Too bad Zeke had wasted his tantrum on the wrong man, the animosity he felt toward Simon would have fueled a good fight.

Picking up the lone dictionary on the shelf, he looked up *animosity* and read Webster's definition. *"Animos'ity, noun [Latin animositas; animosus, animated, courageous, enraged; from animus, spirit, mind passion. Gr. Wind, breath, is from flowing, swelling, rushing, which gives the sense of violent action and passion. See animal.] Violent hatred accompanied with active opposition; active enmity. Animosity differs from enmity which may be secret and inactive; and it expresses a less criminal passion than malice. Animosity seeks to gain a cause or destroy an enemy or rival, from hatred or private interest; malice seeks revenge for the sake of giving pain."*

Zeke sucked in a slow breath through barred teeth and whistled. Animosity did not describe his feelings toward anyone. A touch of enmity perhaps, but that was all. He slid the book back on the shelf and meandered around the store until it was time to meet Sam at the livery.

Stay or go. Take the job or leave it. Pursue or not to pursue. There were too many what-ifs that haunted him. For now, he would take care of Sam. It was the easiest of all the things rattling through his brain.

The air slapped his face when he left the mercantile, and Zeke crossed the street just in time to take Suzy Girl's reins. Sam was windblown, but a smile spread across his whole face. Zeke wasn't sure who expended more energy during the ride, the boy or the horse. Without waiting for an invitation, Sam launched into a detailed account of their adventure together. Not much else was required from Zeke than an occasional, "You don't say?" Leaving far too much space available for thinking about another pair of rosy cheeks he'd much rather be looking at.

Jessica and Roy were seated at the dining table with a board game between them. Zeke knocked on the window from the porch, and the couple waved him inside.

"Hiya, Zeke!" Roy called to him. "We're about to start another round; want in?"

Playing games was more appealing than confronting Simon at the moment. He tapped the side of Rachel's letter on the table. "What's the game?"

"Sit down," Roy said, "and we'll show you. It's called Chinese Checkers. It's similar to checkers, but more people can play." He handed Zeke ten glass marbles. "Put yours there, and the winner is the first to get them to the other side."

"I've beaten him twice already." Jessica rubbed her hand along Roy's arm.

Roy snatched her hand and held it. "You've been cheating, dear."

She giggled. "Have not."

Roy looked at Zeke. "She cheats."

"Sit, Zeke," Jessica said. "A lady never cheats."

"Nobody was arguing that point." Zeke pulled out a chair, ignoring her gasp.

Roy asked, "Staying for dinner?"

"Is that allowed?"

"Sure, it's allowed. Though you can pay for yours. Mine is free on account of courting the daughter of the establishment."

Jessica kicked him under the table. "You work enough for it. That chicken house didn't fix itself yesterday."

"Chinese Checkers?" Zeke asked.

Once Zeke got the hang of the game, it wasn't a bad way to pass an hour with friends, and one game turned into three, and he lost track of time. Even with Jessica trying to cheat, Roy won two rounds and Zeke one. Soon, Helen was shooing them from the table and setting up for dinner—putting Jessica and Roy to work with the final preparations.

Simon appeared at the foot of the stairs and eyed Zeke suspiciously. "You," he said and turned to go back to his room.

Zeke rolled his eyes and followed him up the stairs and through the familiar hallway. His old room was open again. The other boarder had only stayed two nights while waiting for the coach. "Simon, wait. We need to talk."

Simon continued to his room and slammed the door in Zeke's face.

That makes two in one day. Zeke took the wad of money from his pocket and tried to smooth the bills flat on his thigh. "Simon?" He considered shoving the money one at a time through the crack under the door. "Simon, I just want to say . . ." He nearly choked. "Thank you." He cleared his throat. "You were very generous and helpful, but I'm returning your money. I'm doing well now. Boss doesn't even have a bruise on his face anymore. All's well that that ends well."

Zeke took each bill and lined them carefully together and folded them in the middle. They were not the crisp bills he'd been given, but they would spend. "Even Eloise has forgiven me, so that's good." He brushed away her *Please leave*, and thought instead of the pancakes and the meal they'd shared as a family. *Tobias, Luke, Eloise, and me.*

The door in front of his face jerked open and Simon stood glaring at him. "You do not know anything about anything, do you?"

Zeke stepped back.

"You do not deserve her. You would do well to leave her alone."

The jealousy in Simon was strong enough that Zeke was surprised his skin hadn't turned a shade of green. The realization cleared up things in his mind regarding the man, but Zeke's hackles were raised now. He'd always felt like a dog trying to defend his territory when Simon was around, and now he knew why.

"I know a lot of things," Zeke said. "I know that after Philip died, she had a hard time. She's been struggling and—"

"Died." Simon spat out the word with a cold laugh. "Is that what she told you?"

"Not in so many words," said Zeke, feeling defensive against Simon's aggression. "But there aren't so many ways to say it. A widow is a widow, no matter how it came about."

"Philip shot himself in the head," Simon said. "Took his own gun and killed himself."

Zeke grew cold. He stepped back as if slapped. He closed his eyes and took a deep breath. "Oh, Eloise," Zeke whispered. What she must have been dealing with all this time. His heart went out to her. Her question ran through his mind: *What about those who don't wake up?* She'd been asking about Philip.

But Simon wasn't finished. "I have been here for Miss Eloise for years. I have been her friend since childhood. I was the one who carried her books home from school when all Philip did was pull the ribbons from her braids, and yet she followed him around like a puppy and went wherever he led her. I spent years waiting for Eloise to look in my direction, but she had eyes on the oaf who sat behind me. The ironmonger she chose over me did not even have the honor to stay with her. He did not cherish her like I would have. He made it clear in the end that he did not want to be with her."

"That's not—"

"—and then you show up. A nobody from nowhere. And I will not stand for her plunging into another situation she cannot get out of."

"Now see here!" Zeke didn't like being referred to as a situation.

Simon jabbed his finger into Zeke's chest. "The best thing for Miss Eloise is for you to leave. Go find the West you want so badly. Just because she thinks she is in love with you does not give you the right to dazzle her with your lies. Let those of us who know her take care of her."

It took all of Zeke's restraint not to slug the man. He probably would have, if he hadn't spent the afternoon mentoring Samuel against such foolishness. He settled for shoving Simon's hand and his bony finger away from his chest. "Eloise can take care of herself. She doesn't need you or me to do that for her." Wadding the cash into a tight ball, he shoved it in Simon's shirt pocket. "Take your money. I won't be needing it." He spun on his heel to stalk down the hallway but stopped. A smile crept over his face. He angled back to Simon. "Did you say she was in love with me?"

Simon scoffed. "You are obscene." He slammed the door to his bedroom.

Tripping down the stairs, Zeke felt a break in his spirit. No longer at odds with himself, he knew what he had to do.

Chapter 24

Eloise stayed in her room throughout the remainder of the day, but it didn't provide the solace she was after. She flung open her window to let out the stuffiness, but the icy gusts brought no comfort. After a minute, she banged the window shut and sulked on her bed. A tear escaped, which opened the river until she was sobbing. Burying her face in her pillow, she screamed into it.

Tobias tapped on her door. "El?"

"Go away!" She didn't need his pity anymore.

Turning Zeke away was the right choice. But it hurt. He said himself that he was still in love with Rachel. Regardless of what he'd said to sweet-talk her, his sights were elsewhere. She knew better than to let a man kiss her who hadn't made his intentions clear. Tobias would never approve of Zeke's behavior if she told him the half of it. Desperate to be loved, she'd almost let him get away with it. Another wave of grief washed over her. She was ashamed at how badly she wanted Zeke's kiss.

Laying on her side on top of her bedding, she stared at the floral wallpaper until her vision blurred, and the flowers appeared to come off the wall and slide down but never reach the floor. She closed her eyes against the mirage and eventually fell asleep.

Waking sometime during the night, she was hungry. Her face was swollen, and her eyes were salt-crusted with dried tears. Lighting her lamp, she tiptoed down the hall and was careful to avoid the boards that creaked.

The mess the boys left in the kitchen did not surprise her. The dishes had been moved from the table to the dishpan, but the table had not been wiped, nor the floor swept. Poking around in the cupboards, she found a package of store-bought crackers and a new jar of peaches.

Leaning her hip against the counter, she stood to eat. The bowl of flour she had filled sat by the dishpan. Rather, the bowl of flour she and Zeke had filled . . . with his arms around her. She stuck a finger into the powder and twirled it around. Then brushing off her hands, she searched in her work apron that hung on the wall for the letter Sam had delivered. The page with the verses scrawled on it called to her. She angled it toward the lamp and ran her eyes over the list again, but none of the references brought any specific verses to mind. She'd never memorized very many of them.

Bringing the lamp with her to the front room, she found the family Bible in its proper place on the top shelf. It was right where it sat most of the time, except for Sundays when Tobias carried it to church. She settled into her wing-backed chair, the one belonging to her mother, and flipped through the pages for Zeke's first verse: Isaiah 41:10. She'd needed to use the table of contents to find it.

Fear thou not; for I am with thee. That was a good start. The passage went on with more words of encouragement, and she wasn't able to stop at the one verse. Completing the chapter, she went to verse one and read it through three times, letting it sink in. The chapter was filled with words she wanted to pull out and paste all over the walls of her bedroom. *Courage. Strength. Be not afraid. My friend. Help. Uphold. Chosen thee.* She had never considered God to be a friend.

He was the Creator. Ruler. Omniscient. Majestic. She knew all of that. But a friend? No.

She checked Zeke's note, squinting at his smeared ink, and looked up the next verse in the book of John. *The thief does not come except to steal, and to kill, and to destroy. I have come that they may have life and they may have it more abundantly.* Again, she found herself pouring over the whole chapter. Jesus spoke of sheep and shepherds, and it was rather confusing, but the bit Zeke mentioned in verse ten . . . *abundantly.* What kind of life could that be? It wasn't what she had right now. Living in fear was not an abundant life, but how was she supposed to move toward that promise? Fear was a shield. She wasn't living abundantly; she was safe.

The Bible was heavy on her lap, though the pages were thin. She thought of her parents reading through these same words. She had memories of her mother taking it off the shelf and silently reading in the mornings and of her father carrying it to church each Sunday as Tobias did. When her parents were alive, it didn't live on the shelf for the six days in between Sundays.

Fifteen was too young to lose a mother, and Eloise had always felt robbed of the last few years of her childhood. The thief had come and killed, and she'd been left. Now Jesus tells her to live abundantly?

Absorbed in her study, Eloise was surprised to notice the change in the light out the window. Surely she hadn't been sitting here for hours. The black night turned gray as the white and dreary clouds on the horizon made an appearance. She watched evidence of the sun rising with hues of pink and gold before closing her eyes.

She snuggled deeper in her mother's chair.

She must have dozed, for Luke woke her, giggling at her jerk of surprise when he slapped his hands on her lap.

"Morning," she said, finding Tobias watching her from the kitchen table with a ledger from the brickyard in front of him. Pulling the toddler into her lap, she cuddled him, and he wrapped his chubby hands around her neck.

"Eat?" He pointed to the kitchen.

"Yes, buddy. Let's eat." She ignored Tobias's questioning look when she came into the kitchen.

"You look better." He cast his eyes over her rumpled dress. "Sort of."

A laugh burst out of her from his honesty. It bubbled out without thought, so no offense was taken. Her hair was still in its pins from yesterday, half up and half down. Her skirt was thoroughly wrinkled. But she knew what he meant.

"I feel better." She eyed him from the side, knowing she owed him some hint of an explanation. "I'm sorry. About last night. I was rude."

Tobias grunted, fiddling with his shirt cuffs. She translated it to his implied, *I forgive you, but you still haven't told me what's going on.*

Once Luke was settled in his chair, she gave him a spoon and an empty bowl to play with. Eloise got out the pot and oats and pumped water to make oatmeal and coffee for breakfast. While she filled the percolator with water, Tobias busied himself by building a fire in the stove. "I should have started the fire when I came down," she said. "I didn't realize how cold it was during the night." Eloise peered out the window at the hazy sky. "Think the sun will come out today?"

Tobias put his face to the window, squinting at the dull sky, "Hope so." He shuffled to the lean-to for the broom and walked around the table, sweeping last night's dinner crumbs into a pile.

A knock at the door startled them both. Nothing less than an emergency would warrant a visitor at this hour. It was not yet seven o'clock.

Eloise took the broom from Tobias. "You go." Her heart tightened at the prospect of bad news.

He returned promptly to the kitchen, unwrapping the paper from around a loaf of bread. "Save your oatmeal," he said with a huge grin on his face. "There's bread in the house again."

"Who was there?" Relief filled her.

Tobias shrugged. "Nobody—just this sitting there." He laid it on the table and went in search of the bread knife.

"You didn't look down the street? Whoever left it can't be far off."

"Eat first, ask questions later," he said, "That's my motto." And then he had the audacity to whistle—as if he didn't have anything else on his mind but bread for breakfast. As if he wasn't bothered by fresh, warm bread appearing at their door.

She knew it came from Zeke. Who else could it have been? But to leave a loaf of bread after she'd clearly told him to leave . . . was he making amends or toying with her still? She didn't have the energy to muddle through the hidden meanings this morning. She had work to do. The least of which included washing the dishes from Tobias's dinner yesterday.

"I can have it ready for you before closing," said Jacob Davidson after inspecting the bit rings. "The crack is small enough that we can repair it without trouble."

"Thank you, sir, that's good news," Zeke said. Everything was coming together. He'd spent time shining his saddle and tack with the borrowed can of saddle soap from Frank. Samuel had done well with Suzy Girl the past few days, and her coat shone from the extra rubdowns she'd been given. Thankfully, he'd noticed the crack in the bit ring on Suzy Girl's bridle before he'd left. Once that was repaired, there was nothing else to be done.

Zeke watched Isaiah Sage in the back of the smithy, bent over the second anvil, focused on his work. Even so, Zeke lowered his voice. "Mr. Davidson, I hope you'll excuse me. Is it true? About your son?"

"Depends," Mr. Davidson said. "What have you heard?" His jovial demeanor was in contrast with the topic of conversation.

"Mr. Oakfield shared with me the method of Philip's death."

A scowl washed over Mr. Davidson's face. He tossed the bridle on a pile of other projects to be mended and waved Zeke to follow him outside. The cool breeze was a welcome relief from the heat of the smithy.

"It isn't Simon's place to speak of it. But, yes. It's an event we don't often bring up." Mr. Davidson sighed and smacked his leather glove against his thigh, sending a cloud of black dust into the air. "I don't know what went on in Philip's mind or what kind of demons he was fighting." He relaxed his expression and stared across the square at the groups of kids who had just been let loose from the schoolhouse. "We trust that God is merciful."

"Yes sir. I'm sorry to have brought it up. I only asked due to the nature of the accusation, and I doubted the source."

"Eloise is a fine woman." Mr. Davidson turned to Zeke. "Florence and I gained a daughter when Philip married her. One of the best choices Philip ever made. But I've seen the way she looks at you."

Zeke toed the ground and dug his hands into his pockets. He couldn't tell if Mr. Davidson was threatening him or not. "Yes sir." Zeke opted for the noncommittal and safe answer.

"You could do worse." Mr. Davidson thumped him on the back.

The force of it caused Zeke to stumble forward, and his hands came out of his pockets to steady himself.

Mr. Davidson laughed at Zeke's stumble. "I have work waiting. You can pick up the bridle tonight, or we'll have the doors unlocked before sunup tomorrow."

Chapter 25

The rest of the week was quiet for Eloise. There were no more bread deliveries and no more questions from Tobias. She spent the days at home, busying herself with whatever needed doing, and in her moments of rest, she worked her way through the list of verses from Zeke, digging into the chapters, and returning again and again to read Isaiah 41.

On Saturday morning, she'd been downstairs an hour before Tobias and Luke made their way to the kitchen. The stove was hot, the coffee percolating, and the sizzling bacon ready to come off the pan. As long as she didn't walk away from the stove, bacon was something she was able to serve with no apologies.

"Morning boys," she said to them with a smile.

Father and son alike had puffy eyes and hair that stuck up in the back. Tobias settled Luke in his chair with a picture book and shuffled to the stove for the coffee. While breathing in the fragrant steam with both hands around the warm mug, he looked out the window. "Might snow."

"Tobias, do you know anything about a Rachel?" Eloise fiddled with the end of her braid, waiting for the water in the pot to heat for the oatmeal.

"Nope," Tobias said. "I don't know any Rachels." He took the corner of the book out of Luke's mouth. "Don't eat that." Looking at Eloise, he asked, "Should I know a Rachel?"

"Never mind," Eloise said. The facts just didn't line up. She hadn't imagined that letter. The words were clearly stated. *All my love . . .* and the letter meant enough to Zeke that he'd kept it in his overcoat, likely pulling it out to read over and over again. What kind of man was Zeke at heart?

She'd almost given in to his persuasions. He obviously felt something for her, too, unless it was all physical. She blushed, remembering the way he'd caressed her face, drawing her to himself while his lips brushed against her temple.

But if he was still in love with Rachel, why did he stay in Ockelbo? Why did he make advances? She couldn't bear to think that he was using her for physical pleasure. Was he interested in her only to fulfill a base need? She felt disgusted at the thought. But she also thought of the conversations they shared and the friendship between them. Those things didn't stem from his physical desires. Did they? Was she that blind?

Her heart couldn't take much more thinking about Zeke. She'd sent him away. For good this time. Yet through her Bible studies this week, she didn't understand how a man who called God a friend could be capable of that kind of malicious behavior. If he loved Rachel, why did he confess he wanted more from Eloise than friendship? He'd practically spelled it out. Maybe not in so many words, but the message was clear.

She wasn't going to be his plaything. If he wanted a toy, he could look for something above the saloon. If that's what he thought of her . . . for shame! She felt the heat rising in her cheeks just thinking about it.

"Hey!" Tobias shouted at her. "The stove!"

Eloise jerked at his cry and tossed her braid over her shoulder. "Ope! Sorry." The oatmeal boiled, and the foam rolled over the edge, sizzling down the side of the pan and burning to the iron stovetop. The acrid smell bit her nose.

What she wanted to do was pour her heart out to Jessica and let her friend talk some sense into her. She'd been brave enough to bring up the question of Rachel to Zeke, and though she hated the truth of his answer, she didn't regret asking. Knowing was better. Jessica was blissfully preoccupied with Roy, and as much as Eloise was happy for her, she missed having Jess all to herself.

"Tobias, I'm going out." Sprinkling a touch of cinnamon and sugar on the oats, she served two sloppy bowls of oatmeal to Tobias. "Feed him, please. You'll clean more off his face and floor if you let him do it himself." Luke was content gnawing on a strip of bacon. The drool traveled down his arm to drip off his elbow. Eloise made a face and brought a rag to Tobias. "You'll need this."

"You're going now?" Tobias glanced at the clock.

She followed his gaze. The clock read half-past seven. She

looked around at the mess in her kitchen and realized she was still wearing her robe and stockings. "You're right. I'll need to change."

"You eating any of this?" He craned his head around to follow her.

"I hate oatmeal," she called, already halfway up the stairs.

She took her time getting ready, deciding on the luxury of a bath, letting the warm water settle her nerves. Saturdays were glorious. Having Tobias around to wrangle Luke was the gift of the weekend. She loved the kid, but it was wonderful to stay in the bath until the water cooled. Even washing the dishes without tripping on the child underfoot was a pleasure.

Eventually, she came down the stairs in her favorite blue dress, her long underwear underneath, prepared to go out. Tobias had attempted conversation multiple times, giving up when she had trouble putting a string of words together in answer. He was clearly confused by her cryptic departure, but he didn't question her. She must have snapped at him more than usual over the week. She smiled while tying her bonnet next to her ear. No matter, he would get over it.

"I love you," she said, and kissed him and Luke. "Enjoy your day. Don't hold lunch for me."

At half-past nine, Eloise was finally on her way to Jessica's. Her hair had been brushed and coiled against her head. She'd used a few of her mother's combs, adding a touch of flair on an otherwise typical outfit.

Tobias was right about the prediction of snow. It hadn't started yet, but it was cold enough that she had pulled her winter coat back from where she'd stored it in the trunk. Under the thick wool, she was well-protected. The cold weather had blown into town over the past two days of little sunlight. During the night, a white sheet unrolled overhead and it hung low in the sky. It almost blocked the sun from rising. It seemed to imply that it was prepared to stay. Thankfully, there was little to no wind. She took comfort in that. The brisk temperature was bearable when the wind didn't suck the breath from her lungs.

She took the longer route to avoid walking by the bakery. A chance encounter with Zeke shouldn't happen until she knew what she would say. And for that to happen, she needed to talk to Jessica first.

Despite the chill, it was a beautiful morning. It was cold but in a delightfully crisp way. If the leaves on the trees weren't fresh and bright, ready for spring, it would have been the perfect autumn day. The sky was a vast white expanse that hung over Ockelbo like a down comforter, shielding and protecting.

Two blocks from the boarding house, she was happy to see Jessica walking toward her. They waved at each other like long-lost companions.

"Good morning!" Jessica pulled her into a tight hug. "I was thinking about you. You have been avoiding me." Jessica waved her finger under Eloise's nose. "Zeke has been by to visit more than you, and he doesn't even live there anymore. We could have had a good game, the four of us." Jessica linked elbows and turned Eloise toward the square with an envelope in her hand.

Eloise caught the name on the front: *Rachel Donnely*. She snatched the letter from Jessica. "What is this?"

Jessica shrugged. "Zeke left it. I'm sure he meant to post it, but he must have forgotten. It's already sealed and addressed. I'm taking it to the post office." Jessica plucked it out of Eloise's hands. "What's the matter, friend? You look half dead. You feeling okay?"

Eloise was not feeling okay. She knew this heart-healing business would take time but being constantly reminded of her problems was not helping. "You've seen Zeke this week?" she asked. "How is he?"

"Oh, fine. He and Roy get along swell. We had loads of fun, talked about everything. Books, politics, childhood adventures. You'll come next time. Could we meet Monday?"

Eloise couldn't get over the hump. "Do you know who Rachel is?" Because if she didn't find out soon, she would burst. The Palmers may know more about Zeke than she did, depending on the conversations shared around the dinner table during the week he had lived there.

Jessica held the letter high and waved it like a flag. "Rachel!"

"Stop that." Eloise grabbed at her friend's arm. Embarrassed that she'd make a scene.

"Rachel Donnely," Jessica said in an exaggerated whisper.

Eloise jostled her friend but couldn't help but laugh. "You know I love you, but honestly. Do you know anything about Rachel?"

"Sure, baby. Sorry, I thought you knew. You and Zeke seemed all friendly-like." And then she launched into her presentation voice that Eloise knew well from their school days. "Rachel Donnely, soon to be Mrs. Daniel Rhys, is Zeke's older sister. Adopted sister. She is the oldest daughter of the Donnely family who raised Zeke after the death of his mother." She coughed into her closed fist. "May she rest in peace. Rachel and Zeke had a disagreement about the timing of his trip west. Apparently, she thought he needed to stay through spring planting, but all agree, Zeke, Roy, and myself, that timing had more to do with the upcoming wedding. I don't know the rest." She giggled and pulled Eloise close. "I confess to being overly interested in another man at the table. Roy pestered him about the whole thing, but I wasn't listening. We can go find him and ask, shall we?" Jessica's face lit up at the prospect of seeing Roy again. She flashed another smile. "Roy kept ahold of my hand under the table. It was practically indecent."

If Eloise weren't holding Jessica's arm, she would have sat down in the middle of the boardwalk. Instead, she pulled Jess to a stop. Zeke loved Rachel like she loved Tobias. She'd assumed terrible things about Zeke with nobody to blame but herself. Jessica was still talking, oblivious to Eloise and the fact that they'd stopped walking. Eloise didn't hear a thing.

Eloise retracted her arm from her friend. "I have to go. I'll catch up with you later." Leaving Jessica calling after her, she made a beeline directly to Anderson's Bakery. Her mind was a whirl of emotion, but the foremost being elation. *He loves me.* He'd tried to tell her. He'd practically spelled it out, begging her to ask him to stay, and she'd told him to leave. *Please leave.*

Pushing into the bakery, for once not bothered by the bells that announced her entrance, she scanned the room for him. But he wasn't there. Agnes greeted her instead.

Eloise offered a thin smile and a curt reply, but she had no patience for pleasantries. "I need to speak with Zeke. Can you let him know, please?" She kept her eyes on the door to the backroom. "It's rather urgent."

Agnes frowned. "Sorry, honey. He's not here."

"He's gone?"

"He left before dawn, though I made sure he had a warm breakfast and hot coffee in him. It's a cold one this morning."

"Yes," Eloise said. "Thank you." She backed up to the door. She was too late.

"Need anything?" Agnes pointed out the large cinnamon rolls in the display. "He managed to put together quite a spread for the Saturday rush before he left."

Eloise shook her head wordlessly and wandered back outside. So that was that. Four weeks, almost. And she'd ruined everything.

She thought of Zeke's verse from Lamentations. *It is of the Lord's mercies that we are not consumed.* In place of crumbling into tears, she straightened her shoulders and walked resolutely across town. If Jeremiah could look over his entire nation in rubble and speak words of comfort, the least that she could do was hold her head up and walk through town without falling to pieces—a town full of people who cared for her, whether she noticed them or not. Ockelbo had been a shelter for her all these years. The people had never shut her out, even when she tried to close herself in. Agnes . . . Helen . . . Tobias, Jessica, Jacob, and Florence. She tried to remember all the blessings that had been showered on her since her parents died.

When her lip began to tremble, she clamped it down. She kept walking. Kept moving. She meandered without thought of direction, going where her feet led. When she came to the street that led to the cemetery, she stopped. She didn't need to go there today.

There was nothing for her there. No answers were found in the grave, and no comfort either.

For a fleeting moment, she considered begging Frank for a horse and riding after Zeke, but he was hours ahead, and she would never catch him, even if she knew the direction he had gone. Hadley Springs was only seven miles away, but there were other routes to the ocean.

Standing near the edge of town, with the cemetery in view, she tipped her head back. Her lip quivered, and she did everything in her power to keep the tears from breaking loose.

Chapter 26

Her boots made no noise while she walked. The spring growth was still soft and green. Last season's grass lay underfoot and provided a layer of protection for the new growth—shielding it until it was ready to brave the harsh wind and sun.

The morning was still cold, and the sky was still a white sheet.

Barely visible, flecks of snow drifted down. The predicted snow had come at last. A few flowers were in bloom and green leaves budded from each tree, and yet the snow came. She'd thought they were out of winter. The last few weeks had teased them with a string of hot days, but the falling snow carried with it a reminder that her human plans accounted for little. *Oh, God.*

I have a plan for you too.

A tear squeezed its way out before she could stop it. Did she trust God's plan? That was the question. What if his plan included her parents dying and her husband leaving her. Was that part of the plan? What if his plan included things for her that were hard to swallow?

God's plan was hidden from her, whatever it was. She didn't have a hint of it, not one tiny inkling. But like this spring snow, whether she fought against it or welcomed it, it was there. Eloise walked throughout the morning, tucking her hands deep in the pockets of her coat, mulling over the new ideas that were growing in her heart. Coming to the place where the stones made a crossing along the creek, she sank onto a large rock at the edge and watched the water as it flowed between each stone.

"I miss you, Philip," she whispered. She missed his slow, easy smile when he woke up next to her each morning. And as often as she'd told herself that it was his own decision to take his life, it was only recently that she'd been able to believe it. It was not her fault. It wasn't.

Oh, that she could go back in time and share with him what she felt now. Could he have found freedom in this life? What if they had studied the promises offered in the scriptures together? Would they have filled the void in him that she'd never been able to fill? Those questions would never have answers.

Eloise found a small stone and tossed it in the water. It plunked to the bottom of the creek, hardly disturbing the path of the water. The ripples disappeared in the current. The water was on its way to join a larger body, which might flow all the way to Zeke's ocean. It didn't have the time to worry about a rock she threw in its way. She let out a deep breath. Looking at the sky, she closed her eyes against the brightness of it. The sun wasn't visible; the sky was completely overcast. But the sun was there, she knew it, simply because she knew it! Even though she couldn't see it, it burned her eyes to look where she knew the sun to be. The flakes of snow melted on her upturned face, but she hardly felt them because they were so small.

Finally, she stood and arched her back. She'd been sitting so long that her legs had lost some of their feeling. Long enough that her nose grew cold. It was past time to be going home. Tobias would be worried if she stayed away much longer.

With another wistful glance over the creek, she said goodbye to Ezekiel James.

She squeezed her eyes shut, almost believing she could make him reappear. She'd tell him she'd been a fool and beg for another chance. But she was too late. Turning, she took a step back toward Ockelbo when her ankle turned on the uneven ground, and she almost fell. She chuckled, remembering Zeke's clumsy antics, from his first fall into the creek bed, their blunders in town, and his feet tangling with the blanket in the jail. She sent up a petition for his safety. *Lord knows he needs it.*

She heard a voice in the distance. She cocked her head and listened. Someone was singing—a man. Only a few steps from the creek, she turned back. Her heart pumped as if it could run along ahead of her. She knew that voice.

Was he really there?

Taking the stone steps carefully over the water, she crossed the creek. Struggling up the other side of the bank, grabbing roots and tufts of grass as she went, not caring about the dirt being ground into her dress. She made it to the high ground.

There he was, only fifty yards away. His head was ducked, and he was walking toward her, swinging his arms and briskly marching through the grass. And singing. Just barely, she could make out the words.

His voice carried to her. "Where seldom is heard a discouraging word and the skies are not—"

"Zeke!" She called to him and waved, albeit frantically.

He glanced up, squinting against the snowy glare of the white sky. "Would you look at that? Chipmunks in the wild." He pointed up. "It's snowing! In April!"

His smile brought a swarm of butterflies to life in her middle. Restraining herself from running to him like a child, she waited for him to come to her. At his brisk march, it wouldn't take long.

He burst into a new song, drawing out the words in dramatic fashion. "As I was walking down the street, down the street, down the street." His eyes never left her as he sang, striding ever closer. "A chipmunk I chanced to meet, oh she was fair to view." Nearly ten feet away, he asked, "What are you doing out here?"

"I wanted to say goodbye," she said softly.

"You going somewhere?" he asked. He'd stopped in front of her with his shoulders hunched against the cold and his hands deep in his pockets.

She looked at him, speechless.

Zeke draped a hand over her shoulders and turned her back toward the creek. Taking up the chorus of his song, he sang loudly. "Buffalo gals, won't you come out tonight, come out tonight, come out tonight."

When they entered the shelter of the trees, Eloise interrupted.

"Zeke, I thought you were leaving. Gone. Agnes said you'd left. Left before dawn."

"Of course I did. I had to get Suzy Girl to market on time. Didn't anyone tell you? I got $215 for her and the saddle together." He whistled low and leaned toward her. "I didn't tell them how ornery she likes to be." His face broke into a huge smile. "I was going to tell you all about it. Oscar wants to retire one of these days, and the Andersons have given me a full-time position." He shrugged. "I thought you'd be interested, but you kicked me out before I could tell you."

He jumped down to the creek bed and started singing again, "Aaaaand dance by the light of the moon." He reached for her hand. "Coming?"

Eloise stayed on the bank, dumbfounded. "You're not leaving?"

"Sorry to disappoint." He beckoned her with his hand.

"I'm so relieved. And Zeke? I'm glad that Rachel is your sister. When I read her letter, I flew into a fit of jealousy."

Zeke's mouth hung open for a moment before the smile flashed across his face. "You snooping, busybody. Serves you right for reading my mail."

"You're not mad?"

"Darling, if you will come down off that bank, I'll never be mad again."

He grinned that cheeky grin—the one she would never tire of seeing. Holding tightly to the hand she offered, he guided her down.

Needing to get a few things straightened out still, she skipped any preamble. "The other day, when you said all those sweet things. You really meant them? For me?"

"Every last word."

"But what about the ocean? I don't want you to blame me for crushing your dreams."

He brushed a lock of hair behind her ear and smiled. "You are my only dream. I was scared to admit it even to myself, but I've discovered something wonderful about Ockelbo. There's a woman here that I'd like to be beholden to. If she'll have me."

"She will," Eloise whispered.

Zeke ducked his head and led her a few steps before turning toward her again. "Hey, I was thinking we should—"

She stood on her toes and kissed him squarely on the mouth, surprising them both. But before she could pull away, he came to his senses. Wrapping his arms around her waist, he kissed her back, none too shyly.

Her hands found the back of his neck, and knocking his hat from his head, she ran her fingers through his hair. Eventually, and out of breath, she pulled back. "I'm sorry I interrupted. You were saying? What were you thinking?"

"Hm?" he grunted. "I'm thinking 'bout kisses." He angled his head to hers for another round.

They both laughed, which made kissing difficult.

Zeke pulled her into an embrace, his cheek pressed against hers. "Let's go home."